MAGNUS AND A LOVE BEYOND WORDS

DIANA KNIGHTLEY

For all my babies — Och, twas such a joyful noise. I thank ye for it.

CHAPTER 1

$\mathcal{M}$agnus jostled my shoulder. "Kaitlyn? Wake up, we needs..."

I pried my eyes open and looked around the Great Hall, it was dark. Cold. The fire barely warmed the room. There was stirring as huddled people around us awoke, a noise at the end, loud voices from outside the door.

"What?" I rubbed my bleary eyes as Magnus pushed me off and lurched to his feet from his spot as my comfy warm bed.

His face was worried glancing up and down the hall. "Stay here, right here, daena move." He jogged down the room to the doors at the end. Other men were headed there too and slipping out of the room. Magnus slipped out of the room too.

I looked around, there were only a few women left together, hugging their tartans around their shoulders. There were whispered words I didn't understand. I hugged around my linen-skirt-covered knees, listened to my breathing, and watched the door.

A long few moments later Magnus slammed through the door and rushed down the hall toward me. I stood to meet him on my feet. He grabbed my arm, picked up my backpack, and hustled me to the closest exit. He was quiet and earnest so I didn't ask any questions, I just let him lead me down a dark room and through a hallway and out a door. The chill pre-dawn air hit me like a slap across the face. Cold. August. *What the hell?*

We kept close to an outer wall racing along the side, then pulled short beside a bush. Magnus situated me between the cold stone wall and the branches. He wordlessly pressed me to the wall and put his finger to his lips.

I gulped in air and searched his face. *How scared are we?*

His eyes said, *We are afraid, my love.*

He nodded his head and rushed away. So apparently this was what I was to do, stand behind this bush.

It was dark and shadowed. Cold and damp. I leaned against the stone, pulled my tartan tight around my shoulders, stared into nothingness, and hoped Magnus would hurry.

CHAPTER 2

A while later stealthily quiet Magnus returned leading two horses outfitted with packs on their sides. Wordlessly he moved me toward the horses and hoisted me up. Then he climbed on behind me and with a quiet syllable set our horse into motion. Leading the other horse we followed a path that ran along the wall for a while, then turned away. He picked a trail down a grassy slope into some woods and then wove our way through brush and bushes and around trees until the river was ahead of us. Magnus turned our horses and kept the river on our left, choosing a path through the trees.

After about thirty minutes of quiet travel, the woods opened and our path climbed. Magnus shifted to look behind us and watched for a moment: the path we had left, the woods, the river, and farther along, presumably, Balloch.

I glanced over my shoulder but saw nothing.

Magnus said, "I need ye tae get on the other horse so we can cover more ground." He led the horses behind a small outcropping of rock for our dismount.

I dropped into his arms and he hoisted me to the hard leather saddle of the smaller horse. Then he showed me with a gesture where and how to hold on and wrapped the leather reins around his right hand. He mounted his horse again and led mine as we picked our way up a wide treeless hill. We rode along rocky crags, clifflike edges and a high ridge.

I could see the river far below, but I didn't want to look down too much. I focused instead on the wide strong back of my husband before me, as he led us to safety.

Finally, after such a long time, he said, "Thank ye, mo reul-iuil."

"You're welcome." Then I teased. "For what?"

"For listenin' without needin' me tae speak on it."

"Of course. What was it — what was happening?"

"Twas men approachin' the castle." He shook his head. "My cousins have been causin' trouble with the Donalds. They were of a mind that the Donalds were returnin' tae skirmish at our walls, but I daena..." He shifted in his seat. "Why would they want tae fight on Lughnasadh? Tis the harvest festival. I daena believe any Scot would choose tae fight on this day."

"So you think it's..."

"I think ye have been followed. Twas safest tae leave."

"Where will we go, should we jump?"

"We canna. They would see the storm. We're goin' west tae Castle Kilchurn. After we will decide where tae go next."

"How long, an hour or so?"

He grinned. "Tomorrow."

I laughed. "Fun!" And adjusted my ass on the saddle. It was already sore.

CHAPTER 3 - MAGNUS

I dinna think we had been followed, so I was able tae relax. This route, across rocky highlands, was a favorite of mine, had been since I was verra wee, and the weather was perfect for a ride. I was verra glad tae be takin' Kaitlyn tae my childhood home.

We had been ridin' in silence for a while. I checked behind me tae see her deep in thought. I loved that about her. She could be so animated, but also quiet when she needed tae be. I had missed her so much while I hadna had her and here she was, suddenly, when I hadna expected her again.

She sensed I was looking on her and her face lit in a smile. A smile I hadna seen in many long years.

She asked, "What are you thinking about?"

"You. How I missed ye. How ye have come upon me so suddenly and now tis as if ye were never gone."

Her smile went wide.

A wisp of her hair floated on the breeze beside her face.

I steered m'horse around a grouping of boulders and we fell back intae companionable silence.

My thoughts turned tae Archie, now four years auld. He was always wantin' tae follow me tae the stables tae see the horses, especially this one, black in color, strong and graceful. I carried this stallion with me now whenever I traveled tae the past.

A hawk circled above us, then silently dove toward the horizon. Archie would love a ride like this, a high ridge, an open path, a wide sky, and would wish tae ride on his own, but he was still a wee bairn. I would have him on my horse and teach him how tae hold the reins in front of me.

Twas hard tae reconcile that young boy with the man I kent, Tyler.

I was still havin' trouble understandin' the truth of it. There had been so many years thinkin' Tyler was one kind of a man. Tae ken now he was a different man, my son, was tae make me regret much of the time I spent with him. I needed Kaitlyn tae tell me once more.

"It all happened because ye died?"

"Yes."

I faced front hidin' m'face from Kaitlyn so she couldna ken what I was thinkin'. I was so full of shame I hadna protected her. "Did he tell ye what happened?"

"He said I died on the dock."

"How? What did I do?"

"Tyler said they ran me through with a sword and then you tried to loop around twice to save my life. He said each time I died. He said it kept getting more brutal."

I shifted sideways in m'seat and watched her face as she spoke these words.

"I tried three times?"

"Yes, that's what he said."

"Och," I said. The shame settled on m'shoulders and was a heavy load tae carry. I shifted around tae face forward again. "Och, nae."

I couldna continue without stopping, without holdin' her, without tellin' her I was sorry tae have let it happen. I slowed m'horse with a word and dismounted to the ground. Kaitlyn's horse stamped impatiently because it was nose to nose with mine.

I stepped between the horses and held my arms for her.

She swung her leg around and slid down.

I held her. I pulled her tae m'chest and said intae her hair, "Och nae, mo reul-iuil."

We embraced for a verra long time. Finally, I said, "I am sorry, Kaitlyn. I should have kept tryin' I dinna—"

She steadied my face and looked up into m'eyes. "You did exactly what you were meant to do, Magnus. I don't know the whole story, but I can imagine how it went — you tried to save my life three times and that was all you could do without breaking our hearts. You would never quit unless you had to quit."

I shook my head. It couldna be true.

She said, "And Archie said you were heartbroken. Twenty-some years later, still heartbroken. He said even though you had the power to go back and see me, you knew you couldn't use that power and it was tormenting you. You had to quit, you couldn't keep trying."

"What if I had gone back further?"

"Every time you loop back you take a chance of erasing some of our lives together. When I was coming to find you yesterday I was so worried — what if somehow I found you before you met me? What if I erased all of our memories?"

She reached intae the handbag secured at her waist and pulled out a wee photo. "I brought this to show you in case you didn't remember who I was."

The photo was of us with a horse in the snow in Scotland. Twas the year 1702. We were both smiling.

"Why did ye pick this one?"

"Because I was worried you might not even remember Florida or me or our marriage or..."

I brushed some wayward hair from her cheek and tucked it behind her ear. "I canna imagine nae recognizin' ye. You are a part of me. When you appeared in the Great Hall, I felt ye before I saw ye. I said tae m'self, 'Kaitlyn is...' and afore I finished with 'here', there ye were."

"Can you imagine how awful it would be if we erased part of that? If you had gone to the past? What if we had lost our wedding night? Or when you were holding me in my hospital bed after we lost the baby?"

"Och, ye want tae keep that one?"

"Yes. I want that memory so much. You held me through our hearts' breaking. I wouldn't trade it for anything. It's the saddest moment of our lives and we love each other more because of it." She straightened the shirt across my shoulders while she spoke. "I wouldn't trade it." There was a considerable deal of sadness in her eyes, but twas in her voice I kent she meant it.

I took the photo from her. "Can I keep it?"

"Of course."

I unbuckled my sporran and placed the photo inside. "So ye think I tried hard enough?"

"Yes. You did everything possible to save me but you couldn't. But you didn't loop back and destroy all of our memories, instead you lived your whole life heartbroken over me. I hate the idea of you living on in a super-sad state, but also, dear Magnus, this is a win for me. I get you in a second lifetime, knowing there was a first lifetime where you loved me that much."

"I love ye even more."

A smile spread across her face, a mischievous glint in her eye. "I can't imagine that could possibly be true."

"Tis added tae everyday, with every movement."

She arched her brow. "Really? That's a lot of 'adding to'."

"See, just then, the little tilt tae yer head, the jest, the smile? It has doubled my love."

"Good lord, so easy? What happens to your love when I climb on your lap and—"

"Och," I tapped a heartbeat against my chest, and with m'hands I shewed her m'heart burstin'. "So much."

She smiled and twas all I ever wanted tae see. I tilted her chin, kissed her, and lifted her tae her horse. I mounted m'own again and we continued tae walk.

"What is your kingdom like?" She asked later, "I mean, the day to day, now you're the king, because the only thing I know so far seems completely barbaric."

"Och aye, it has been verra barbaric. Donnan was a brutal king. When I came tae power, I was told I couldna change his rules. I was told that challengin' the crown was how the king kept his power and it had always been that way. Did ye ken, Kaitlyn, the future kingdom was created by men from the past? I daena remember if I ever told ye that before."

"I think you did."

"Twas, my great-great-great-great-grandfather traveled tae the future tae gather weapons and an army then picked a year and invaded it. He overpowered them with weapons they had never seen. There was a terrible loss of life, over many lands. Tis why there are parts of the kingdom that are verra advanced and parts that seem verra auld. The kings ruled over machines and weapons they couldna understand and tis as if history stopped. For centuries there were nae new inventions, only theft from the past and the future and tryin' tae survive."

"So they didn't come up with anything new because they could just go steal it?"

"Aye." I steered my horse around a boulder and hers followed dutifully. "Lady Mairead winna go tae the future from my kingdom anymore. She said they have killed most of the world, stripped it of everythin', and now tis a brutal wasteland."

"God, that sucks."

"Aye, I have secured most of the vessels but I haena been able tae find them all and there are still sons of Donnan who want tae challenge me."

"You haven't been able to change that law?"

I shook m'head but tried tae smile because I dinna want tae scare her. "I have changed the law but they still insist on challengin' me. Tis hard tae ken how tae answer a challenge from a usurper. If I ignore him I look weak. If I kill him unfairly, I look barbaric. An arena battle is many times m'only resort. It tells the kingdom I will kill my challengers and the kingdom loves tae watch me do it." I drew a deep breath. "All I want is tae make the kingdom less brutal for Archie. I daena want him tae have tae fight."

"It sounds like you've had to deal with a lot."

I urged our horses forward and joked, "That bein' said, the kingdom has excellent ice cream, ye will like it verra much."

CHAPTER 4

A while later, we followed a gradual descent from the mountains through a pine forest and lower into a woods with many ash trees. Here it was a wet kind of cool compared to the dry breezy cold of the higher land.

My horse was walking behind his. "I did kind of screw up something."

"What?"

"Tyler, I mean Archie, wrote out a list for me: everything you knew after fighting the guy you're... What was his name?"

Magnus shifted in his saddle to look back at me, his brow drew together. "General Reyes."

"Archie made me a list for you. Maybe some of it would—"

His face grew dark. "I was still fightin' General Reyes after twenty-five years?"

I wished I could put my arms around him. "Yeah, but now you have more information, earlier, because Archie wrote it for you. The only problem is I didn't bring it. I left it in our safe in Florida."

"Och." He turned back to facing forward. He was quiet for a

moment then said, "Tis okay, Kaitlyn, we will go back for it somehow."

I chewed my lip. This was all so complicated, full of what ifs and other strands of time-ness, and not-really-but-still-totally-happened things. And what would we do to solve it? The fresh morning sky soared overhead lightening with the sunrise and the midges weren't out because of a gentle breeze. It was still a little chilly as we climbed higher into the hills.

He was quiet for longer. "I needs tae get Quentin as well."

"Really?"

"Aye. I have advisors in my kingdom, but they daena ken my mind as he does."

"Okay, we will go back and get the list and Quentin. Chef Zach will cook us dinner. And then we will vanquish your enemy."

He smiled over his shoulder. "Twill be easy now ye are here."

"Definitely. I'm nothing but skills. Look at me riding this horse like an expert."

He jokingly pulled my reins so my horse drew near his and leaned across from horse to horse and kissed me sweetly on the lips.

"You should have these." He passed the reins to me and gestured how to hold them.

"Are you sure?"

"She is gentle, mo reul-iuil. She winna do anythin' but follow mine, tis why I chose her."

A few moments later, Magnus turned to check me.

I grinned. "I'm doing it! Look, I'm doing it!"

He chuckled, "Aye, ye are doing it." He made a haw kind of noise and our horses moved faster; I squealed a little and held on.

CHAPTER 5

I was watching the stretch of linen across his shoulders as his arm held the reins and his back rocked with his horse's gait. I said, "That's a beautiful horse."

He stroked his horse's neck. "Aye, he's an each-cogaidh. I like him so much I travel with him now, tae my kingdom and here. He is always verra angry when we jump but soon forgives me on it."

"What does that mean — eck-cogade?"

"A war horse." He patted the stallion's neck proudly. "He is gentle, but in a fight he will bite the other horse. He verra much likes tae win."

"What's his name?"

"Guess. Twas named after somethin' we used tae hunt."

"Hunt? I don't hunt."

He smiled. "I named him Shark. Tis funny because he daena like the water much."

I laughed. "It's very funny especially if he's a biter."

We slowed; the path was steep, the terrain rocky and our horses were picking their own way.

He said, "Up ahead is a burn. We should stop and let the horses rest. Tis early yet, but we traveled verra far this day."

"What's a burn?"

"A stream."

"How can you tell?"

"See the falcon above us? He told me."

Sure enough there was a bird circling, but when Magnus pulled our horses to a stop, the stream was rushing, noisy rushing. There was only about three inches of water, but it was moving over the rocks at a fast clip. "You heard the stream. I have never known you to converse with birds."

He dismounted. "I haena shown ye? I speak tae birds all the time. The gulls in Florida are particularly good friends. I had them watchin' over ye while I was away."

I put my hands on his shoulders, swung my leg over, and dropped into his arms. It was all very sweet and romantic, but as soon as my feet hit the ground I was — "Ow, ow, ow, owie." I duck-waddled a few steps. Then wailed, "Owiiiiiieeeeeeeeee. My whole—" I gestured around my whole crotch area. "Is very very very ouchie."

Magnus chuckled. "The whole?"

I nodded and pretend-wailed again. "Owie-ouchie, plus I am so hot for you right now — the horseback riding... Is that a thing, to get turned on while horseback-riding?" I held my skirts out away from my thighs.

His smile spread under his bushy moustache and the crinkles under his eyes crinkled more. "Aye, mo reul-iuil, tis a thing."

"I mean, I guessed it was. Every time I ride with you I am so hot for you, but this time I was on a different horse, watching your back and your ass and your... but it's so ouchie!"

Magnus raised his brow and laughed. "I can be gentle."

I pouted. "I don't think you can be this gentle."

"Show me."

I pulled my skirts up in the front and Magnus stooped over to investigate my upper thighs. He gently turned my leg to see the inside skin.

He winced. "Aye, mo ghradh, tis especially 'owie.' Ye need thicker skin there."

"I don't want thicker skin there, I want soft delicate skin there." I tried to look past the bundle of skirts but I could only see a bit of red raw skin about halfway down. "Is it all raw?"

Magnus nodded solemnly. "Aye, ye needs tae go tae the burn."

"Why?"

"Tae dangle yer arse in the water."

I squinted my eyes. "Sounds cold."

"May be cold but twill cure your malady, m'lady."

He led the horses and me down the small rocky slope to the edge of the stream. The horses drank from the water while we took off our shoes. Mine were leather boots with laces. I stripped off my socks and tucked them inside. His were leather, tall and expensive looking, I guessed he had them made in the future to wear here in the past.

"Do I completely undress?"

"You daena need tae go swimmin'; the water isna deep enough. You just needs tae get yer arse submerged."

I stepped out onto the rocks along the edge.

"Careful, twill be slippery."

I put a toe in. "Cold! It's so cold!"

"Tis comin' from the snowy mountain."

My foot slipped a little and I squealed. "It's too cold!"

"Tis nae too cold, ye just have tae lift yer skirts and dip yer arse." He grinned and stepped into the water beside me and joked, "Tis cold! I am glad I daena have tae do it. I will help ye hold your skirts."

I stepped my other foot out on a wide flat rock with a couple of inches of water moving across it. My left foot slipped again, but I pressed it against the rock edge until I was stationary. I held my skirts, but my feet felt frozen. I puffed air. "I don't think I can do it."

"Ye can. Drop yer arse lower."

I shivered. My pale white feet were submerged in the ice water.

I talked to myself: "Why? Why are you letting him talk you into this, Kaitlyn? He's a freaking highlander. He takes his one bath a year in water this cold — by choice. When you met him all his showers were this cold, but you're a Florida girl. You like humid days and hot showers..." Talking took my mind off it. I dropped to one knee on the smooth rock. Water rushed around my calf. I puffed and puffed and dropped the second knee with a squeal.

Magnus laughed as he scooped up my skirts to keep them from getting wet. I settled my whole hips, ass, thighs, and crotch into the ice cold water. "Oh my god oh my god oh my god! Cold cold cold cold cold."

"Wriggle your hips."

I dutifully wiggled my hips while he chuckled. I crouched there for one more moment and jumped to my feet and leapt shivering and splashing to the shore. "Freezing!"

Magnus was practically guffawing. "Twas a breac splashin'!"

I dropped my skirts and put my hands on my hips. "A breac?"

Magnus wiggled a flat hand.

"A fish? Like a trout? Magnus, are you comparing my ass to a trout?"

He splashed back to the shore and swept me into his arms. "I missed ye."

"I missed you too. So much. And you were barely gone, but still."

"Let me build a fire and get our dinner."

CHAPTER 6

We cleared a space under a tree. It had a flat spot to sleep and a view of the trail in case someone was following us. I gathered sticks for a fire.

"Dost ye have a flame?"

"Yep." I dug in my pack and brought out a little wax envelope full of matches. Striking one on a stone, I quickly lit the kindling and adjusted sticks until we had a roaring little blaze.

"What's for food, Highlander? We've eaten all but one of the protein bars I brought."

"I have some bread and some dried meat." He dug through one of his packs and carried over a small burlap bundle and two thick wool blankets. "The night is growin' cool."

"I love sleeping outside with you, but this can't be night. It's still pretty bright out here in the wide open."

"Aye, tis latha fada, we have tae sleep in the long day and we daena have curtains tae close. I am sorry for the lack of a roof, when I married ye I promised ye one above your head."

I wrapped one of the blankets around my shoulders. "I do not remember that in our vows."

He grinned and tapped his heart.

"Well see, I heard your heart say you would be my shelter, so this is not a broken vow..."

Images flashed through my mind, Magnus on Bella, his hand holding hers. I pulled the blanket tighter around my shoulders and drew my head inside.

Magnus leaned his head on my shoulder. "What are ye seein'?"

"I don't want to tell you." Then I asked, "Do you have to see her? Do you talk to her?"

His voice was close to my ear, but the blankets between us muffled it. "Only in the beginning. We had tae talk of Archie, but even those conversations became too difficult. I had tae ask the courts tae intervene. Now we only speak through lawyers."

I peeled the blankets away to see his face beside mine. "How did it become difficult?"

"She was usin' Archie against me. Tae see me..."

I pulled my hand from inside my blankets to stroke his cheek. "I'm sorry you had to deal with that alone. When I decided it for you, I truly thought we would be doing it together."

"Me too, mo reul-iuil."

"So you have four years of your life I don't know about?"

His head nodded against my shoulder.

"You built a government? You have advisors and you did so much, a whole four years you lived without me. You figured so much out without me there to help."

He pulled away and opened the burlap bundle laying out the food in our laps: crusty bread, some dried meat. I picked up a piece of meat and tore into it with my teeth.

He said, "Twas nae really living. I was fighting and..." His voice trailed off. He bit into the meat first and then bit off a hunk of bread. With his mouth full he said, "Mostly fightin'."

He chewed and chewed then grinned. "Tis a tough dinner tonight, m'lady."

"And why are we going to... Where are we going again?"

"Kilchurn on the Loch Awe. Because I ken the location on the map and tis safe tae jump from there, but even more, I have always wanted tae shew it tae ye. Tis where I spent much of my time as a young lad. When I was with your grandparents in Maine, it reminded me of Kilchurn and I kent I needed tae take ye someday."

"Good, I'm excited to see it." I chewed some meat, a bite of bread, and took a long draft of water. "And so I'm not feeling left out and sad about all I missed, you have to tell me about everything."

"The whole history of it?"

"Everything, from day one: what you ate for breakfast."

"Och. I was in the hospital from day one. The fight against Samuel almost killed me. The food was terrible. I decided right then tae go tae Florida tae get Chef Zach."

"And me!"

He chuckled mischievously. "Aye, and ye too, but the food was verra bad. Twas the first time I tried tae reach home. I traveled tae the dock but General Reyes's men were waitin' for me. I barely escaped."

"I didn't see the storm on the weather. I was watching."

"I daena ken why, perhaps because it was so fast. I wasna on the ground for long, but I am glad ye dinna come tae the storm, ye would have been killed for sure."

"Like the first time."

"Aye, like the first time." Magnus shook his head slowly. He repeated, "I am glad ye dinna come." He chewed off another hunk of bread. "When I got home I had tae lead the army against the insurgents on the western border. That took some time."

"You were at war?"

"Aye, I commanded from the front. Twas necessary and I dinna have anywhere else tae go. After that year I tried tae get tae ye in Florida again. I took weapons with me. I had a plan, but again General Reyes was waitin'. I escaped, but he followed. Our battle at the walls of my castle killed many of my men. Some verra good soldiers. Twas where I learned of his name and that it would be verra difficult tae defeat him."

He leaned against the boulder and I snuggled under his arm. "He told me he kent whenever I arrived in Florida. I couldna tell if he had knowledge of the year or the place, so I was tryin' tae decide what tae do on it." His face relaxed. "Twas nae all bad though, I spent time with Archie. Last year he spent two full months with me. I am plannin' tae see him when I go back — when we go back."

"I'd really like that, I look forward to meeting him."

I tucked what was left of my dinner into the burlap bag and carried it to the horses and tucked it inside a saddlebag. I returned and sat facing Magnus leaned on one arm across his legs.

I put my other hand on his chest. "You told me you had 'many a wound' while you were gone. I was thinking you could introduce me to them."

"My wounds?"

"I plan to kiss each one to make them feel better. I didn't get to kiss you for four years so I'll do all of them now. Each day I'll do it again until, I don't know — maybe four years should be right."

He pointed at a scar across his left palm, between his thumb and forefinger. I took it in both of mine, spread it flat, and kissed the scar. "Where did this one come from?"

"My fight with Samuel."

He pushed the blanket back from his arms, pulled the neck of his shirt aside, and showed me a healing gash on the top of his shoulder. His point was off, because he couldn't see it, but I could: pinkish purple, raised, and long.

I ran a finger along it. "How?"

"Reyes's blade."

I leaned in and kissed.

He pulled up the front of his shirt exposing a wide straight scar on his abdomen. I brushed my fingertips along it. "Who did this?"

"Twas the blade of Samuel. It stabbed deep. There had tae be a surgery because of it."

I adjusted to kiss his lower abdomen beside the ridges of his muscles. He was so taut and solid and strong. I marveled he was also injured and harmed. As I brushed my lips across his skin, he was soft, delicate, and so vulnerable. Just a man. That's all he was but he had to endure so much pain.

There was an area there, rough skin, textured. I ran my tongue across it. "What's this one?"

"Twas a burn. There was an explosion near the front, I was burnt along here..." He twisted a little. "It goes up here." I saw it extended around his back, meeting his scars from the whipping years ago.

I kissed the scarred skin from the burn, a slow press that wanted to linger.

When I met his eyes, he gave me a small half-grin. "I have another one that needs kissin', tis under here." He gestured toward his kilt.

"Oh you do, do you? Well, it will wait for last. We would get distracted and I have all these others to kiss first."

Magnus pointed at a gash between his calf and shin. It looked like a hunk of him had gone missing. "That looks very painful."

"Twas. That happened when I was at the front, two-and-a-half years ago. It has only now healed."

I shimmied down and kissed him there.

I put my head on his knee and watched him while he checked his arms for one he might have forgotten. Then he smiled and it was so full of melancholy. He tapped his fingertips to the middle of his chest.

"What happened there?"

"Twas my heart, when I couldna come home."

I crawled up his body slowly and pulled the front of his shirt down and kissed the space of skin over his sternum, guarding his heart — plainly not guarding it well enough. I rose, crossed a leg over him, and sat gingerly on his lap. "I will kiss you on every scar, I promise, but I did really want to kiss you here."

He tilted his head back and I settled in on his mouth, kissing deeply. His hands clutched my bottom and pulled me close. "Does that hurt ye?"

My mouth on his I said, "Your sporran is lumpy."

He said, "Och," with a laugh.

I raised so he could unhook his sporran from around his waist. He tossed it to the side.

I teased as I settled back on his lap, "Now it's not lumpy—wait, yes it is."

"Tis much more majestic than lumpy."

"Och," I joked. "Tis majestic and pokey." I kissed his lip and nibbled it.

His hands clenched tighter on my arse. My lips drew down to his throat and then—

CHAPTER 7

*H*e smacked my butt. "Off Kaitlyn, behind me. Grab your knife. Guard the horses. Go!"

I stumbled off and dove behind him as he jumped up and crouched by the fire.

His voice low and dangerous, "Friend, I am telling ye tae turn around and walk away afore I make ye."

I dug frantically through my pack for one of my knives, finally finding it and clutching it pointing out at chest level. I grasped for the horse reins and held both, watching the trees. A small man, dirty and gross, stepped closer to the fire.

He didn't seem phased or worried at all about Magnus, crouched quietly, his back tensed, eyes leveled, a second away from springing. My hands shook with fear while I tried to be the kind of person who could guard horses.

Another man stepped from the woods on the other side of the fire.

I said, "Magnus."

"I see him, tis one more tae the left." He held his position but slightly shifted his weight. The hilt of his sword was at his finger-tips, but he wasn't threatening with it yet.

Fear settling in my stomach made me want to throw up — it was Magnus against three men. He raised his voice to speak to them all. "I see ye and am tellin' ye tae move along. I am nae in a mood tae share bread or warmth."

The man who entered our glade first sneered. "Tis nae the food or fire we are wantin' tae partake of."

The two men who had remained hidden stepped into the clearing. They were bigger, foul smelling, menacing and gross.

One leered at me and licked his lips.

Magnus remained calm and still. He said simply. "Tis my wife ye are speakin' on. Ye best move along, I have killed men for less than the words ye just uttered."

One of the bigger men laughed a laugh full of spite and malice. My eyes flitted from man to man, searching their faces, trying to decide what to do, how to help.

The man on the right edged toward me and the horses. Magnus said, "You daena want tae move again."

The man on the left moved a step closer. I held my knife higher and tried to look tougher than I felt.

Magnus swept up through the fire aiming a burning stick with a spray of sparks at the smaller man's face. Then he wheeled around and swung his blade toward the man on the right.

Fury filled me. I aimed my knife point at the other man. "Don't come near me, asshole." He took a step closer and another. The horses stamped and whinnied behind me, pulling at their reins.

Magnus spun around and charged the man who was looming over me, swinging left and down slicing almost through the man's arm.

Then rotating and slicing his side so that he crumpled to the ground.

A second man ran at Magnus and slammed his elbow into his side, but Magnus pivoted, threw his full weight on him, and forced him back. Magnus was enraged, bellowing. He swung his blade back and forth while the man cowered. Suddenly Magnus lunged and the man emitted a high and loud screeching sound.

I couldn't take it, any of it: Magnus's anger, the blood, the dead man, the screams.

I dropped to the ground still holding my knife facing out as if I was helping, nonononononoooo.

The last man begged for his life.

Magnus turned on him, his bloody sword held high. "I told ye tae leave." Every square inch of his flesh was holding in a bulging fury — like the Hulk about to smash some shit.

"Daena kill me."

"I told ye tae leave!" Magnus's face was red, wet, enraged.

I clamped my hands over my ears.

"No, please stop please." The man cowered and begged as Magnus thrust and stabbed him through.

Magnus kicked the writhing body from his blade and yelled at it, "I told ye tae leave, I told ye!"

I lurched to my feet, stumbled through the dirt, and pulled his arm back. "Stop. Stop Magnus, please don't."

Magnus looked at me like he couldn't see me. His breaths were ragged. His chest heaving. "I told him tae leave."

Tears streamed down my face, obscuring my vision. I stroked the sides of his face, his temples, smoothing folds of anger. His eyes clamped shut. I sobbed and tried to calm him, myself. "You did, you warned him and they kept coming."

"I warned him, I did, I told him." He opened his eyes and they were so full of pain.

He collapsed down to his knees in front of me and clutched my skirts. "I canna stop, Kaitlyn. I canna stop killin'." He pressed his face to me so hard, so rough, he almost knocked me to the ground.

I braced my feet and held on around his head and gripped his wide shoulders. They heaved with his breathing and it felt a lot like anguish.

"I canna stop, tis all I do. They come from every direction and I warn them. I tell them I canna let them live but they keep comin' and I canna do it anymore, Kaitlyn. I canna stop and I need ye mo reul-iuil. I need ye so much."

His hands bunched my skirts and pulled me closer pressing his face to me. "I need ye, every day. I dinna ken what tae do. I dinna ken how tae survive without ye and it tore me apart and I think I may be broken. I lost what made me who I am. I am nae longer the man ye love."

I clutched his head. "I love you, Magnus, I do. You're still the same man, I—"

"Nae," he wrapped his arms around me and held us together. "Nae. I canna be. When I meet a man, I decide how I will kill him. While I am smilin' at him, while I am charmin' him with my wit I am decidin' on it. I have a plan how I will kill him because everyone I meet wants tae kill me. I needed ye so much. I couldna get tae ye, tae ask ye for help."

I pulled his face up to look into his eyes.

"I'm here now. It's not too late."

He closed his eyes and moaned. "Tis, mo ghradh." A bead of sweat rolled down his face. "I needed ye so much. You heard Archie. He said I fought General Reyes for a quarter of a century, how can I bear it, mo reul-iuil? I have been fightin' four years and I am breakin'."

"Oh Magnus." I knelt in front of him and clasped his hands. "Have you been praying?"

He wouldn't meet my eyes.

"Why not?"

"God has turned his back on me."

I tried to look in his eyes to bring him back. "I'm so sorry. I'm sorry you were so alone. I wanted to come to you but I didn't know how."

"Tis nae your fault." He looked away.

"It's no one's fault, but I'm still so sorry I wasn't there." I steadied his face, looked in his eyes and spoke assurances. "But it will be okay. I have the list. We'll get it. It will show you how to fight him. You'll be able to end it once and for all."

He closed his eyes and pressed his cheek to my hand.

"Aye."

He sat back on his heels and looked down on his bloody hands. "Aye I can end it." He wiped the blood on his kilt. "I'll end it." He glanced into my eyes but quickly looked away. "I can. I will." He wiped his hands again. "I am sorry about this... Twas havin' ye back that caused me tae remember how I used tae feel when we were together. I had forgotten."

"What do you mean how you used to feel?"

"I was strong and at peace. I had hope."

I took a deep breath. "Now I'm back, you'll feel that again, you'll see..."

He winced. "I canna believe it, mo reul-iuil, when I feel this dark and hopeless inside." He clutched his chest.

"If I pray will you join me?" I asked.

He hung his head. "Nae. I am forsaken."

I chewed my lip as I closed my eyes, bowed my head, and decided to pray anyway. I knew it was his comfort. I also knew of everything he said, his inability to pray scared me most of all. It was a part of him, what he did. If he hadn't been praying, then he had been shaken to his core.

I began with "Dear God," not much more than a whisper. I asked for his infinite wisdom to guide Magnus and me as we rebuilt our life together and as we fought the darkness growing in my husband's heart. As I asked for guidance Magnus's voice joined mine.

I peeked. His eyes were clamped tight, his face wearing a mask of pain.

He begged forgiveness for the deaths he had caused and for not praying.

I clutched his hands between us on our knees.

And I quieted.

And I listened.

And I cried.

The actions he needed forgiveness for were many.

Hearing them was a burden that weighed on my heart. He had become a warrior and it was all that was expected of him. The one identity he had never really wanted. He had been born to make war but had grown to love peace. I had fallen for his easy humor and his kindness and the grace that filled his life.

I had chosen for him to become a king but then wasn't there when his kingdom demanded he fight and fight and fight.

Finally his breathing calmed, his words slowed.

His head bowed—

I pressed my head to his shoulder.

Do you feel better?

Aye.

If you could tell me the one moment, the moment you needed me the most, I could go to you then. I would.

I pressed my forehead to his beard and stroked across his shirt linen across the planes of his chest, around his shoulder, and down his arm.

I needed ye when I was bein' treated in the hospital. The day after I fought Samuel.

From the first day?

The very first day.

Okay, my love, that's what I'll do.

Magnus wiped the tears from my cheeks with his thumbs. He kissed me and I rose and hugged his head to my chest. "I love you."

"I love ye too, mo reul-iuil." His voice came from near my heart.

I held him for a moment more then said, "So I will go, but there are things we have to deal with here."

"Och aye, we needs tae get some distance from this battlefield."

We gathered our things, packed the bags, loaded the horses, kicked sand on the fire, and left our glade to head further west while the sun continued to shine.

CHAPTER 8

*W*e rode for another three hours. My thighs had gone past raw to numb which was good. It had finally grown dark, but we kept walking in the moonlight. I must have eventually fallen asleep because when I heard Magnus's voice, "Kaitlyn, we are stopping for the night," I had to struggle to open my bleary eyes. Magnus had his arms out for me.

Then while I stood to the side wrapped in a blanket yawning and barely staying awake, Magnus tied the horses to the closest branch. He wrapped in another blanket, sat leaned against a tree, and held out his arm for me.

I tucked my head to his chest, and wrapped my fingertips in his beard. His strong arms wrapped around me and the sounds of the wind rustling the trees, the nearby stream rushing down from the mountaintop, and the insects with their vibrating hums, all lulled me to sleep.

The next morning I woke slowly: comfortable, warm, wrapped in

Magnus's arms. Slowly I tilted my head back and he dropped his head forward and we kissed — the best way to wake. I tucked my head back under his chin, not wanting to speak until my mouth was well away from his nose — morning breath and all.

Magnus ran his hand down the back of my head, still wrapped in the warm woolen blanket. "I have been thinkin' about it, mo reul-iuil, and I am worried about ye goin' back. I was in the hospital and there was a long and complicated transfer of power. I daena ken if I will be able tae protect ye—"

"Do you have someone there you trust?"

He looked off into space. "I have one man, Hammie—"

"Hammie?"

"Tis short for Hammond Donahoe. He stationed men about the castle during the transition from Samuel's government tae mine. He has since fought alongside me many times. I trust him, but when I was there after my surgery I haena met him yet."

"Does he know about the vessels?"

"Aye, he does."

"Then tell me something only you can know about him, and I'll tell him you said he needs to protect me."

"Aye. Let me think..." Magnus stared off in the direction of a group of trees and squinted, thinking. "He greatly admired a singer by the name of Shona; she is verra famous. You could tell him I said tae protect ye and in return I will introduce him tae her. She often came tae the castle and he would get verra excited around her."

I twirled the bottom edge of his beard.

"What will happen to you?"

"I daena ken..."

"You are here, alive, I don't think I can bear leaving you if it means..."

His big strong hand held my head, his thumb brushed my cheek. "Twill be okay, twill be a relief, Kaitlyn."

"Oh." I nestled into his arms. "It will be so hard to leave."

"I ken it will, mo reul-iuil." He kissed my forehead and next thing we were rising, brushing ourselves off, folding the blankets and packing them away. We shared the last protein bar and Magnus finished his breakfast with some hard bread and dried meat.

CHAPTER 9

*B*efore we descended toward Loch Awe, I took a bathroom break and then Magnus had me join him on his horse. His arms around me, he began to talk of the landscape, the undulating hills and craggy peaks, using ancient sounding words like beinn and creag, uaine meaning green, and ghorm for the blue sky. The sky *was* ghorm and endless and high, with puffy clouds speckling it, or as Magnus told me to call it, bhreac.

We talked about the weather, our horse traveling slowly on a path through the hills.

His voice rumbled as he told me what he saw — the entire landscape reminded him of being young, happy, playing with Sean through the hills. The path turned and ahead of us the loch glistened in the sun. With barely a breeze it reflected the sky. A brighter blue below, sky in the water. Surrounding it a green, so vivid it seemed unreal. The castle seemed not to rest on the land, but to float within the loch, taking up most of a far point on an island out in the water.

The surrounding land was green and lush and was

connected with a low causeway to the shore. The castle was a tall five-story tower surrounded with fortified walls. It looked magical, fairytale-like. "It's beautiful... this is your childhood home?"

"Aye, though we spent a lot of time at Balloch, tis Kilchurn I am most fond of. Tis the highlands, mo ghradh, my Scottish home."

"I've never seen any place this gorgeous. It's vivid, like it was painted by an artist. It's beautiful."

Magnus said, "Aye. Twas painted by God." Our wide and worn trail led to the shore. Magnus brought the horses to a slower pace. "I had many adventures climbin' the hills here. Sean and I would climb tae the top and yell, 'Cruachan!' and run and roll down the slopes."

"What is Crewakan?"

He pointed at one of the peaks. "That majestic beinn is named Cruach na Beinne or ye might call it Beinn Cruachan. We Campbells believe tis formidable, so we have made it our war cry."

"So little Magnus was yelling a Campbell war cry while playing with his brother on the hills here?"

"Aye."

"I'm really glad you're showing this to me."

We approached the long, low, thin path that stretched across the water to the castle. Men on horseback were coming and going along the causeway. We headed in the direction of the stables.

Magnus stabled our horses speaking first to a few of the men tending them. He unlatched our bags, slung them over his shoulder and carrying the bundle of blankets under his arm led me from the stables along a path and through the main gate to the walled courtyard. There he spoke with the guards for a few moments before we were allowed to pass through.

The castle was very different from Balloch, older, more

fortress-like. I spun to take in the towers and the main building that loomed at the far end. "It's so medieval looking."

"Twas built a verra long time ago, even for me."

"I want to see your room, where did you sleep?"

"Everythin' is older, m'uncle made improvements afore I was born, but I can show ye the rooms." Magnus deposited our things under a low roof along the wall and led me through the main door.

He led me down long halls and up a staircase. We had to press against the stone so some men could descend. He showed me through large doors on the second floor, the Great Hall, cold, big, and impressive. A wooden table stretched the length of it. There were long benches instead of chairs. This seemed the kind of place where people drank mead, clutched turkey legs in their fists, and said things like Argh, or Och. People like my husband I supposed.

Then we climbed another two floors and down a small corridor to a room with rugs and some very small wooden beds. "Tis the room where the bairn would sleep. We were only here in the summer with Uncle Baldie. Twas his favorite place from his own childhood. He has never cared much for Balloch."

He ducked inside and crossed to the window, not much more than a sliver, open to the weather. "See there? We have a clear view of Beinn Cruachan. I dreamed a lot about what adventures lay beyond that beinn."

"If you only knew Florida awaited you, huh?"

"If I only kent ye were waitin' for me on an island in the New World — twould have truly been a marvel tae the young Magnus."

He turned from the window. "Let me take ye up tae show ye the view."

We climbed two more flights of stairs and stood on the rooftop, the breeze pulling my skirts behind me, pushing my hair from my face. The sun was warm on our skin. "Point me to north."

He turned my shoulder so I was facing due north. I marveled at the mountain range.

"East." We both turned to take in the pass between the hills we had traveled through a couple of hours before. "That's where we came from?"

"Aye, mo ghradh."

"South." We turned to look south.

Magnus pointed. "Verra far off there is the home of Kaitlyn Campbell, wife of Magnus Campbell, on the shores of the Atlantic Ocean in the year two naught seventeen."

"Your home too."

"Aye, tis. I hope ye will help me get back there."

"I'll do everything I can."

We turned to take in the west. "What's this way?"

"Your grandparents' house, with the lake and the dock and if we think on it, tis only one ocean and a wee bit of land separatin' that dock from this dock here." He pointed at a dock below. "Tis almost as if we could sail from the one tae the other."

"I like thinking of it that way. And we need to put a toe in the water. You can't visit a shore without getting your feet wet."

Magnus led me down the five flights of dark stone stairs and across the dusty courtyard through the guarded gate and around the high walls to a simple wooden dock jutting into Loch Awe.

We had the dock to ourselves, though there were boats sprinkled across the loch's surface, and men fishing in the glorious weather.

I stripped my boots off and then my woolen socks and stuffed them inside.

Magnus took off his leather boots and placed them beside mine.

I got close to the edge, clutched his arm, and knelt to dip my toes in. "Cold! So cold!"

Magnus grinned and dropped beside me and dangled his feet in the water. "When we would go fishin', tae ensure we would catch a great haul of fish, we had a tradition tae throw someone in the water. Twas the spring when I was eight-years-auld and I dinna ken twas my turn. Uncle Baldie and some other men crept up behind, picked me up, and tossed me over."

My eyes were wide. "It must have been freezing!"

He laughed, "Aye, twas nae warm like this."

"What did you do?"

"I tried tae breathe until they pulled me from the loch and then I tried tae laugh so they would think I had the strength tae bear it. Then I tried nae tae shiver in my wet clothes. Twas a difficult day and I was feelin' verra ill-used until Baldie came tae fish beside me and said tae me, low, so only I could hear, 'Last year we sent Malcolm over the side and he carried on like a bairn for the rest of the day. I am proud of ye, Young Magnus.' After that twas a verra good day."

"That does sound like a good day."

We both lost our thoughts to the sparkling surface of the freezing cold water. I said, "When I was a kid I swore that I would always jump into the lake first thing without thinking about it, but here I am breaking that rule, cannon-balling into this ice water is out of the question."

"Aye, also the men of the castle would be aghast at your brazenness. I haena got it in me tae fight them all."

I nudged against his shoulder and dropped my head there. "I don't want you to have to fight over things like that. Not anymore."

"Nae anymore, mo ghradh." He kissed the top of my head.

I swung my feet back-and-forth splashing water-sprinkles on our clothes.

"I know I said it before but this is all really beautiful and I can imagine a little Magnus running on the hills here, chasing Sean, splashing through the freezing water—"

"Fishin'."

I nodded. "Fishing." I added with a smile, "For trout."

He grinned. "Your arse is all better now, m'lady?"

"Much." He put his hand on mine and we entwined our fingers and both looked out over the wide, gently glistening loch.

"I wish I could stay here with you. We could live here in this castle..."

Magnus said, "Let your eyes follow the loch as far as ye can see, farther still is a small house on a lake in Maine in a new world called America. We should live there: Magnus, Kaitlyn, and our bairn."

"I would like that. I would really like that a lot."

"Tell me when ye get tae my hospital bed. Tell me tis what we should do and I will make it happen. I promise ye, I will."

Tears spilled from my eyes and rolled down my cheeks. I ducked my head to his shoulder and held his bushy, bearded jaw and brought his lips to mine and kissed him with tear-glistened skin and wet lips.

"I could stay. You think this is past your control, but we can—"

His cheek was close to my lips, his breath on my skin. "Nae, I ken this is the right decision."

"Do you want me to spend the night? We could make love one last..."

He ran his fingers through a tendril of hair hanging by my face, then brushed his fingers down my cheek, concentrating on the places where my skin met his. "I fear, mo reul-iuil, it might break me completely tae say goodbye after... I couldna bear it."

He kissed me then pulled away. "Twould be easier tae do it now than later..."

I enclosed his hand in both of mine and brought it to my lips and kissed it. I watched his face while he stared out over the lake.

After a long time he asked, "Where do ye think I will go?"

"I don't know." My face was covered in tears. "But you deserve the best place, wherever it is."

He pulled his hand from mine and stood. "We should go. The weather is goin' tae turn and..."

I dried my feet on the bottom of my skirts. Then Magnus and I both held onto each other for balance while we pulled on our boots.

CHAPTER 10

$\mathcal{W}$e walked quietly down the dock to the castle following the path around the walls and passed through the gate to get my bag. Then we walked along the causeway, warm in the sun. I had been overusing the word beautiful today, but it all was, like being immersed in a movie — full of extra special effects, vivid colors, and more details. Even the sounds were lovely: water lapping, grass rustling, bugs and birds. My breathing was louder but nature put up a good fight for dominance. And the smells: the Scottish breeze rolling across the land mingling with loch and castle and stable and as we ascended to a grassy hilltop, the smell of the upper levels of air, clear and crisp and cool. A cloud crossed in front of the sun and when the cloud danced away the warm sun baked the air around us the smell warm and friendly.

My hand in Magnus's, protected and loved. I really didn't want to go. I didn't know how I was going to leave him.

The more we walked the more tears rolled down my cheeks, until I was a blithering, sobbing, wet mess.

We came to a small crest on one of the lower hills with a

stand of trees blocking us from the view of the castle. Magnus pulled to a stop. "I should put your knives on ye." He pulled two knives from my backpack. I raised my skirts and he strapped one to my upper thigh and the other to my waist. He paused for a moment with his hands on my hips and then shook out of it and dug through the bag some more.

I said, "I'll leave my bag for you, there's not much. Some matches. We ate all the food, I'm sorry."

"Ye daena need tae be sorry."

"You always say that."

He smiled sadly. "Tis always true."

"Not always, like now, this here — this is awful. I can't leave you."

He brushed hair from my cheek and tucked it behind my ear. "You can, ye must. I need ye so much, mo reul-iuil. I ken tis hard but I need ye."

I sobbed and nodded. "Okay. I know. I love you though, so much. I would never leave you if I didn't have to."

"I ken how much ye love me, because ye are willin' tae leave me tae save me." He dropped his forehead to mine. "I thank ye for it."

"What if I can't save you? What if I can't stop all the fighting or the bloodshed or the danger? What if it's all the same?"

"It might be, but ye will be with me through it."

I nodded and sniffled and leaned forward pressing my forehead into his beard against his chest. "I love you so much this hurts."

"Aye." His arms held around me, pulling me close to his chest. "Aye," he said it again.

He added, whispering into my hair, "You have given me a gift with your life Kaitlyn, and I am so grateful for it."

I pulled my arms in and let him really hold me, protective and strong. I said, my voice small and weak, "I'm grateful for your life too." I cried in his arms for a very long time while we clung to each other on a hillside in Scotland, the shores of his childhood home, in the way, way long ago past, just before I left him, in this time, forever.

Finally I pulled away and brushed my hair from my face. "I need a napkin." Then, "What the hell, it's a mess, anyway." I pulled my skirts up and blew my nose and wiped my face on the inside. It smelled like horse and sadness and the dirt of centuries.

I dropped the hem, straightened my skirts, and smoothed them as if somehow I could become presentable though I was a splotchy, swollen, filthy, broken-hearted mess.

Magnus dug the two vessels we owned out of his sporran and handed them both to me.

"You won't keep one, just in case?"

"Nae. I daena want tae use it."

"Okay, yeah, that makes sense."

He told me the numbers to add, the order, to include this castle and his castle in the future. I repeated them back to him twice, to make sure I had them all. Then he said, "The castle will be in turmoil. There are factions loyal to Samuel who fought against my ascension, I daena think ye should trust anyone but Hammond Donahoe. Demand tae see him and convince him tae keep ye safe and bring ye tae me."

"Okay. I will. Is there anything else you need, that you needed to know, that I can tell you?"

"Tell me I need Quentin."

"But we can't go to Florida?"

"Aye, General Reyes will be there, but tell me tae figure it out. Tell me tae get Quentin and Tyler's list and tae figure out how tae defeat General Reyes."

I nodded.

"And tell me ye love me again."

I brushed my fingers down the side of his cheek, the length of his beard. "I do, I love you so much. I don't think in the history of the world there is anyone that has loved someone as much as I love you."

He shook his head. "Tell me when ye see me. I will be needin' tae hear it."

Then he said, "I will go sit over there while ye jump."

Tears welled up again and speaking was impossible.

He kissed my hairline and turned, scooping my pack up and walking about ten yards away. It hurt to watch him with his back turned, his footsteps carrying him farther, and farther still.

Instead I looked at the vessel. I twisted the ends of it and brought it humming to life.

I burst into tears, more tears, streaming down my face. I looked across the hillside at Magnus. "I can't leave you. Don't make me."

Magnus's voice carried across the Scottish hills, "I canna live without ye, mo reul-iuil. Please go tae me."

I sobbed and said I love you one last time.

I clutched the vessel to my chest and kept my eyes locked on his across the way, standing still and solid like the mountain he grew up beside. I turned the dial and said the numbers. The storm grew above me as the wind rose around me and the force of the jump slammed into me and tore me through time.

CHAPTER 11

*J*was yanked to standing between four men. There was one security floodlight on the high rooftop, but my eyes were blinded. It's how I figured I had arrived at the castle, because other than that I was simply raw nerves and fear.

Behind me an explosion blasted so loud I had to clap my hands to my ears. All the sounds were deafeningly loud. Someone shoved me from behind causing me to stumble and bang my knee. I was pulled to my feet and forced to walk.

I mumbled, "Hammond Donahoe..." My head felt wobbly on my neck, it was hard to see, and my ears were buzzing from the noise.

"Where are you taking me?" My voice wasn't much more than a whimper. "Where?" My head lolled forward as they unceremoniously grabbed me by the underarms and dragged me down the hall. "Hammond Donahoe?" I managed to say again.

At the end of a long hall a door opened. I decided to struggle, but the soldiers overpowered and shoved me in. The door slid shut and I was alone.

The room was small and bare. A bed stood to one side, exactly like the room Donnan imprisoned me in. I recoiled to the door and banged, three weak bangs. "I need to speak to Hammond, *please.*"

An outside explosion rattled the windows of my room. Through the door I heard footsteps run down the halls, more footsteps ran the other direction. I needed to lie down. Loud gunfire emitted from the ground outside. I ran to the window to see.

I was about eight stories above the dark landscape, but there was a fire on the horizon and to the left three vehicles raced along a road. Footsteps pounded by my room again.

I went back to the door and banged. "Someone! Anyone! I need to see Hammond Donahoe!" I pressed my ear to the door. The hallway sounded empty. "Anyone?"

I stumbled to the bed and collapsed on it. I didn't want to touch it — who knew what kind of berserker things had happened here? I wasn't going to sleep; I had too much to do, but I couldn't stand anymore.

I woke to another loud explosion. Furious with myself for falling asleep, I crept into the bathroom and yanked open every drawer and cabinet looking for something, anything, a weapon, some food, some freaking clean clothes. It was wishful thinking though, everything was bare.

I drank water from the faucet. My hands were really disgusting and there wasn't any soap.

When my eyes looked at my reflection in the mirror a

memory flashed: punching the mirror, collecting a shard, murdering the king. His naked shoulder against my mouth, bucking as he died.

I was imprisoned again.

I didn't know for sure if they realized who I was or if they threw me in jail to deal with me later. I only knew my position was precarious. If Lady Mairead learned I was here, she would come and I would have to deal with her without Magnus to protect me.

Gunfire rang out nearby, glass shattered from one of the floors above. I peeked out the bathroom, raced across the room, sank to the floor beside the bed, and curled into a ball. I covered my ears, waiting for someone to remember I was here.

A small panel slid open within my door and a plate of food was unceremoniously thrust into my hands. "Please tell Hammond Donahoe I'm here, please, Hammond Donahoe!" I yelled as the door slid shut. Footsteps ran away down the hall. It would be nice if they were running to go tell him, but it seemed much more likely they were running to or from a battle. More gunfire from the end of the hall. Great, whatever was going on had breached the building.

There was a possibility this room was actually the safest place for me right now.

But that was also cold comfort.

Like the food: cold, leathery meat and bread with a small smear of butter. A paper cup for water from the tap, finally.

I slept some more and tried to conjure a plan beyond: lay here and wait for Hammond to stumble on me... And where was Magnus? The hospital. *Was he safe?* He survived this once already, but hadn't my arrival given it all a new trajectory?

What if he died?

What if this was one of those looping-back-on-yourself-makes-shit-go-screwy kind of things?

And was the Magnus in the past gone now? Had I killed him by leaving him?

And it was all a moot point: someone had confiscated my vessels. I couldn't go back now.

Hours passed. It sounded like the battles outside were escalating. There were drones and helicopters buzzing all around. The noise was deafening.

My door slid open. A thin man entered looking harried and confused. His uniform looked important because it was covered in medals.

"Are you Hammond?"

"I am not. I am Lewis, First Lieutenant. Explain to me where you got the vessels?"

"I was given them. Whose side are you on, Magnus's side? I don't know so I'm not talking to you."

"I'm on the side of the crown."

I folded my arms across my chest to look firm. "I'm still not talking to you. I want to talk to Hammond Donahoe."

"Understand this, Kaitlyn Campbell, you won't be the one making demands. You are under arrest for the murder of King Donnan the second."

Crap. He knew my name.

I reminded myself: *don't talk about Magnus, don't talk to*

anyone. "I'm not making demands. I'm simply stating I won't speak to anyone but Hammond Donahoe. If he comes, I'll tell him how I got the vessels. I won't tell anyone else."

I tried to glare straight ahead. I got the distinct impression he wanted to punch me. I tried to ready myself as I continued to glare.

Finally he said, "Suit yourself. The castle is going to fall anyway, and Magnus won't survive the night. You'll have no king to protect you. Hell, we don't even have to feed you." He turned for the door.

"What do you mean Magnus won't—?"

The door slid closed behind him.

Magnus wouldn't survive the night.

I banged on the door. "Let me out! I need to talk to Hammond!" I tried to control my breaths. I banged again and yelled more. And banged more. Then I yelled even more.

CHAPTER 12

A helicopter flew very close to the window; the glass vibrated. I dropped to my knees and huddled there. What if that sonic window blast thing happened again?

The door opened.

A man, big, a little like a football player who had gone soft from his athletic youth, barged in. He was wearing a soldier uniform in a dark gray camouflage-pattern with gold accents. His left chest was covered in medals. He crossed the room, yanked the shade on the window aside, looked out, then let the shade drop back.

"I'm Hammond Donahoe. You have two minutes." His hair and short beard were red, his cheeks round like he might laugh, sometimes, but he had that pale skin tone that flushed red when angry and right now he looked furious.

He hadn't really looked at me and I was relieved at that. I wished I had figured out some way to put on better clothes. I needed to make a case that I was worth saving while my life and Magnus's life hung in the balance.

"I'm Kaitlyn Campbell, I was sent here by Magnus. I mean, you know about the vessels right — the time travel machines?"

"I do."

The fact he was listening made me gather my wits to make a better case. "Good, so Magnus sent me. I was with him four years in the future. He was the king at the time, and he told me to come here to this time. I need to see him in the hospital. He wants me to."

Hammond's expression was skeptical. "I'm supposed to believe this story?"

"He told me to ask for you, to tell you that you helped protect the throne for him. He said you're good friends and he trusts you." He looked even more skeptical.

I added, "He gave me the vessels."

"I haven't met Magnus," he glanced at his watch, "and from the looks of it he won't make it until morning."

"But he does, he makes it, and you help him and he calls you Hammie."

His mouth twisted — that meant something. "He also said you like a female singer — I can't remember her name — but he said if you'll help me he promises to introduce you to her."

He leveled his eyes on me. "If you left Magnus in the future why are you dressed like a medieval peasant?"

I glanced down. "It was four years in the future but actually in the past — look this is not the important thing. The important thing is I'm Magnus's wife and I need to see him..."

"I know who you are." He glanced at his watch again. "The kingdom is in total chaos, the throne is for grabs, Magnus won't make it to morning, and you, Kaitlyn Campbell, are a murderer. I saw you the night of the Gala. I was in the ballroom. You can't deny you did it. I don't know what will happen with Magnus, or the kingdom, but I know this: for months I have been under orders to have you arrested on sight. Why would I take your side against direct orders?"

I racked my brain and could only come up with one reason. "Because the orders came from a dead man? Magnus is the next king, I promise you he wants to see me..."

He stood firm, his boots wide, his back straight like he was at attention. "I have a crisis to manage and a lot of bullshit stuff to accomplish that I have no instructions for — this is one of them. I have a new king who arrived without you. You arrive while he's in the hospital and want to be taken to him but I've already known you to murder a king. I have no way of knowing your motives. How do I guarantee his safety? I can't."

I opened and closed my mouth while he walked to the door.

"You'll stay here until Magnus wakes and tells me to bring you to him."

His hand was on the door. "Please? I promise he'll repay you for doing it."

"He can repay me for keeping you alive, here and safe, while he's in recovery."

I got on my knees, folded my hands together and pleaded, "Please Hammond. He told me he needed me in the hospital. He sent me to be with him. I know you don't know me, you haven't met him, but we are fiercely loyal to our friends and we will both be forever in your debt..."

"I'll take you to him as soon as he wakes. It's all I can do."

I huffed, stood, and brushed off my skirts. "Fine. I understand. When he wakes though, when you tell him I'm here, you make sure you tell him I begged you to let me see him."

He turned to leave.

"And please don't let Lady Mairead learn I'm here. I need guards outside the door. If she knows I'm here, she'll kill me."

His face clouded over. "Lady Mairead is a threat to you?"

"God yes. Just keep it quiet please, and I need guards, that's all I—"

He stared at me as if thinking it over. "Why does she want you dead?"

"I don't know why. Maybe because she can't control him—"

"I was under the impression Lady Mairead completely controls Magnus." He spoke like he was carefully judging everything I said, turning it over.

"She tries to but she can't. She sees me as a threat so she would prefer me dead."

He scowled.

I asked, "Shit, are you friends? Please don't tell her I said any of this."

"I won't say anything and we aren't friends. She used to ask me to do things for her. Things that would have been treasonous. She doesn't ask me anymore. " He sort of laughed.

"Well yeah, she is a total bitch. Magnus told me never to trust her in anything and we don't. Not really. I mean, she can be useful. She has helped Magnus stay alive for a long time, but I promise you, if you are loyal to Magnus he will protect you from her. He would want you to protect me too."

He looked at me long. "And how would she feel if I take you to Magnus's hospital room?"

"She would hate it."

"Okay. Do you have all your things?"

I spun and realized I had nothing. "I'm ready when you are."

I followed Hammond Donahoe out to the hall.

CHAPTER 13

With the nod of his head two men fell in beside me and I was led down a very long passageway to an elevator and taken up three floors. There was an explosion and for a short terrifying moment the electricity flashed off and on and then off again and the elevator lurched. When the lights sputtered back on, I was blinded momentarily. My eyes watered. Hammond's face remained calm and cool.

I, on the other hand, was about to totally freak out.

The door slid open. We stepped into another hall. The lighting was 'hospital at night' style, small lights along one wall, the other wall projected a video of a battle: soldiers shooting, helicopters, soldiers racing over rubble in an alley, tanks rolling along an empty city street. Was this today? Right now? It was all filmed with a shaky aerial camera and loomed very very large. If I looked at it my head hurt, but at least the sound was off.

A startlingly loud amplified voice asked, "Can I help you?"

"I'm Colonel Donahoe, I'm escorting Kaitlyn Campbell, the king's wife, to his room."

We stopped at a wide ornate door. Two men were guarding

it. From further down the hall a man headed toward us wearing what looked like surgical scrubs.

I asked Hammond, "Is there anything I should know about, the fighting, that I need to tell him? Samuel's forces are fighting against him? Will we win?"

"Why don't you tell me, Kaitlyn from the future?"

"I've got nothing."

"So don't say anything, if he wakes I'll brief him."

The doctor reached us. His face was pinched, tired, and irritated. "I'm the Royal Physician, John Abercrombie, at your service." His expression was distasteful as if he didn't want to be of service to me.

Hammond said, "Kaitlyn Campbell is to be taken to the king."

"He isn't in any condition for visitors — I sent his mistress away just a few hours ago."

My fury rose. *Breathe Kaitlyn, just breathe. Get to Magnus, he needs you.*

Hammond said, "She is not solely a visitor. She needs to be protected during this interregnum and I don't have the manpower to protect both royal personages. She will be staying here with King Magnus so we can concentrate our guards in one place." He checked his watch for the fiftieth time. "I will come to see to her in the morning. When will the king wake?"

"He's likely to sleep for many more hours. Are you sure this is..."

"Yes, definitely, Kaitlyn is wanted at the king's bedside." He added, "Notify me as soon as he wakes. I need to brief him on the current situation."

He moved to leave and remembered to say, "And Doctor Abercrombie, the king isn't to have any other visitors while Kaitlyn is with him."

The doctor said, "Of course."

Hammond said, "Queen Kaitlyn, it was interesting meeting you." He left down the long hallway. The doctor's gaze traveled over my attire. "You can't attend the king in those clothes..."

"I completely agree."

He huffed. "Follow me."

I wanted to go into the room to see Magnus so badly. I was only feet away, but I also had to be covered in bacteria from the freaking 18th century. I needed to protect him from germs. I had just now used the first toilet paper I had seen in at least four days.

So I followed the doctor past the doors. I couldn't tell where exactly I was — in a hospital, was I still inside the castle? So far in my travels to this kingdom I had been on the helicopter pad, dragged through hallways, chased around the grounds, and trapped in Donnan's prison rooms. I wasn't at all a fan of this place. It was very hard to believe it would be my home. *If Magnus survived.*

The doctor jerked his head toward a door. "There's a bathroom with a shower. I'll have someone deliver something clean for you to wear."

I pushed open the door onto a large bathroom. Everything was there I needed: water, shower, soap. I turned on the shower but had to figure out how to unlace my bodice in a hurry. I pulled at any lace I could get my fingers in contact with, then wriggled and squirmed and twisted, and just about threw my back out doing contortions to get it open enough to pull painfully up and off my body. I tossed it to the ground as someone tapped on the door.

"Yes?"

A woman's voice said, "I have some clean clothes for you, Mrs Campbell."

I stuck my head out to receive a small stack of brown clothes, baby poop brown clothes. I tried for a nice, charming smile but the nurse didn't seem impressed.

I ducked back into the bathroom and checked the mirror. Yep, since the struggle with the bodice I was even more insane looking. My hair stuck up all over. Something was smeared on my cheek. Talk about first impressions — *Hi, I'm the king's wife. Also a murderer.*

I tossed the pile of clothes to the counter by the sink, pulled my shift off, and stepped into the warm water. Thank god. There was nothing better than a shower after a trip to medieval Scotland. There were bottles of shampoo and conditioner, also a bottle of shower gel. I lathered every square inch of my body, rinsed it, and then lathered it all again.

When I felt sufficiently clean, I wrapped in a towel and tried to figure out the clothes. They were made of a thin, silky material, but incredibly plain, like surgical scrubs. The shirt was tunic-style colored brown. The pants were pajama-style, tied at the waist, also in brown. Not particularly how I wanted to see my husband for the first time in centuries, but seriously, this was plenty of time wasted already.

I needed to see him, *now.*

I rubbed the towel all over my hair trying to dry it. It wouldn't. Crap. I blew my hair dry for a few seconds to take the drippiness off then declared myself officially done. I kicked all my gross clothes, boots, socks, and towels into a pile in a corner and didn't give a shit if I ever saw them again. I crept barefoot down the hall.

There was no one else except the two guards in front of Magnus's door. I had no idea what time it was, but it seemed like the middle of the night.

Gunfire sounded outside and a helicopter swept past the building.

At the double doors the guards wordlessly allowed me to pass into Magnus's room.

The room was darkened, a few over-bright lights along the

side. A machine near him, making the comforting beeping sound of ICU rooms: this patient is breathing, this patient's heart is beating.

Magnus.

His face was drawn. He was asleep flat on his back. A bag of fluids dripped into his arm.

I crept to the bed. "Magnus?"

There was no answer or shift, just silent solid Magnus. I placed my hand carefully under his and waited.

I folded my hand around his. "Hi," I whispered. I pushed a lock of hair from his forehead, his skin too cool, his eyes closed, eyelashes down, an etched grove by his mouth, a sadness to his face. I brushed my fingers down his cheek and added, "It's me, Kaitlyn," in case he could hear me and needed to know.

Tears spilled over my lower lids and streamed down my face. I pulled his fingers to my lips and breathed him in. His smell now mingled with antiseptic and strangers. "I love you. You asked me to come and I'm here now, so you're going to be okay." The machine went beep, beep, beep. A drone flew by the window.

"I promise." I wrapped around his hand and rested my head on his shoulder and sobbed into his blanket. "I promise. I'll do everything in my power to keep you safe."

I needed to be closer, had to be closer. I climbed onto the bed. It was wide enough if I lay on my side on the edge. I curled along his left arm, being careful to slide under the IV tubing attached there, and knowing the stab wound, the reason for the surgery, was on his right side: low, deep, and life-threatening. I pressed my face to his shoulder. "I'm here now and we're going to get through this together, I promise."

I massaged the back of his hand with my thumb. "I was with you, my love, in the year 1679. I found you and you took me to Kilchurn Castle. It was beautiful. I'm really happy I got to see it."

I ran my fingertips across his shoulder. "We put our feet in the water and I saw the room where you slept when you were a bairn. I wanted to stay with you but we talked it through and you said you needed me here today. You said you couldn't live without me and the truth is I can't live without you either. I totally understand. So I didn't argue, not really, though I cried a lot — leaving you is the hardest thing in the world."

I listened to the beep-beep of his monitors for a moment. "You said to me once it took all the pain you could bear to leave me. That everything about me begged you to stay. I understand what you meant now because you were saying goodbye to me and it was so hard to leave."

An explosion happened in the far off distance. I clutched his hand. "Because what if it was the wrong decision? What if I screwed something up by trying? I think now this is a new history and I don't know what happens from here on out. You survived before, but what if something about me makes the timeline happen differently? I came because you need me and so I'm here but please don't die. Please. I love you and you have to survive this because it will kill me if I left you when I had you. It was a huge risk and — Please. Please don't die."

I lay there for a lot longer and then I said it again, "Please don't die. I'm here to rescue you."

CHAPTER 14

a woman's voice woke me. "Mrs Campbell?"

"Huh? What?" I raised my head from Magnus's shoulder with a glance at his face.

He was as deep and still as he had been when I fell asleep, but the room was brighter — just past sunrise I guessed. A helicopter roared by the building.

"We need to take his vital signs, we'll be busy for a few moments. Would you like to step into the hall?"

"I need to go to the bathroom, anyway."

I climbed off the bed and padded across the room to the door and pushed through for the hallway.

In the bathroom I looked in every drawer for a toothbrush and toothpaste or any kind of makeup, with luck a hairbrush. What kind of place has a blow dryer but no hairbrush or toothbrush? I sighed, thanked the universe for the toilet paper, and apologized to the ether for complaining, because whoever stocked the bathroom with shampoo and soap was a literal angel. I left the bathroom.

The hallway was empty. The guards weren't at Magnus's door anymore. The doors stood wide open.

I raced into the room as the doctor, the nurses, and the guards were hurriedly wheeling Magnus on a gurney into another room. "Where are you taking him?"

A nurse said, "Mrs Campbell, his vitals have dropped; we're taking him back to surgery. We'll let you know as soon as we have information." The doors began to slide closed behind them.

I slipped through the doors after them. "Excuse me — he had a thing once — his heart stopped, just be careful, he—"

They passed through another set of double doors.

I didn't know if I was allowed to follow them or if I was allowed to wait here in someone's office so I returned to Magnus's room. Daylight streamed through the windows, yet outside still sounded like a war zone.

What if that was it?

What if that had been my last moment with Magnus? A loud explosion vibrated the glass, another helicopter hovered over the building, loud and terrifying.

I stood watching the door, waiting, chewing my lip, occasionally my fingernails.

The doors behind me slid open. Hammond rushed in with four men, weapons drawn. "Where's Magnus?"

I pointed, because I lacked words.

Hammond barged through to the surgical room commanding, "We have to go, now!"

From somewhere in the building, gunfire, loud, close, possibly on the floor below. Footsteps in the hallway running by.

Suddenly Hammond rushed back through the doors, followed by the physician, two nurses, and the gurney with

Magnus on it. A nurse was pulling a fluid bag from the stand and tossing it beside Magnus on the bed. I stepped back as they all rushed past me. Soldiers fell in around the gurney. Wires and tubing trailed behind them.

I jumped into action, picked up the wires, rolled them around my fist, and put them on the end of the bed while trying to keep pace. I held onto one of the corners as we all rushed following Hammond.

Dr Abercrombie said, "I can't guarantee the king's life if we leave the palace. He isn't stabilized—"

Hammond reached the door and slammed it open. "We have to move him to safety, the palace is about to fall to the insurgents."

a large military helicopter waited for us with its rotor blades spinning — noisy, windy, and overwhelming. I had only been in a couple of helicopters, both times under extreme duress, and there was nothing now that made me want to go into it. Except Magnus being wheeled there.

The men slammed the gurney against the helicopter folding the front legs and sliding it across the floor. Two soldiers jumped in after it. The nurses and Dr Abercrombie climbed in and began buckling into seats.

I took the closest seat I could get — the one next to his legs. I buckled my seatbelt and wiggled my bare foot under his thigh. It felt crucial that I be touching him.

The helicopter lifted into the air with bumps and jolts. I gripped my seat.

The rooftop we just escaped was now swarming with soldiers. Loud gunfire aimed at our helicopter sent showers of sparks past the windows. Bullets hit the metal with a ting ting ting noise. A soldier beside me returned fire with loud continuous blasts and it was so completely terrifying. I clamped my hands over my head and focused on the lump under the blankets that was Magnus's knee.

Everyone held on. Nobody spoke because it was so loud. Awful loud. And I for one was concentrating on keeping us up in the air. *Please fly, please fly, pleasepleaseplease fly.*

We were going very very, very fast. Like well over a hundred miles per hour. I took glances through the windows: city to the right, sprawling suburbs to the left, drones and other things flying by all around. Two other military helicopters pulled beside us and seemed to escort us before they peeled away headed in opposite directions. We continued: past the suburbs, past forests, to a coastline, then along it for a while, until we turned away and descended toward an opulent palace nestled against a forest. We landed on a wide green lawn surrounded by well-groomed showcase gardens.

The palace was gray brick, three stories high, with rooftops that went higher. There was a double front stair sweeping up to a large glass front entrance. The roofline was all finials and cones and higher and lower so that it totally resembled a sandcastle, the drippy kind. It seemed like someone might call it their 'Grand House, ' as in, 'Mummy, will we be summering in the Grand House with the Kennedys this year?' But how would I know? I never saw a grand house up close in my life and here we were landing on the lawn in front of it.

Hammond jumped off the helicopter followed by two soldiers. Another helicopter landed behind us, six men jumped out and entered the house with their weapons drawn.

They were gone for thirty minutes. Fifteen minutes in, Hammond said, "My apologies, Your Highness, we are sweeping the house to make sure it's safe."

When they returned they were leading three men and one woman, with their hands bound behind their backs. The prisoners were loaded onto another helicopter and then it rose into the air and flew away.

Hammond waved us out of ours.

I climbed out first and waited while the doctor and the two nurses climbed out and Magnus was pulled from the helicopter. In a group we pushed his gurney up the giant grand steps and in through the doors.

Men stood guard at the windows and doors while I stood in the gigantic foyer and was introduced to what was left of the staff: a man and one older woman. Hammond said, "Your Highness, I'd like you to meet Mrs Johnstone, the head of your household, she's been here for thirty years." Mrs Johnstone was in her late sixties and had an expression on her face like I had interrupted a really good sit-down day. I curtseyed like an idiot, because I didn't have any idea what I was doing; I was being addressed like a Queen while I was barefoot and wearing brown pajamas.

Plus I was suffering extreme duress, the doctor and the nurses were setting up Magnus's bed through far doors in the middle of the living room and we were here, standing under a giant painting of Donnan's mean-ass face.

To the gardener, I didn't remember his name, I mumbled something about, "Nice to meet you," as I started to head into the living room.

I asked Hammond, "What happened to the rest of the staff?"

He said, "They no longer wanted to work here."

The nurses were organizing Magnus's IV pump and their other

equipment right in the opulent, white and gold accented living room. The room was full of antiques and art and things that looked very precious. The luxury was contrasted with a giant projection of street battles along one wall: explosions, gunfire, more shaky video. It was very loud as if the battle was right here in the living room. Along another wall, doors of glass looked out over the sprawling grass surrounded by woods. The other two walls were covered, floor to ceiling, with small paintings interspersed with large framed photos of Donnan: Donnan in a uniform. Donnan laughing with a sneer. Donnan beside a boat. Donnan the Terrible in one direction, horrific explosions in the other.

Dr Abercrombie had gone and slumped down on the couch in the middle of all that luxury.

I walked over and stood in front of him. "When do you think he'll wake up? He's been asleep for a really long time. Is it a coma? Is that what's happening?"

The doctor ignored me. I crossed my arms across my chest.

"It doesn't seem right he hasn't stirred at all — are you sure you're giving him the right dosage of whatever it is you're giving him? What are you giving him?"

"I'm administering antibiotics. The weapons they use in these battles are ancient and of course I'm giving him the right dosage, Ms Campbell." His voice dripped with condescension. "He'll wake soon enough." He dropped his head back on the couch as if he planned to take a nap.

CHAPTER 16

*H*ammond returned from making his rounds and called me over. "Your Highness, we have men stationed around the perimeter. You don't have anything on you, anything that can be tracked?"

"No, nothing. I don't even have shoes."

"There might be some here, you could go through the—"

"Nope. I can't go through any of Donnan's things. At all." I looked around at all the photos leering at me.

Hammond followed my eyes. "Ah, yes. Sadly, there was no where else safe to bring you. I think Samuel knew about all the other houses. You should be hidden enough for now and I'm trying to get you both moved back to the castle as soon as possible."

"Sure, that sounds good. And anyway, he should wake any minute now."

"Yes, he certainly should. In the meantime I'll be stationed outside. Tell Mrs Johnstone if you need anything."

"I don't want to be a bother.... Can we turn down the

volume? It's really really—" I really wanted to turn it all the way off but thought that might sound too complain-y.

"Of course."

Hammond lowered the volume as he left and I returned to Magnus's bedside. I watched the nurses fidget with tubing and wires.

I asked the younger nurse, "When do you think he'll wake up?"

"I can't really say, um, ma'am. With the medicines..." Her eyes flitted to the other nurse and she continued looking over a chart.

"What medicines? Can you tell me—?"

The older nurse asked abruptly, "How long have you been married to him?"

"Something like two years. I would need to see a calendar to know exactly."

"Oh, and will his mistress be joining us here too?"

"Excuse me?" I asked.

"His mistress, Bella, she was in his room during his surgery."

I leveled my gaze. "She isn't his mistress and no, she won't be."

With a shrug she said, "Oh, I thought... my apologies. She's carrying his child. I thought you must know—"

"I do know. You don't need to tell me."

I clutched his hand and tried to swallow my fury. The war scenes on the projections looked terrifying: the camera zoomed low over a body laying partially in rubble.

The nurses joined the doctor on the comfortable couches and chairs in the sitting area.

It was incongruous: the medical staff in their uniforms sitting relaxed in this lavish house while the king slept on a gurney with scary looking liquids dripping into his arm.

I pulled a barstool beside Magnus's bed, clutched his hand, and whispered in his ear, but my fear was rising. He was too still. This sleep had been going on for too long. There was no movement or anything and I was starting to really freak out. This was not at all what I thought the medical staff should be doing.

"Magnus? Can you hear me?" I massaged his fingers and up his wrist. "Magnus? Can you wiggle a finger if you hear me?"

This is what was freaking me out so much: Magnus had been alive. I had been with him and he was alive and I left him to come here.

I knew there were rules — interplanetary, inter-dimensional rules about folding back on your own life, but I thought this would be safe, coming here to Magnus.

But what if it wasn't?

When I left him, he was so sad but alive and here, he was technically alive but lying there completely still, and...

I was beginning to tingle, like the 'before you pass out' kind, the skin-crawling kind, the full-blown panic kind. "Magnus, can you wake up?"

The nurses left for the kitchen to see about some food.

I was famished but couldn't imagine being able to eat.

They returned later with plates of eggs and toast and beans and ate theirs on the couch. Mrs Johnstone delivered a plate of food and a mug of coffee to me on a tray and asked if I wanted to sit at a table; I refused deciding to stay perched on the barstool instead.

She said vaguely, "I didn't think you'd be so young."

"Oh, yes, I'm twenty-four," I said awkwardly.

She watched Magnus's sleeping face. "He looks just like his father. Now *that* was a gentleman. He always treated his staff very well."

She said, offhandedly, "You need some proper clothes."

"Yes, but I don't know where I would..."

She huffed. "I'll see if I can find you some. If you need anything ring me through this." She handed me what looked like a very small remote control. "This button." When she gestured at it she whispered, "Don't tell anyone I said this, but the doctor is on Samuel's side."

My eyes went wide and my stomach dropped to the floor, but I couldn't ask a single question because she abruptly left the room.

My hands shook from fear.

Samuel's side? Shit. I looked at the remote control wishing I knew how to push a button to conjure Hammond.

The doctor stood, stretched, approached Magnus's gurney, and sifted through a box.

I crowded him looking over his shoulder. There were a couple of basic medical kits, a few bags of fluids. I asked, "What are you looking for?" because he had the look on his face of someone who wouldn't want to say.

He ignored me. He pulled a bag out and put it on Magnus's mattress and began unscrewing the tubing from the bag hanging beside the gurney. I wedged myself between him and Magnus.

"What is that? More of the same? Is that... What is it?" I grabbed his arm so I could read the writing on the label but couldn't make out the names. "Tell me what it's for or I'm not letting you put it in him."

He leaned over me so I was arched back above Magnus's chest. "I don't have to answer to you. I'm the royal physician—"

"Yeah, well, I'm Magnus's wife and I'm not to be pushed around." It was an empty threat though because I was basically pushed.

He glared into my eyes.

The nurses rushed over. The older one said, "Your behavior is shocking, Ms Campbell, please move."

"No," I spread my arms out over Magnus. "Not until I understand what's being done, no one touches him."

Doctor Abercrombie's grin grew even more malevolent.

Our ruckus alerted the two guards who rushed in with their guns drawn.

The doctor said, "She attacked me. She killed King Donnan. The fact she's even allowed access to Magnus is unbelievable."

"That's not true. I'm just—"

"I'm trying to administer fluids to the king."

One of the guards tried to pull me off Magnus.

"I just need to know what—" I started kicking.

I kicked the tray of food and coffee off the end table and it splashed to the ground all over one of the nurses.

I kicked Dr Abercrombie really hard in the knee and he yelled and clutched it like I had done serious damage. Stupid asshole.

They yanked me off Magnus's bed. "I just — I'm trying to protect him, I think he's on Samuel's side—"

He looked outraged.

I twisted out of the guard's grip and threw my body across Magnus's legs and held onto the edges of the bed. The gurney rocked dangerously. I knew I looked insane in my bare feet and pajamas but—

Both guards tried prying me from the bed. "Call Hammond, I'll go if you'll call him first." My left fingers lost their grip but I struggled hard to get it back. "Call Hammond!"

Dr Abercrombie was replacing Magnus's fluid bags.

I leapt from the bed and grabbed hold of the doctor's arm. "Stop!"

"Get her off me."

The guards pulled me off the Doctor. "I'll go quietly, only

nobody do anything, stop the doctor until Colonel Donahoe comes back, *please.*"

They bound my hands behind my back but finally, thankfully, one said, "Doctor Abercrombie, please stop what you're doing until Colonel Donahoe can make a decision."

He said, "You're going to take the words of a murderer over mine?"

The guard answered, "Colonel Donahoe told me to make sure she was comfortable. I don't think he's going to be too happy I've handcuffed her. Don't do anything else until he returns." He turned his back on us to use his radio.

The other guard held me ten feet away from Magnus while the doctor stood at Magnus's bedside, glaring at me furiously. The tubing connected to my husband was laying at the doctor's feet and blood flowed from Magnus onto the floor.

"Please pick up the tubing, please, I beg of you."

The guard said, "Pick up the tubing, Dr Abercrombie."

He picked the hose up grudgingly.

I had my answer, this doctor wasn't putting anything inside of Magnus, not anymore.

CHAPTER 17

A few moments later Hammond bustled into the room, his face flushed and stern. He nodded brusquely toward me and asked, "Dr Abercrombie, what's happening?"

Dr Abercrombie said, "This person—"

He corrected, "Queen Kaitlyn, the king's wife."

"—has attempted to block me from administering treatments to Magnus. I am the royal physician and to perform my duties I had her restrained. Your guards ordered me to discontinue treatment until you give me the all-clear."

I interrupted, "Please don't. He's on Samuel's side, I'm sure of it."

Hammond turned to me, his brow raised. "He's been the royal physician for twenty years. What would make you think—?"

The doctor interrupted, "This is outrageous!"

"I just, I have my suspicions. When I asked him what he was giving Magnus, he wouldn't tell me. I think Magnus should be awake by now and I'm worried."

"Worried enough to be arrested over it?"

I nodded. "Yes."

Hammond looked around the room. He seemed to be judging the area more than the people inside it.

After a moment he asked, "Queen Kaitlyn, have you any idea what is going on in the kingdom right now?"

Crap. I was the queen apparently and I knew nothing about the people, the kingdom, the reason for the fighting. I was Marie Antoinette-ing this whole thing and not doing a good job of it.

I searched my brain for anything but didn't have enough to even bullshit with. "All I know is Magnus was next in line for the throne after Donnan. About this war I have no idea. My guess is Magnus's uncle Samuel has followers who are angry Magnus killed him in the arena. Maybe he has a son..." My eyes grew wide. "Does he have a son? Wait, Hammond, is Bella in a safe house?"

He nodded. "Yes, Bella has been moved to a safe house."

I said, "Good."

Hammond turned to Doctor Abercrombie. "Would you like to fill in the gaps in Queen Kaitlyn's knowledge?"

Doctor Abercrombie said, "Samuel's son, Roderick is fighting for the throne."

Hammond said, "See, Queen Kaitlyn, it's a simple matter. And Doctor Abercrombie has been treating kings since... Can you remind me the kings you've treated, Doctor Abercrombie?"

He straightened his back. "There was Donnan the first, Donnan the second, Samuel, and now Magnus."

Hammond explained, looking directly at me. "And here we are in the interregnum period between the reign of Donnan the second and Magnus the first. And while the kingdom has been between the two kings, Samuel attempted to usurp the crown. He failed, of course, and died in an arena battle against Magnus and yet... the rebels are still trying to overthrow the rightful king." He shook his head. "They are trying to take the palace by force and many people have lost their lives." He added, "Finding where one's loyalties lies is sometimes very difficult."

He added, "So that's why, Doctor Abercrombie, I'm going to have to ask you to step away from Magnus. You're under arrest—"

"You have no right! I'm the royal physician, what am I being accused of?"

Hammond raised his brow. "You listed Samuel as a king."

The guards closed in around him.

The older nurse said, "You can't arrest him for saying Roderick fights for the throne, it's true!"

"Oh I can. I have no proof. I'm no judge or juror but I can let the courts decide. I only know that if the doctor was on Magnus's side he would have described this all much differently and he wouldn't be speaking to Magnus's wife, the queen, with all this disrespect. You're relieved of duty as well."

He turned to the younger nurse. "Do you think I'm being unfair?"

She shook her head. "I think this is a good decision."

"Queen Kaitlyn, are you comfortable with only one nurse while I try to replace the doctor?"

"I am."

"Okay, then we'll make do with one nurse."

Doctor Abercrombie said, "When Roderick is king and I'm reinstated as Royal Physician you'll regret this move."

"I won't regret it because I won't be alive to see it."

The soldiers arrested them and shoved them out the front door and I could see through a window their helicopter rise into the air.

Hammond scrubbed his hands on his face making his beard stick out in crazy directions. He looked unkempt and very tired.

"Queen Kaitlyn, it's been twelve hours since I met you and I've placed a great deal of trust at your feet. I truly hope you haven't lied to me."

"I haven't. I have one goal — protecting Magnus."

"That's my goal too. So let's get to it."

He cut through my bindings then left to return to his post. I asked the nurse. "What's your name?"

"Tess Daniels."

"Can you tell me what he was giving Magnus?"

"A concoction to bring on coma. I think he planned to kill him last night, but then Colonel Donahoe brought you and I don't think he had a plan after that. I think he was desperate and decided to do it today in front of everyone."

"Can we safely stop it?"

"If we monitor him closely, probably."

"Okay, let's do that then, but he will wake up?"

"I think you stopped the doctor in time, but I don't really know for certain."

"Great." I massaged Magnus's hand, working my way up and down the fingers. Wishing Emma was a phone call away so she could research in her hippy manual some kind of remedy for coma brought on by an evil doctor.

Tessa said, "I'm really sorry about all of this." She turned her attention to the machine beside Magnus's almost lifeless body.

Mrs Johnstone entered the room. "How is the king?"

"Thank you for telling me."

"Well, Donnan's son is the rightful heir to Donnan's throne, god rest his soul."

"Oh yes, of course. You did it for Donnan's son. Perfect."

Mrs Johnstone left Donnan's living room for Donnan's kitchen in Donnan's grand house.

I focused on Magnus, stroking my fingers on his cheek, brushing some hair from his forehead. "She's wrong. You're not Donnan's son, you're your own man, Magnus. You're kind and generous and funny and you're my husband and — I'm so tired.

Please wake up. Because I'm kind of overwhelmed by all of this. I miss you so much."

I massaged his hand some more.

"You know, there are a lot of moments in our life when I have to explain the world to you. And when we go to Scotland, you have to explain the world to me, but here — I don't have a guide to this place. I need you to yell 'Cruachan!' and fight this. Come on. Cruachan, my love, please."

I was perched on the barstool. My eyelids were heavy, so heavy. I leaned forward over Magnus's hand, my forehead on the edge of his abdomen, my eyes closed and within a second I was asleep.

I slept so soundly I dreamed. I was standing on the side of a mountain. Magnus was farther up, forty feet or so — he was looking right at me though he wasn't moving or speaking or — he looked so desperately sad, like his heart was breaking, but he was holding it all inside.

And I was yelling, "Magnus, don't leave me!"

But he didn't move.

And I couldn't get closer — I couldn't move. So who was leaving? Both of us? Neither of us?

And so I dropped to my knees. "Please don't leave me."

I put my hands in the grass in front of me, stalks and sticks and thistles and weeds and I dug my fingers down into the base of them, the thick soil around, the rock and solid mass of the mountain and I held it in my grasp and begged, "Please don't go."

CHAPTER 18

There was a movement under my head. Slight. A very small twitch of the fingers clasped in my hands. I had a moment of confusion, where was I? Oh yeah, the living room of a grand house in some future world. Why? Because the kingdom was falling or some other bullshit. And who?

Magnus.

His face had changed from the sleep mask of the last twelve or so hours to a wince. A furrowed brow. "Oh my god, you're waking up." I kissed his fingers, pressed my cheek to his palm and kissed them again. I looked at his face. "Are you waking up?" There was another twitch. I kissed his fingers then I kissed his wrist and his forearm to his elbow. "Magnus?" I pushed my barstool back from the gurney. His fingers twitched more. I pressed my lips to his shoulder and watched his face. "Magnus?"

He groaned.

"Oh my god, Magnus!"

I kissed his fingers and then I climbed a leg onto the edge of his bed and then both knees and I kissed his collarbone and his chin and I leaned over him, a few inches from his face. "Magnus?"

I put my left leg across his hips, careful not to sit and hurt his injury, crouched over him like a tv doctor performing that chest-thumping technique, except I was kissing and cajoling. "Magnus?"

His eyes fluttered.

I pulled both his hands to his chest and clutched them in mine, kissed his knuckles and peered at him like a ravenously hungry vulture, not at all sure I wouldn't scare the hell out of him when he came to full consciousness.

I whispered. "Magnus, wake up, it's me, Kaitlyn."

The living room was completely empty. Tessa must have gone to sleep somewhere. Hammond was out guarding which was good. We needed guarding. Magnus was waking up.

I kissed his chin, his short beard. I kissed his Adam's apple and checked his face. Another flutter of his eyes and another wince. "Hey baby, wake up, this is Kaitlyn and you need to wake, okay?"

His fingers wiggled. His eyes opened and closed tight. He winced again.

"Magnus?"

"Tis bright."

"Oh my god, Magnus!" I burst into tears. I kissed his lips, his cheeks, his nose, his lips again. "Magnus, you're alive you — can you move your fingertips for me?"

His fingers moved on both hands.

I happy-sobbed. "Can you move your toes?" I twisted to see a lump under the blanket wiggle. "You can! You can!"

"Tis somethin' quite heavy pressin' on my middle."

"That's me! Oh my god that's me!" I lay my forearms on both sides of his head and held my lips to his mouth. I spoke with my lips against his. "It's me, right here on you."

"Ye must be a figment of m'fancy, yet ye art heavy as a clach-chinn."

Happy tears rolled down my cheeks. "What's a clock-chin?"

"M'headstone."

I shook my head. "Nope, it's really me, my love, open your eyes, you'll see."

He opened an eye and quickly closed it. A smile worked on the side of his mouth. "Ye art a dream."

"I'm not. I swear I'm not. I'm right here on you. I'll pinch you to prove it."

"Nae, kiss me."

I kissed him long and slow and sweet. I groaned from the love of it. Chin to chin I looked into his eyes. "I'm right here, my love."

His eyes opened. "Truly?"

"One hundred percent and you're alive. Wiggle all your parts again. Let me see. I need to know." I looked around at all his appendages. Every one of them moving and even better when I returned to look at his face it held a smile. A weak smile, but one all the same.

I put my head on his pillow beside his ear. "Oh my god, I can't believe it. I came so far and risked so much and I can't believe you just woke up. I was beginning to think you might not."

He turned his head and his lips met mine again and then his left hand raised to steady my cheek while we kissed and oh my god it was the most amazing thing ever to be kissed by Magnus when I was beginning to believe it wouldn't happen anymore.

"How are ye here?"

"You sent me. You told me you needed me, you couldn't live without me. It was the most romantic and terrifying thing ever, but here I am." I kissed him again.

He said, "Och, tis much tae understand, but I am verra hungry."

"I'll ask Mrs Johnstone to bring you something."

I climbed off him and dropped to the ground and reached for the call button.

Mrs Johnstone answered, I said, "Magnus is awake, can you bring him something for dinner?"

He sat with a groan, pushed the blankets off his lower half, and swung his legs over the side of the gurney. He was completely naked except for a bandage taped to his lower right abdomen.

"You maybe shouldn't get up," I said.

"Och, mo reul-iuil, I must pish and I am nae wantin' tae do it here in this..." He looked around the room with bleary eyes. "Fancy house."

"Let me help, you'll probably be unsteady. Do you want to be naked?"

In answer he stood, wobbly and a little like he might fall. I jumped under his arm and held around his side, trying to hold him erect, but he was heavy and gravity pulled at him hard. He shuffled, weaving a little. I held him up but started giggling as we made it to the hall, his footsteps plodding.

"M'lady thinks my plight is humorous."

I giggled again. "Your pikestaff is flopping for all the world to see."

"Tis nae awake fully."

I called, projecting for the upper floors, "Tessa? Tessa, this is Kaitlyn, please don't come out. I have Magnus up and taking him to the bathroom, and he's without proper clothes."

Tessa said from the hall, "You don't need my help supporting him, Queen Kaitlyn?"

"No, I got him, he's actually kind of steady."

Magnus bumped a shoulder against a wall. "Ye art a queen, my Kaitlyn?"

"You're a king apparently, though your pant-less state says differently."

"So I have beaten Samuel?" He collapsed against the bathroom door frame. I propped him there with my hip and turned on the light. I wriggled him into the room and closed the door behind us.

"You got this, highlander?"

He leaned on the counter to steady himself to the toilet. Then he directed a loud stream at the bowl. I smiled. He was alive for five minutes and already naked in front of me. There was a sort of happiness in that even with the bandage and the pissing and the wince. "How are you feeling?"

"My head is verra painful." He finished peeing. I turned on the water so he could wash and passed him a towel. He stopped drying to check himself out in the full large mirror. "I am a mess, mo reul-iuil."

"A mess? You might be the most beautiful thing I've ever seen."

He rubbed along his stubbled jaw. "I have the beginnings of a beard—"

I grinned.

"Bandages, bruises." He inspected an angry bruise on his hip.

I reached out and brushed my fingers along it. "I'm glad he didn't hit your ribs."

"Aye," He gingerly rubbed the area where he had been broken not that long ago.

"I have a lot to tell you about the beard too, but let's get some food in you first."

We padded together barefoot to the living room, he was steadier now. I grabbed the sheet off his gurney and wrapped it around him as a kilt for his royal nakedness.

We entered the kitchen.

Mrs Johnstone said, "Good lord! I meant to bring you this meal to the bed!"

I said, "My apologies, Mrs Johnstone, he needed food and to walk for a moment so we just walked here. If you'd like to head to your room, I can finish up with feeding him. Oh, and this is Magnus. Magnus, this is Mrs Johnstone."

She bowed and left, leaving a large tray with two plates filled with steak and mashed potatoes. The full wall of the kitchen displayed videos of battles on city streets. There was a large photo over the sink of Donnan smirking with a flower in his lapel.

I poured a glass of water and passed it to Magnus. He gulped it down. Then I filled it for myself while he stared at the videos.

"Och, tis a war, mo reul-iuil. This is because of my ascension?"

"Yes. I think so."

"There will be many people losin' their lives."

He struggled to cut his meat, so I sat on the counter and cut it for him.

He ate ravenously.

While he ate, his sheet slid down exposing half his ass. "Ye haena wrapped m'kilt correctly, mo reul-iuil, how are ye a proper Scottish wife?"

"I properly prefer the unwrapping." I grinned at him happily.

He put down his fork with a moan. "I needed food." He moved between my knees, kissed my lips, and licked the corner of my mouth. "Ye had a bit of steak there."

"I put it there, so you'd kiss me."

"I will always kiss ye." He held my hand in my lap. "So tell me how ye are here?"

"When I got to Florida, I waited for you for three days. I knew that meant you were dead, and I..." I smiled sadly. "I couldn't accept it. Until one night I woke remembering Old Magnus. Lizbeth told me about him. He was often around when she was a bairn. Old Magnus is the reason they called you Young Magnus, but I looked him up once and there was no Old Magnus in your clan. So I got to thinking — what if Old Magnus was you?" I grinned. "So I went."

"By yerself? What year did ye go tae?"

"Yes by myself. To 1679."

"Before I was born. Twas verra brave of ye. Why dinna ye take Quentin?"

"That is exactly what you asked me when you saw me there, and my answer was, I thought it was too dangerous for a black man to be wandering around with me in the 17th century. I might have been wrong, but I wasn't wrong about you being there. You were! You were in the Great Hall. And this is something big I need to tell you of — you had a beard to here." I pointed at his chest.

"I did? What did ye think of it?"

"I thought it was sexy."

"Really?"

"Och aye," I joked.

"So ye rescued me in 1679... how much time had passed for me?"

I put my hands on his cheeks. "Four years, Magnus, four long years."

He winced. "Why hadna I come home?"

"There is a very long story, something we need to figure out, but the short version is there's a man named General Reyes. You had been fighting him the whole time and he has a way of monitoring when you time-jump into Florida. We can't go back. We have to figure out another way."

His brow furrowed. "We have much tae do, mo reul-iuil."

"True that. I think once you said to me 'we arna used tae easy.' It's so terribly true, but at least we're together while we solve it."

"Tis verra hopeful of ye, I am glad ye are still guidin' us." He stroked the empty space on my ring finger. "You haena your ring, I dinna get it for you? Tis unlike me..."

I rubbed his ring, turning it on his finger. "No, you didn't. You hadn't gone to see Lizbeth or Sean yet and we didn't have time to, not really." I smiled. "We did have time for a few things though..."

"Like what?"

I raised my brow mischievously. "We had sex standing against the wall!" I giggled.

"In castle Balloch?"

"Yes, on that one circular stair to the left of the Grand Hall, you know the one?"

"Aye, I ken it." He winced. "I daena think... I daena want tae think about it, tis verra much like hearin' ye speak of another man."

"Oh yeah, that makes sense. But I should also tell you — you took me to Kilchurn."

A smile spread across his face. "Kilchurn castle?"

"It was summer, you showed me the loch, the mountains, the water, and where you slept. We sat on the dock and dipped our feet—"

"Twas like ice I would guess."

"It was. It was really beautiful. I understand why you think of it as your past home. I could imagine you playing with Sean on the mountains there. It reminded me of Maine and you told me to tell you we should go to my grandparents' lake house. He promised me you'd get me there."

"Consider it done," he joked, "as soon as I find m'kilt."

"And then we walked into the mountains, found a beautiful hidden spot, said goodbye, and I jumped from there to here."

Hammond entered the kitchen. "Oh, excuse me, your um, Majesty."

Magnus pulled the sheet up and closed it in the front with a laugh. "Och, tis a fine way tae greet me when I am standin' naked in the middle of a strange kitchen."

Hammond bowed his head. "I am Colonel Donahoe, sir."

I dropped from the counter. "Magnus, this is Hammond, or Colonel Donahoe. When I left you in the past, you told me to find him, to ask him for help. You told me you trusted him. So when I got here I demanded to see him and he brought me to your hospital room. He has helped me so much."

Hammond said, "The rebels are laying siege to the castle, Your Highness. I moved you and Queen Kaitlyn here to Donnan's safe house. My apologies the household is so small, I had to arrest half the staff and most of your medical team because they were siding with Roderick."

"And Roderick is..."

"Samuel's son."

"Of course, there is always a son tae deal with." Magnus asked, "How is the battle going now?"

"Are you ready to be briefed on the encounters?"

Magnus shook his head. "Nae. I am feelin' the weight of living in my limbs. I needs tae be in the bed. Can it wait until the morn?"

"We won't need any big decisions until tomorrow."

"Thank you Hammond for the care and attention ye shewed Kaitlyn. I appreciate it and winna forget it."

Hammond said, "Yes, sir, thank you, sir." He left the kitchen.

I said, "He's a good man. I think you'll end up being friends." Magnus looked a little green. "Let's get you back to the bed." I put my arm around him, trying to hold him up as we shuffled.

Magnus groaned, "I daena want m'bed in the midst of the Great Hall."

So we continued shuffling until we found a small unused guest room. The bed was covered in fancy pillows and a luxurious silk cover. I helped him to it, pulled all the decorative pillows to the ground, yanked the covers open and helped him lower. I pulled the covers to his chest.

The nurse found our room then. I sat to the side while she fussed over him, checking his vitals, giving him some painkillers, and examining his wound. She left telling him to get some sleep and making me promise to get her if anything was wrong.

I climbed next to him and curled against his left side. "Do you need anything?"

"Nae, only some sleep, mo ghradh, I'll feel better in the morn."

$\mathcal{M}$y night was fitful. I hadn't eaten enough, had to get up and pee, had to turn over the three framed photos of Donnan and pull one off the wall. Then I lay awake for a while and wondered if Magnus was going to be okay, wondered what we were going to do now we were in exile — Old Magnus had told me to trust Hammond, to get Quentin and the list, and not to go to Florida, so there was a shit storm of stuff there to worry about. And I had so much to tell Magnus.

When he finally woke, daylight streaming through the curtains I had forgotten to close, I was already awake. "Do you need to get up?"

"Aye, but I daena need help. I will go slow."

He stood with a moan and plodded around the bed to the bathroom, completely naked, his spectacular ass out for the whole world to see. I was really happy to be the small circle of people who had ever seen it. He pissed in the toilet.

A few minutes later he came plodding out. "What are ye thinkin' of?"

"Your arse." I grinned.

He chuckled. "And I was thinkin' on yours." He climbed into bed beside me. "Tell me the rest of it, I was laying in bed thinking ye haena told me enough."

I teased, "Oh really? It looked a lot like you were sleeping."

He grinned. "I am verra glad you are here, but why would my future self send ye away?"

"Because all you did was fight. There were arena battles, wars, and you had to fight General Reyes every time you tried to come see me, it was a lot."

"I daena like tae fight but I think I could have fought well enough. It still daena sound like me tae send ye away."

I leaned on an elbow and watched him for a second. "Do you want the full story? Because there are many layers I need to tell you about. I can't tell you all at once. You need to hear it bit by bit."

"I want tae hear it."

"You and I were riding between Balloch and Kilchurn and by the way I was on my own horse."

"Ye were?"

"I was." I nodded solemnly. "You told me I was almost perfect. Even though most of the time you held the thingies." I gestured for holding the reins.

"I held the thingies for ye?"

"Yes, but I was amazing — we stopped for the night because I had chafing all over here." I gestured on my thighs. "We built a fire and we were sitting beside it and these three men crept into our camp."

His brow drew down.

"You told them to leave but they wouldn't. They made a remark about wanting some of me and you went ballistic."

"What dost that word mean?"

"Like crazy, violent. I mean you needed to, they weren't backing down, you had to fight them, but they..." I remembered the fight, the ferocious glare in my husband's eyes, his beard adding to his crazed wild look.

He stared at the ceiling. "Tell me."

"You killed them. All of them. Even though the last guy was begging you to spare his life. It was like you couldn't stop and then you broke down and told me you were broken. You said you didn't pray anymore because God had forsaken you and... You begged me to help you."

"Och."

"And by the time you were calmed we had decided to send me here. We didn't really talk about it, we both just knew."

"Twas dangerous for ye tae come alone — the last time ye came... Ye must have been verra afraid."

"I was but Hammond was exactly the right person for me to ask for help and well, the... Here's the other thing." My voice caught. "The doctor was trying to kill you. I had to stop him and they were going to arrest me and if I hadn't gotten here in time, you might have died..."

He turned his head to look on my face. My chin was trembling I chewed my lip to try to control it.

"Twas a tremendous burden tae place at your feet, mo reuliuil. I am sorry for it."

"I would do it again, in a red hot minute. I will rescue you over and over again if I have to, but thank you for noticing that it was hard, because it was really hard and — the nurse, such a bitch, she said Bella was in your room while you were in surgery."

He said, "I daena ken why, but I will make sure nae one puts her above ye again."

"Thank you." I gave him a sad smile. "It was all really hard. What did you have to do, fight to the death?"

"Aye. Sounds like the first of many battles though."

"We'll try to figure out how to keep that from happening."

After a soft knock, Mrs Johnstone came in with a tray of food. "Breakfast for you, Your Highness."

I wiggled under the covers so she wouldn't see how frightful I must have looked, crazed hair, days with not much sleep. I asked from under the blanket, "Is there coffee?"

"Yes, Your Highness, coffee, eggs, and beans. There isn't much I know how to make, it isn't usually my job you see. I was more Donnan's personal assistant, but now I am almost the only person left." She put the tray on the dresser. I peeked. She stood one of the framed photos of Donnan back up again.

I went back under the covers. "Is there a carafe somewhere? I'm going to need four or five cups of coffee this morning."

"I'll bring it, Your Highness. I'll see about finding you some clothes."

Magnus said, "I need some too."

"Yes, I meant you, Your Highness."

"Then Kaitlyn will need some clothes as well." She left with a bow.

Magnus and I looked at each other. "Twill be difficult tae get used tae titles like this."

"I know, Hammond kept calling me Queen Kaitlyn and I thought he was talking about someone else."

I got our plates, put the photo face down again, and we ate in bed. I explained about the food, "This is basically an English breakfast. She served me this yesterday too. It's a little rubbery, because I don't think she's the normal cook. I'm not sure what happened to the cook, but I saw people being arrested and taken from the house and now we're here."

He chewed a bite of eggs dipped through beans. "Och, we need Chef Zach."

"Yes, definitely." I sighed then ate a bite of toast with butter. "What I really want, my love, and you've probably never had this because Chef Zach would never serve it to you, is Lucky Charms cereal. It has marshmallows which makes no sense at all, but someone did it. Or Cookie Crisp, a cereal that tastes like cookies, again, no one knows why. Or Cinnamon Crunch. Cereal like cinnamon toast. What I'm saying is it's a big world of food out there and you've only had a small taste of it. There's so much more for you to try."

"I am glad ye saved my life for the nonsense cereals."

"Me too." I dipped a forkful of the egg through my beans. "This on the other hand tastes like feet and is lacking the best part of Chef Zach's breakfasts: whipped cream and strawberries."

Mrs Johnstone returned minutes later with two stacks of clothes. "You could sleep in the master bedroom, Your Highness."

He glanced at me then asked her, "I believe twas Donnan's room?"

"Yes, Your Highness."

"Well, I am nae interested in sleepin' there. Maybe if we move out all of his things first."

"Oh I see, I'm sorry to say these are his clothes."

"Well, I will be naked without, so twill be necessary." He grinned, but she had a look on her face that seemed like she wasn't used to smiling. She hustled out of the room.

I said, "I don't think she's going to like us, we're not at all what she's used to. And I think she had a crush on Donnan. I can see it in the way she looks at the photos when she's talking to me. It makes me want to throw up."

Magnus said, "I think she is scared of me with my giant majestic naked—"

Mrs Johnstone slipped back into the room with the carafe of coffee I asked for. She bowed. "Your Highness."

Magnus and I tried mightily to suppress our laughs.

When she left I giggled. "Your big majestic — what?"

"You ken, ye have met it afore."

"I don't know, I think I may have forgotten." I blew into my coffee mug trying to cool it. I hadn't mentioned I also needed a lot more milk than this, not wanting to be a bother.

CHAPTER 20

*T*here was a soft knock and the nurse bowed into the room. She fussed even more than last night, looking at Magnus's abdomen, giving him another dose of painkillers, checking his temperature, and asking whether he defecated yet. The whole time she called him 'Your Highness' and it was all very surreal. Finally she said, "Your Highness, you will need to wait for at least a week before resuming any kind of intercourse—"

He looked at me confused.

I explained, "Sex."

"Nae couplin' for a week?"

She said, "At least."

"Och, tis a long time."

I said, "You've gone longer."

"But nae with ye in m'bed, twill be an immense amount of trouble tae keep m'self from—"

The nurse said, "You'll have to restrain yourself, you might open your injury and then we would need a doctor and they're in short supply."

Magnus groaned. "I daena like the sound of that."

I said, "Me neither. That's okay, we'll find something else to do, like, is there a PlayStation here?"

The nurse shook her head.

"Fine, we'll come up with something, I don't know — knitting."

We all laughed.

Even with that terrible news it was so nice to be on the safe side of a very 'big and dangerous thing' and now we were in bed together. Talking about things. Happy.

The nurse left. We kept looking at each other smiling.

I asked, "Where did we leave off?"

"Ye were bein' a good wife tellin' me somethin' about my magnificence, but now we need tae get m'mind off my magnificence. Ye should maybe tell me more about what messages I sent through time."

"You said there were many many battles and one of the warnings was we needed you to do that a lot less. You said you trusted Hammond, but you called him Hammie. Oh, and you said you wished you had gone to get Quentin."

"Yet, we canna go tae Florida."

"Maybe we could land somewhere else and travel there, like on a plane—"

There was another soft knock on the door. "Your Highness, Colonel Donahoe is here to meet with you if you can."

"Tell him I can, I will be out in a moment."

I said, "Looks like the world is upon us, ready to be dealt with."

"Aye." He got up and began to dress.

CHAPTER 21

*M*agnus was gone for hours tucked away in an office with Hammond and three other men I hadn't met. I missed him and was very bored so I wandered around. There were plenty of intricate nicknacks and things to look at, porcelain figurines and old books. There were many photos of Donnan to be taken off walls and shelves and tabletops. I stacked them behind doors, out of sight. The house was very incredibly grand, but also there were reminders everywhere that it once belonged to Donnan. I didn't want to go too deep into the closets.

I took a very long shower and blew dry my hair. The shampoos were all scented like freesia or something beautiful and floral and totally necessary after the length of time I had gone without. I dressed in the simple wrap dress I was given. It fit nicely, but I was dying for some makeup and jewelry.

Mrs Johnstone seemed to think I would want to move into the master apartment but I swear to god I couldn't even look at it. What if there was — I don't know, his gross underwear in there?

And it didn't feel like my home, this didn't feel like my staff. I couldn't imagine telling them to get rid of anything, to clean it out. I felt like a guest. Probably made worse by the 'staying in the guest room' thing, but that couldn't be helped.

It struck me this plan had seemed so normal when I was deciding for us. Yet here I was in the decision, inside an unreal, crazy, war-riddled world. I wandered past the giant projection of the war on the living room wall to the kitchen, suffered Mrs Johnstone bowing and calling me 'your grace' or something, to ask if she could show me a map of the kingdom.

The video projection of the battle scenes shifted to a gigantic map. She pretended to be busy scrubbing the counters while I looked over the familiar outlines of England and the European continent but with unfamiliar colors and strange borders. There had been a serious shakeup in the last 300 years. "Where are we, right now?"

Mrs Johnstone wiped her hands on a towel, approached the projection, and pointed.

I asked, "And what about all of this?" I gestured around continents that were colored gray and barely marked.

"There's nothing there."

"All of this? Like this whole area? Where did all the people go?"

She irritatedly said, "You can see this in your room, Your Highness."

"Oh, okay, thanks."

I returned to my room and with trial and error figured out how to get the map to appear on a wide bare wall. I asked the computer questions and spent time researching locations and being surprised by how wide the kingdom was, but also, how small compared to the whole world. The whole desolate and ruined world. I asked to see some photos of what lay beyond the kingdom and quickly asked to have them turned off. There was some shit that once seen I could not unsee. It was like the future of the world had entered a dark ages.

We had to live and reign in a kingdom that had not much else beyond its borders except the last dredges of what used to be civilization. Two other kingdoms and that was it, barely anything. It was terrifying and would have shaken me to my core if not for the fact I was a visitor here. I hadn't been a part of the apocalypse or whatever that was.

This was what was left, this. All I could do was try to figure how to make *this* work.

And to do that I'd need to learn a lot about the politics of this place.

CHAPTER 22 - MAGNUS

The meetin' lasted for many hours and I was pained from sittin' up for that long. There were men there though that I had never met afore. I had tae earn their respect. I couldna allow them tae see me as weak; twas a time when loyalty was verra important.

Madame Johnstone brought lunch tae the office, but I wanted tae see Kaitlyn so I took my leave.

I found Kaitlyn in our room leanin' on the pillows lookin' at the projected map of my kingdom. I sat on the edge of the bed, my elbows on my knees. I greatly wanted tae lie down but I feared I would nae return tae m'feet. "I have a break but must return, mo ruel-iuil, there is still much left tae discuss. Have ye been studyin'?"

"I have, it's a big kingdom."

"Did you see, Kaitlyn, Castle Don—"

"Is that what it's called?"

"We will want tae rename it."

"Good."

"Did ye see tis verra near the River Tay? When I was living' there I recognized the mountains through the windows but dinna trust m'eyes."

"I noticed."

"Hammond was shewin' me a map and I learned that the castle is near where Balloch castle once stood. Hammond told me the Balloch ruins are on the grounds." I ran a hand through m'hair. "He shewed me photos. There is nae much left but some crumblin' walls."

"Was that hard to see?"

"Aye, twas a verra difficult meeting. Roderick has raised a considerable army. He has the upper hand in two of the five closest shires. I am worried there will be a great many lives lost."

Her face turned concerned. "Are you tired? This has been a lot to do today, maybe you should rest?"

"I feel good enough, I am askin' men tae fight for me, tae possibly die for me. I should hold on long enough tae ken the details of the war."

"Then again, you just had a surgery."

"The stitches are holdin' me taegether." I laughed tae prove I was nae so grave. "I have many deep scars, mo reul-iuil."

She crawled across the bed and wrapped around m'arm and tucked her head against my shoulder. "You should have seen how many you had four years from now."

"Och. We shall try nae tae let that happen again." She kissed me, a pleasant sweetness on m'mouth. "I have tae go back, the head of Royal Affairs wants tae stage the coronation on the morrow. He wants tae broadcast it. Dost that mean tae show everywhere like the cat videos? I wasna sure I kent what he spoke of."

Her hand clasped mine, twas warm and soft and comforting. "Yes, exactly like the cat videos. But really? With the battles going on in the streets and...?"

"They think they have the worst of the fightin' closest tae the castle under control and crownin' me is the highest priority. Once I am crowned, the discussion will change — I am the natural successor tae Donnan. They will put a crown on m'head and twill be difficult tae take it from me."

"Will men come to fight you for it?" Her words quickened with her fear. "You aren't able — I mean, you aren't ready to fight. You need to change the rules about challenging your reign."

"Daena worry, Kaitlyn, I will change the rules. Why do they get tae challenge me? I am the king and what are they? The unclaimed sons of Donnan?" I scoffed. "I am prone tae consider all challenges illegitimate. Who are they tae make me fight? Donnan liked tae have his sons fight for the glory of it."

"He was a really craptastic father."

"Aye. I have higher hopes for my sons." I chuckled and folded her hand in mine. "And once my son is born they winna have a reason tae challenge."

She said, "Your son... I actually have a lot to still explain... So much really."

I tried to read her face, but it told me nothin' of what she meant. "Twill have tae wait for longer, mo reul-iuil. I have the second part of the meetin' still."

CHAPTER 23

I wandered more around the living room, looking out the tall windows at the gardens outside, not sure if I had permission to go out there with the danger and all. Growing braver, I investigated the cabinets and bookshelves, everything exquisite and antique and beautiful and collected. I wondered if Lady Mairead had been involved, but this wasn't hoarded. It looked chosen: the best of the best, the private quarters, the extra special. The books were very very old. I dusted off a few and opened them to see inside, but wasn't much into reading the Iliad or the Epic of Gilgamesh or whatever.

There were some china pieces, dancing figures, small boxes, a shelf of antique spoons and a box with antique coins. I looked at those for a long time sifting them through my fingers investigating the words on them.

There was an antique writing desk with paper and a quill pen. I looked over my shoulder to make sure no one was coming and opened the drawers to investigate and in one drawer I found a book; it said Robert Burns on the spine. I flipped two very delicate pages and found the published date: 1786. Whoa. I gingerly flipped the book open to a poem that read like my husband sounded, so I kept it to read later. Under it was another leather bound antique book, smaller, more ornate. I opened it and saw it was filled with calligraphic handwriting. I flipped through. It belonged to a man, Johnne Cambel, and there was a date: 1558. Double whoa.

I carried the two books to my room. I lay down to read some poetry finding a wonderful romantic one I loved. I loved it so much I read it, laid the book to the side to think about it, then read it again.

And that was how I passed some time until Magnus returned before dinner. He sat on the bed again with a groan. I had barely left it all day. He ran a hand down his face, his other hand pressed to his side. "I am verra tired. Twas much tae discuss. My head is spinnin' from it all."

"I'm glad you're back."

He smiled. "Me too, I have a strong desire tae be inside ye."

"Well, as you know, we can't. You were told not to."

"I daena care what the nurse said, I want tae. I think I can decide for myself."

"Oh really?" I arched my brow. "This is how it is — what about my opinion? You decide for yourself and I'm just supposed to be ready?"

His smile faded and he looked very tired. "Tis exactly like that. But is also that I love ye and I have proven in another lifetime I canna live without ye. I need ye, and twas a verra hard day. I just want it tae be okay for me tae be quiet with ye for a while."

"Oh." I put my hand on his. "Of course, my love. We can if you feel up to it. We can go slow." I pushed the books under the pillow and put a hand against his face and kissed him then pressed my forehead to his. "You tell me if you need to stop." I climbed off the bed, stood before him and dragged the string of my wrap dress out to the side slowly untying it. "Lie back, Master Magnus."

I pulled my dress open, slowly away from my body, and let it slide down my arms. The filmy fabric floated to the ground. I was braless, one hadn't been offered, my underwear was loose and wide-hipped, not at all my style and probably borrowed, which was really kind of upsetting, but there was plenty of fabric to hook my thumbs under. I slowly glided them down my legs. Wiggling a lot.

Magnus moaned and the moan turned past the moan of being turned on and moved into a groan of pain.

"Are you okay?"

He curled onto his side and clutched his bandaged abdomen. His eyes clamped shut. "Aye, I — tis painin' me."

I pulled my panties back up, climbed onto the bed, and wrapped around him. "I'll call Mrs Johnstone to ask the nurse to bring you more pain medicine, but we can lie here quietly for a while. That's good too."

We lay wrapped together until the nurse came. She was kind and never said anything about what we might have been trying to do but instead simply said, "Be careful not to overdo." Everything checked out when she looked, so we hadn't done any damage.

She left and we returned to gentle cuddling. "I am sorry, Kaitlyn."

"You don't have to be sorry. We simply have to wait a week. We're grown ups, we can make it a week. And we can do other things in bed, like — can I read you a poem? I think you'll like it."

I turned for the poetry book half under the pillows and opened it to the page I had marked with a piece of tissue.

"This is by Robert Burns. It's ancient for me but was written after you were born," with my arms around him I read:

O, my luve's like a red, red rose,
       That's newly sprung in June:
    O, my luve's like the melodie,
       That's sweetly play'd in tune.

As fair art thou, my bonnie lass,
       So deep in luve am I:
    And I will luve thee still, my dear,
       'Till a' the seas gang dry.

'Till a' the seas gang dry, my dear,
       And the rocks melt wi' the sun:
    I will luve thee still, my dear,
       While the sands o' life shall run.

And fare thee weel, my only luve!
       And fare thee weel a-while!
    And I will come again, my luve,
       Tho' it were ten thousand mile.

"Och, tis beautiful. I like it when ye talk like a Scottish lass. What did it say of the seas?"

"Till a'the seas gang dry, my dear, and the rocks melt wi' the sun..."

His face nestled into my neck. "Tho it were ten thousand mile?"

"Yep. We always make it back to each other."

"Aye, we do." His stomach growled.

"You're hungry."

"At least somethin' is workin'."

"It will all work, my love, give it a few days."

CHAPTER 24

*M*rs Johnstone fed us at the dining room table. Only the king and I across the short sides facing each other. More steak and potatoes, the exact same taste. It was either what she cooked or what Donnan had liked. Luckily Magnus liked it and I was famished enough to eat anything. The steak was tough, the potatoes mealy.

Magnus ate so fast I didn't think he noticed but then he groaned. "I miss Chef Zach."

"Me too."

After a moment I said, "Not to change the subject, but is there something you want to tell me?"

He chewed slowly, watching my face. "Nae."

I teased, "That phrase I just used means I know you have something you should tell me, but you aren't and I'm about to call you out on it."

"I haena any idea what—"

"You, my love, have been keeping something from me, and because you didn't tell me you lived for four years thinking I was going to do something awful to you and it almost killed you." I held up four fingers. "Four years. So here we are, in this lifetime — you've already been thinking about it for too long. Now's the time to tell me."

"Already been thinkin' about it?" He scrutinized my face. "I daena ken what ye—"

"See, my love, you searched for my future, and you think I'm going to do something. You should tell me what it is so we can pretend like you were being upfront about it." I took a bite of steak having a little fun.

His brow drew down even farther. "I canna tell if ye are bein' funny or angry."

"I'm not being angry. But I tell you Magnus, we need to tell each other the truth if we're making it through this. I have watched a lot of tv and the number one cause of breakups? Not telling each other stuff. So out with it. What did you find out when you looked up my future?"

He put his forearms out beside his plate. "I learned ye are goin' tae have a bairn with Tyler. I haena checked it again tae see if tis still true, but it has been true. Twas true when I was preparin' tae go fight Samuel."

"And you fought Samuel knowing I was going to end up with Tyler?"

He nodded, looking at his plate.

"I'm glad you won, I'm very glad you didn't do anything stupid." I huffed, still teasingly, so he could see my smile, but was mystified by it.

"I'm going to tell you a lot of things right now, and I want you to listen to me, beginning with this: you should tell me everything you're worried about so we can work together. Every time always. I've always known you to be truthful, but this is one time that telling me what you were thinking would have saved you so much heartbreak. Seriously. So here it is, my love: In another lifetime we arrived at the dock in Florida and a group of soldiers fought us on the banks of the spring. They killed me. You, devastated, traveled back in time with one of the vessels and tried to rescue me. You were an extra person, Magnus, and it didn't work. More soldiers arrived and I died again. You did it a third time and more soldiers, a bigger storm, and guess what? The other Magnus died and I died. It was all very tragic." I took his hand and ran my thumb along his knuckle.

"How dost ye ken this?"

"Tyler told me."

His brow drew together.

"And I'll get to that." I continued, "So you learned on the banks of the spring, all by yourself, that when you're time traveling, you shouldn't loop onto your own life and try to fix things. So you gave up. You said goodbye to Chef Zach and came to the future and fought Samuel and became a king."

"I haena ever done this afore."

"You don't remember, but you did."

"How can ye ken it if ye were dead?"

"Bear with me. When you were in the future your son was born. You named him after yourself and he went by the name of Archie. He grew up. You kept fighting the General who sent those soldiers to the dock. For twenty-five years you fought, but you were also Archie's Da and he loved you very much."

"I daena understand."

"I know. But this is where it's important. Archie got married and you told him about me and you told him about that day on the dock and how you hadn't been able to win against the soldiers. And so he decided to go back in time and help you keep me alive."

I watched Magnus's face for the moment of recognition. I added, "He assumed a fake name, and it was Tyler Wilson. He wasn't sure of the date so he kept dropping into my life at different times. That's why he was so weirdly protective of me.

Then he was there at the dock and the rest of the story you know."

"Tyler is my son? Did ye ken this all along?"

"No, not at all, I learned it in the usual way I learn everything by being pissed off at someone who's trying to help me and yelling at them and finding out they were trying to help me and having to apologize profusely. I was so furious at him for dragging me away from you, but he was risking everything for his Da. Because you meant that much to him."

He winced. "But he inna born yet..."

"Yeah, and I don't really understand where grown Archie went. But recently I heard a theory about time, that the strands of time aren't one long string, but rather times happening simultaneously so maybe he's back in his grownup Archie time and we're here in this time where he's not born yet and — I don't know it's very confusing."

"Tis." Magnus looked at his half-eaten plate of food. "Twas my son and I mistrusted him. I regret the way I treated him."

"You didn't know, you can't blame yourself for something you didn't know." I patted his hand.

"After he told me the whole story, he gave me his passport and birth certificate, the ones with the name Tyler Wilson on it, so you could use them if you need to."

I asked, "So do you see what I'm saying?"

"That if anyone is Tyler Wilson now, tis me."

I nodded and said, "Aye." I added, "Before he left he gave me a list, all the things you know about fighting General Reyes for twenty years. He thought it might help you begin on a better foot."

"Where is the list?"

"It's in the safe in Florida."

"And we canna go tae Florida."

"Exactly. And this is what I'm saying to you Magnus. This is your third lifetime, third try, because first, Archie, your son, gave you a new chance at it, and now I am giving you a new chance. Not many people get to do things over, and while I think you're perfect in every way, we have to be smart and not squander this chance. And one way we get smart is by telling each other everything, because as you know, if we don't then evil people will use it against us."

CHAPTER 25

*M*rs Johnstone entered the dining room with Lady Mairead jockeying to arrive first. Mrs Johnstone said, "Excuse me Your Highness, the Lady Mairead is here, she is insisting she would like to see you. Would you like her to come in?"

Magnus said, "Aye, I have a few things tae discuss—"

Lady Mairead said, "Daena rise, Magnus. I ken ye are restin' from your surgery. Are you well?" She ordered Mrs Johnstone to bring her a plate of food and placed a dress box on the table beside me. "A gift for you, daughter, I assumed you would be needing it once I heard you were here."

She turned to Magnus. "Your coronation is tomorrow? I have just learned of it and came when I could. I ken ye think ye can do it without me, but I assure you I will be needed."

Her eyes rested on me as she sat at the head of the table, of, freaking, course. "Open the box, Kaitlyn."

Magnus reached across the table for the box. "I will open it."

Lady Mairead sighed. "Fine, if she's incapable."

Magnus untied the string and lifted the lid. He picked up the garment inside, a dress, in pale blue, ornate and luxurious, and very pretty. I really liked it. Magnus said, "Thank you Lady Mairead, I appreciate the kindness greatly."

"There are some jewelry pieces in there as well, Kaitlyn. You will want tae look your best on the morrow."

I said, "Thank you."

She said, "I consider this a peace offering."

Magnus smirked. "Tis nae matter if ye consider it a peace offering, tis only if Kaitlyn and I consider it so. Tis just a verra wee box."

"True. Either way tis a dress, and she needs one for your coronation." A plate of food was placed down for her and with very prissy manners she began to eat. "Are ye pleased with your kingdom so far, Magnus?"

"I have seen the prison cells, a death match, and now Donnan's secluded safe house. I daena think I have much tae judge. I have been many times almost killed."

"That will all change on the morrow. We will go to the palace and you'll meet your cabinet and—"

"I met with them today."

"Oh well, then ye ken the details—"

"You intend tae stay here this evenin'?"

"Aye, I winna be a cause of trouble for ye, I will keep tae myself in one of the extra rooms."

"Kaitlyn and I are stayin' in one of the downstairs guest rooms. If ye want tae stay in a room on the upper floors ye may."

"Thank you Magnus, that is verra kind." We all ate in silence and it was the most freaking awkward shit ever. And then it got really weird.

"How did *you* come tae be here, Kaitlyn?"

I glanced at Magnus.

He answered, "About four years from now I traveled tae the

past tae hide and rest. Kaitlyn found me there. I asked her for help and sent her here tae this time."

"What on earth would ye be hiding from, ye art a king?"

"I was hidin' from a General Reyes, apparently."

She winced. "Oh."

There was a look in her eyes — I asked, "You know of him?"

"Nae." She shook her head. "Nae, I daena—"

"It seemed like you did, like you recognized the name."

"Nae, maybe the name, but nae a general." She folded her napkin and placed it beside her plate. "I am finished." She pushed her chair from the table and forced a smile on her face. "I think I will retire, we have much tae do on the morrow. Get plenty of sleep, Magnus. G'night Kaitlyn." She swept from the room with her back straight, but I saw a tremble to her hands, held tight in front of her.

Magnus and I exchanged a look.

I said, "She's definitely heard of him."

As we passed the living room to go to our room, Lady Mairead was standing in front of the desk, the drawers open, rifling through it. Piles of papers were stacked on top, papers were clutched in her fingers. Her eyes were wide when she asked, "Magnus, have ye removed anythin' from Donnan's desk?"

Magnus said, "Nae."

She looked around with a worried expression. "It should be there, has anyone been here goin' through Donnan's possessions?"

"I daena think so, but I was sleepin' through most of it."

"Kaitlyn?"

Of course, I had gone through that drawer just hours before and I had two books under the pillow in my room. I didn't know which one she was looking for but I could see from the look in her eyes it was very, very important. "I haven't seen anyone go through the drawers. Maybe it happened before we got here? What's missing?"

She took in the room. "Nothing important." She directed her search to the small bookcase along the other wall.

Magnus said, "Then we will leave ye tae lookin' for it."

Back in our room I dove for the pillow and retrieved the books. I wordlessly held them out to Magnus.

"Och," he said, "Tis what she is searchin' for?"

"I think so..." I flipped open the book of poetry. Inside the front cover there was a long looping calligraphic signature: "To my dearest Donnan, yours, Mairead."

I turned the book so Magnus could read it. He winced. "She is nae usually sentimental, I daena think that is the value of them."

I flipped through the whole poetry book, there was nothing more to it, besides my own tissue paper marker. I opened the second book, the fading handwriting, journal type entries, difficult to read, except the name, Johnne Cambel, and the year, 1558. I turned it toward Magnus.

He read and nodded. "Tis the one, tis an ancestor, and must be important. We shouldna tell her of it until we ken the value of it."

I grinned. "I was hoping you'd say that." I dropped onto the bed with the book. "Cool. I have something Lady Mairead wants, got a new dress for your coronation tomorrow, and you're on the cusp of being a king." I opened the book. "Tis a verra good day for me." I began to try to read the difficult writing.

CHAPTER 26

The following morning Hammond, wearing a dress uniform, collected us and took us by helicopter to the palace. Lady Mairead still seemed discombobulated about the missing book — the one that was beside me hidden inside the dress box she gave me the night before.

Magnus's eyes were open, but he faced straight ahead, focused, probably nervous. I watched out the window, trying to get the scale of the country, the kingdom. It wasn't much different from my own time, at least from the air — except small things: a shit ton more air traffic, taller buildings, more streets, more sprawl.

As we approached the castle I asked, "So this is the same area as Balloch?"

Magnus glanced out the windows. "I recognize the mountains. See," he pointed, "tis called Beinn Labhair."

Around the palace were piles of wreckage from the battles the day before. Military trucks drove around the grounds and drones flew through the air.

We landed on the same landing pad where we had landed so many times before as prisoners, but this time as the royals. People bowed, helped, seemed awed by Magnus. I was not trusted, you could see it in most everyone's eyes.

We were directed to the royal apartments. They had been cleaned of Samuel's things and I was pretty grateful Samuel had lived here for a while, putting some distance between me and Donnan. I could safely assume most of Donnan's stuff had been removed for Samuel's and now stripped for us. And I didn't have a personal grudge against Samuel, now that my husband had killed him and all. His son, Roderick, though, he was really pissing me off.

Our apartments were gorgeous and opulent: glass windows, sliding doors, large-scale paintings and sculptures surrounded by lush fabrics and antiques. But here it wasn't piled and hoarded, these rooms were decorated with the best showpieces history had to offer.

First thing on my list: Organize and catalogue the hoard and have it appraised. Maybe make Lady Mairead stand down from further collecting.

Would I need to take it all back to where it belonged? How much of history had already been screwed up?

The next thing on my list: close Donnan's private prison rooms. It was frankly freaky to imagine they were here somewhere — where I had been kept. Where who knows how many women had been kept.

I would close that shit down.

My dress was a perfect fit. I looked dignified and very rich. My jewelry was simple but expensive. I looked like I was born to do this, like Princess Kate — the British one, though of course she wasn't born to be a queen, she started ordinary, but somehow she always pulled it off. I would try to be like that. To pull it off.

Magnus was gorgeous. He was wearing a white shirt, dark pants, a military jacket much like Donnan used to wear. He looked, what was the word, *resplendent*, with his sword at his waist, medals on his chest. "How come as soon as you strap on a sword I want to take it off you again?"

"Because ye quite fancy me, my wife. Tis a verra nice thing."

"I do, I really do, but I will have to overcome it, I suppose. We still have to wait five days and besides my dress is already on."

"I suppose we do have tae wait and we want the crown on m'head before anymore time passes." He leaned in and kissed me and in our fancy clothes it was quite sexy to press against him.

The coronation was a lot like a small wedding. The very large grand room held about thirty people. Most everyone wore military-style coats except for a handful of women in beautiful dresses. Cameras were stationed around the perimeter to broadcast the ceremony. On the walls were large projections of an audience, from floor to ceiling, their faces coming forward and back, in and out of focus. A large chair-like throne stood at the front and a man in deep purple robes waited solemnly beside it. As I was led to my seat in the front row, there was a good deal of murmuring. Lady Mairead was led to the seat right next to mine.

I did not have enough coaching, none really. I straightened my back and tried to look gracious and commanding. I wrapped my ankles and folded my hands in my lap and wondered why in the world I had decided to do any of this ever at all.

Oh, that's right — Magnus.

I twisted in my seat as he walked through the door and across the carpeted middle of the room. All eyes were on him. His eyes on me.

As he passed my chair he paused. Then he dropped to a knee with a grimace, a slight press against his abdomen as he lowered. He took my hands in his. He bowed his head over our hands. His brow glistened, his hands trembled.

I freed from his grip and gently brushed my fingertips down his face. I put my hands back within his and we squeezed.

Then he stood, composed his face into strength, straightened his jacket, and continued his walk to the front of the room.

The ceremony stretched long and most of it was monotone and in Latin, which made some weird sense now I knew this whole royal lineage time-jumped here from the 16th century.

Like everything about this place, the ceremony was full of incongruities — past and future melded. Historical with bits of futuristic details. Latin contrasting with gigantic video projections. The castles, the ceremonies, the clothing, they weren't the future so much as brought from the past.

An entire kingdom created by time jumpers, men who contained within them the brutality of the past and combined it with invincible power. But yet, until now, the men that ruled held tight to ignorance and savagery—

Note to self: add a law requiring ceremonies that involve my fate and life have to be performed in words understandable by me. I will decree it.

Until then my husband was making lots of promises and vows to his new kingdom in words I couldn't understand. Like a lot of this, I hadn't really thought it through.

There was a reception. No one wanted to speak to me, which was fine. Everyone wanted to speak to Magnus. He introduced me and made small talk while I tried very hard to keep all the names straight to coach him later because the last thing we wanted was Lady Mairead doing that for us. So I spent my time while I was left out of conversations inventing mnemonics, like: Colonel Porters. His wife Wendy is portly. She looks like she's eaten a lot of KFC. The chicken colonel competes with Wendy's hamburgers.

I didn't know if it would work, but it gave me something to do.

Food was served as a grand sit-down meal. A weird thing I noticed on this whole weird day, everyone kept complimenting me on the meal. Wonderful dinner, Your Highness. Why thank you, I did not one thing.

It was thrilling actually that I was the head of a machine that could do this without me lifting one single finger or saying anything to anybody.

We ate at a long table in the formal dining room — Magnus at the head, Lady Mairead and I across from each other. I chewed and wondered, was this my life now? One of the long walls carried a projection: shifting video of gigantic street parties, crowds of people celebrating Magnus's ascension.

After dessert was served, Colonel Donahoe came to the head of the table and whispered something in Magnus's ear. Magnus's eyes cut to me. He listened for a moment then said, "Thank ye, Hammond, keep me informed."

Lady Mairead was watching closely as was I.

Magnus leaned to my ear. "Bella is bein' moved here tae the hospital, she is nearin' her time."

"Oh," I said for lack of anything better, smarter, more interesting to say.

CHAPTER 27

*A*fter dessert Magnus and I took our leave and Lady Mairead stayed behind to say goodbye to the guests. We held hands as we stalked back to our apartments, pausing at the end of the hall for a moment confused about which way to go and needing to ask one of the hallway guards for directions.

We made it to our doors and guards opened them without question so I knew we were in the right place.

We entered our sitting room, sofas in brocades, pillows in silk and embroidery, antique tapestries, marble sculptures, intricately carved tables and above it all one of my Picasso paintings. It was comforting — here behind the couch and also back there in 2018. I couldn't imagine how it got here but at least I never sold it to a museum. It was still ours and I loved its timelessness so much.

The other wall, facing our painting, held one of those never ending videos of celebrations. The overall color theme of the room was white accented with gold, like a king named Louis was about to get married all up in here — probably to his mistress.

I did not like the parallels.

Magnus sank into the couch. I sat in the chair opposite him. The skirt of my pale blue dress spread around my daintily clad feet, my elbows on my knees. "What do you know?"

"She is here. She is accompanied by a man, a John Mitchell, Colonel Donahoe daena ken him, and is searchin' his history. The bairn is early."

"Dangerous early, or just exciting early? She looked far along when I saw her..."

"I daena ken."

"Well, we'll have to ask someone for the information." I looked around. "As soon as there is someone to ask."

We looked at each other across the room. "Until then we wait, I suppose." I stared at my hands. "It feels like good news she has a man with her? But I suppose it could be bad news too?"

"Depends on what kind of man he is."

"I guess that's true."

Every few hours a physician named Dr Franklin would come to our apartment to fill Magnus in on the details. All I needed to know was Bella was going to have a baby.

Everything else was shaking my core.

I didn't understand how to advise him or help him because I was completely lost. The Manual for How To Be A Human had been silent on waiting for the birth of your husband's baby. It helped a little that the birth of the baby would help save my husband's life — having an heir improved his chances, but by a slim amount, on both saving him and helping me.

Lady Mairead sent word that all the guests were gone home. I guessed she wanted to come hear news, but Magnus didn't offer any information beyond: we are waiting to hear.

Who was I kidding though, Lady Mairead had been living here for long enough; she was sure to be getting crucial information long before me.

We went to bed early. There was a dresser drawer in my room with some clothes for me, pajamas and underwear, a closet with a few dresses inside. The bed was a four poster, in a deep purple with gold accents, and was very comfortable but still my sleep was fitful.

And then in the middle of the night Magnus rose from the bed. "Where are you going?"

"Nae where, mo reul-iuil. Just tae get the news."

He slipped through our door to the sitting room.

He didn't return, so I got up to see what the news was. Magnus was on the couch. The room dark except for one small table lamp. "What's happening?"

"Tis a surgery."

"Oh, " I sat beside him and took his hand. "That's good though, a decision has been made, the baby will be here really soon."

He nodded.

"Do you need to go to her? I mean, I don't know what protocol is, should be in the room, or like waiting out in the hall?"

"He is a bastard. I shouldna be there, twould raise her standin' above yours."

"Oh. I mean, I appreciate that, but he is your son."

"I will see him after he is born. And I will proclaim him mine in due time."

"How do you know all of this, what to do?"

"I have lived in London, been to court, I have seen this many times. It helps me greatly tae have him as an heir, but the man with them complicates things. If Bella marries him and he is—"

"So we wait some more?"

"Aye."

CHAPTER 28

The physician arrived an hour later to tell us the baby, a boy, had been born. And Bella had come through the surgery well. Bella was with the baby right now, but Magnus should come to the hospital rooms to meet him.

Magnus dressed in dark slacks and a nice white shirt. I didn't have anything casual and comfortable, but I supposed this occasion required a dress. I applied some makeup and brushed my hair. I should look good in case there were photos.

Magnus and I met at the doors to our apartments and Colonel Donahoe met us to accompany us downstairs.

We walked the route I had traveled just a few days before. We passed the room where Magnus had been recovering. Bella was in there, I could sense it in the way the air turned dark and repelling.

We were let into the same office I had been in when they wheeled Magnus away. The room was dark except for a small desk lamp spilling light across the desk blotter. There was a leather couch, two comfortable leather chairs and a wall of books. It looked like the kind of office a New York psychiatrist might have.

A nurse said to Magnus, "Your highness, please have a seat, I'll bring him in a moment." She left through the double doors.

Magnus and I sat in chairs. We didn't talk. I barely even breathed. I didn't know how I passed the time because I may have freaking gone unconscious. I was surprised I stayed in the chair and didn't collapse onto the floor.

Then, after so very long — all my nightmares and dreams came true when a hospital-style bassinet was pushed through the double doors by the nurse. Magnus stood. I stood. Magnus crossed to the bassinet and looked in. The baby was wearing a little blue hat and swaddled in a blue silk blanket.

Magnus whispered, "Och aye, he is verra wee."

The nurse said, "He is early but Dr Franklin said he is in perfect health. Would you like to hold him?" She scooped the baby from the bassinet with the practiced movements of a delivery room nurse and before Magnus could finish with, "Can I?" placed the baby in Magnus's arms.

My chin trembled with tears as Magnus's arms simultaneously strengthened around the baby and relaxed with the comforting of him. He stepped back and lowered into the chair, his eyes on the baby's face. The baby was awake, looking up at Magnus. Magnus repeated himself, his eyes glistening. "Verra wee."

I sob smiled, a confusing clash of emotions inside me, love for my husband and happiness for him with bitter regret and anger at this baby who was so sweet — so there was some guilt there too. I sat in the chair beside them and tried to keep from dissolving into ugly-crying.

Magnus looking at the sweet baby face, Archie, a baby who would one day love his Da so much he would sacrifice everything for him and save my life. Magnus looking at me his face glistening with tears. Me, someone who loved Magnus so much I would sacrifice everything for him, because I knew he would do the same for me. I knew it. Down deep inside.

Magnus's chin trembled like mine. "Tis overwhelmin' me tae meet him."

"Me too. I just went through like one hundred and seventy-five emotions." I gulped some air. "He's beautiful."

"Aye." We both sat and concentrated on that baby face as slowly the baby's eyes closed and he fell asleep.

Magnus ran a hand through his hair. "I should go speak tae Bella."

"Yeah, probably."

"Would ye hold him while I am gone?"

"Can I?"

"Aye, Kaitlyn." I put my arms out and he gingerly transferred the baby from his arms to mine, a weight that was heavier than I expected, much like the arrival — it was all more heavy, big, deep, and destroying than I thought possible.

Magnus slipped through the doors to go to Bella's room as the baby settled into my arms, across my stomach; a pleasant weight, one I wanted so desperately and here it was, borrowed—

I sobbed and tears streamed down my face. I missed my baby. I had never looked into his eyes. Felt his lovely living weight. Never listened to his soft breaths and smelled his sweet baby skin and... and... *oh god—*

My shoulders shook with it as I tried to be quiet. I tried to be contained and controlled, a grown up, a mother, the kind of person who could hold a baby and keep them comforted and could love them and be loved back.

The baby looked up at me.

My first moment with him and here I was devastated.

I gulped down my tears and took a deep breath.

"Hi." I rubbed my thumb gently across the baby's temple. "Did you wake up? You're probably surprised to see someone holding you while they're crying. I'm sorry about that. This was not how I wanted to make my first impression. I'm Kaitlyn." I wrapped his baby fist around my thumb. "I'm going to be your stepmom. Now, before you get upset and go thinking that means I'm going to suck, let me tell you three things about me. First, I do kind of suck. And you and I might not always see eye to eye. As a matter of fact you'll probably think I'm a huge pain in the ass. But I love your Da, and you will really love your Da, so we will have that in common. We can be friends based on that I think. Plus, two, I am very loyal, and you and I just became family, so you can count on me, I will always be here for you."

I stroked a finger down the baby's cheek and there was a little fuzz of dark hair out from under his hat. I pulled the baby hat off his head and leaned in and kissed his forehead. "If you ever think, 'No one listens to me,' or 'No one likes me,' or 'No one wants me,' because I've been there before — when I was growing up it seemed like the only person who really wanted me was my grandmother, Barb, I always knew at least I had one person. Well, you have your Da, of course, and your mom, but you also have me, a third person. And that makes you very lucky, to have three people. Also, I am cool. I know if people say that it generally means they aren't, but I'm saying it because you don't realize it yet. Because you're a baby, but I'm very cool. I understand a lot about how the world works. I'm brave and strong and true. I have fought kings and won. So yeah, I'm your step mom and I'm a little like having a dragon in your corner. Like the good kind."

I sat looking at his sweet face, a lot like Magnus, not enough like Bella for me to care.

Magnus came in a few minutes later.

He said, "Come sit with me." He helped me up and we carefully crossed to the couch, the worried movements of people not used to carrying sleeping newborns in their arms. He sat first and held out an arm and I tucked in against his side and we got the baby into the crook of Magnus's arm.

"What did you say to her?"

He was silent for a moment. "I said, 'Thank you.'" He added, "I told her if she needed anythin' tae let me ken and I told her I wanted his name tae be Archibald Campbell after my uncle. And I would like tae call him Archie. She said she would like that."

"So like Magnus Archibald Caelhin Campbell?"

"Nae, just Archibald. I will save the full name for our son, Kaitlyn."

"Thank you."

He kissed me on my forehead. "Were you introducin' yerself?"

"I was, I told him he can call me Kaitlyn. And I was like having a protective dragon for a friend."

"Tis how ye see yourself?"

"Sure, how do you see me?"

"I think ye are a lot like your grandma Barb. Funny and wise. You are fiercely loyal as well, but funny and wise foremost."

"Oh, I like that better."

"Aye, tis better tae be like Barb instead of a dragon."

"I'll leave the dragon-y stuff to Archie's grandma, Lady Mairead."

Magnus chuckled. "See, I have never met such a witty dragon."

"How many have you met?"

"Verra many, remember, I come from the dark ages, dragons nursed me when I was a bairn."

I laughed, as quiet as I could. "You sir, just made a history joke, I'm very proud of you."

"As I am of you."

"Bella doesn't want him tonight?"

"Nae, she said she needed tae sleep, so I will keep him tonight."

"Good." I was also feeling very sleepy. My eyes growing heavy, I slowly fell asleep beside the baby in Magnus's arms.

CHAPTER 29 - MAGNUS

Kaitlyn fell asleep, a familiar weight along my side, the unfamiliar weight of wee Archie in m'arms. I watched him sleep with soft shallow breaths and then he squirmed, his small fist moved tae his mouth, and his dark eyes opened tae look up.

"Och, wee one, did ye wake?"

His eyes held mine as if in answer.

"Aye, ye have woken tae meet me finally. I am your da. Tis verra nice tae see ye, wee one." Archie squirmed in my arms and I helped him get comfortable.

"Most everyone calls me Magnus, but these days many people call me a king." I smiled down at him. "I too, am verra surprised by the title. I tell ye, twas nae m'intent when I was a bairn in the highlands, growin' up with m'brother Sean. He will be your uncle if I can get him tae come around tae it." I ran a finger along the curve of his perfect ear.

"There is also my sister, Lizbeth. She has always taken care of me and Sean and everybody else without actin' as if she cares on us at all. You will just tell her ye can take care of yerself and ye two can be great friends."

Kaitlyn breathed deep and shifted beside me. I lifted m'arm and waited for her tae settle back tae sleep.

I lowered my voice. "I grew up in a castle called Kilchurn on Loch Awe. I hope tae shew it tae ye some day."

He was still watchin' me so I continued, "I also lived in a castle called Balloch. Twas verra grand but ye winna ken it as anythin' but a ruin. I am sorry for it. I would have liked ye tae see it."

I ran my fingers down his soft cheek. "I also lived in London, a wondrous city, and once I was introduced tae the Queen. What if she saw me now, wee one? Nae longer that young mischievous boy but a king? Twould be a marvel tae her I would think." I chuckled. "Dost ye think ye will be mischievous like your da?"

I watched his expression change. His brow drew taegether as if he were answerin'. "I take that as an answer, aye, but I warn ye will be a great troublin' tae ye if ye are. I canna argue against it, because tis great fun, but if ye do like tae have some mischief ye will have tae stand up like a man after it. I want ye tae tell the truth when all is done. Promise me ye will."

He made a wee noise like bairn do and we watched each other quietly for a moment.

After a long time I whispered, "I heard ye have met Kaitlyn. I hope ye like her because I like her verra much." I pulled his little hand up from under the blanket. "She is verra funny. You will see it when ye are older. She will make ye laugh verra often."

I let out a deep exhale. "Though I have made her cry more than is fair. She needs us, wee one, she needs our protection. She will also need ye tae let her protect ye too. She will want tae love ye and I hope ye will be kind tae her about it. You winna find a better…" I dinna ken how tae finish without callin' her a mother and it hurt me tae say it aloud. "I hope ye will let her. I would consider it a great favor tae me."

He yawned big and wide. "Och, tis a strong expression ye have."

I moved a pillow up and placed it behind m'head. "We have a lot tae do, you and I. We have tae be strong. We have tae be warriors. We have tae fight." I caressed his tiny fingers, his smooth fist, twas hard tae imagine it might someday hold a sword.

"I ken ye daena have the strength yet. We will have tae build your muscles with milk and Chef Zach will feed ye ice cream. Tis a wondrous nourishment. Twill grow ye up tae have brawn like your da." I flexed m'arm tae show him the muscles on it. Archie dinna seem impressed.

I pulled his arm up and bent it and chuckled. "Och, ye will have some growin' tae do. Ice cream is verra grand. Twill also make ye a proud lover like your da too. I hope someday ye have a woman ye like verra much who will make ye laugh and let ye take her tae bed whenever ye want tae. Tis a verra nice thing." I shifted the weight of him more tae the crook of m'arm. "A verra nice thing. When ye find a woman like that ye have tae promise tae love her well, she will deserve all your kindnesses."

Archie's eyes drifted closed then open, then closed once more, finally asleep. "Aye, ye sleep, bairn, ye will need yer rest." I added, "Forget what I said about bein' a warrior. I daena want ye tae fight, wee one. Tis a burden I will spare ye from if I can, I promise it tae ye." A few moments later in the darkness of the room I fell asleep holding Archie and Kaitlyn in m'arms.

$\mathcal{M}$agnus had meetings the next day.

I was scheduled to meet with the house-keeping crew and the kitchen staff to go over the menus. I had to make choices. I had to override my embarrassing lack of taste and pick things to impress strangers. Things that would probably taste awful. I missed Zach. He always criticized what I liked, but he usually provided enough of it without prompting. He fed me. These people wanted me to tell them what I wanted to eat and not just me, Magnus and apparently everyone in the castle too. Hamburgers weren't an option.

Then I had to pick rotations — how often did I want my linens changed? What was the correct answer? Laundry day at home was when I needed laundry done. I wished Emma was here to tell me what I wanted. Because my answers seemed to cause these strangers to be disappointed. I wanted to ask, 'How often do you want to change my bed linens?' But that seemed like a rookie move.

Wasn't I supposed to have some kindly matronly lady to orga-nize everything for me, to guide me through this?

I asked the woman holding a tablet and making marks during the meeting, "How many of you are new here at the castle?"

She looked around at the faces of the staff. "Almost everyone, your highness, there was an um, pretty brutal changeover in the staff after Samuel moved in."

"Brutal?"

"Yep."

"I'm sorry about the brutality. Have you been here the whole time since Donnan?"

"I worked for Donnan for about two years, before—"

I cut her off. "Okay, we can work with that. I'm new, so I'll need some help to figure this out."

I asked her to accompany me to have some coffee and we sat and I liked her; she seemed competent. I dug a little to see what she thought of Donnan and she said she had, "seen some things but wouldn't want to talk about them." I supposed that was a good trait, so I asked her to be my household manager.

And I was really glad she didn't tell me anything. I seriously didn't want to know.

I also didn't want to know what she thought of me so I didn't ask. Everyone I talked to had a look in their eyes: suspicious, judgmental, wary. I had somehow managed to get away without a trial, but there was an everyday trial of public opinion and — where were the public relations people? There had to be some, right? That was a big city we passed over, there couldn't be a big city without a public relations firm. I should ask whoever would know.

I should also ask someone how to get the local kingdom news beyond the giant shifting images that were once again showing the post-war streets. It looked like a bomb had gone off in the kingdom and Magnus would need to clean that up. We needed to learn how to clean this up.

But right now I was trying to read this ancient handwritten

book, a not so easy task. The handwriting was more carved pen-marks and flourishes than letters and when I could make out the letters, it was pretty common for the words to be indecipherable. But, when I stopped thinking and simply read, I sometimes got the gist. The first two pages, basically: this is Johnne's book. Johnne is of the family Cambell. Johnne has many brothers and cousins and uncles.

So far it wasn't really the kind of book Lady Mairead should be desperate about.

After my 'household' meetings I had lunch by myself and read the book some more. Another page, something had happened. There was a battle on Là Samhna. The battle looked like it was called Inchaiden, but the N might have been an 'M' so I wasn't sure.

I asked the surrounding room computer if this was a place it could identify and after a lot of trial and error I came to a place called Inchadney, an old village in Kenmore. On further research I realized Kenmore was the location of Balloch Castle as I knew it, later rebuilt as Taymouth Castle, and finally now, a new castle built on the grounds. This one. Castle Don — a name Magnus needed to change first thing.

I looked at the book, okay, hundreds of years ago there was a battle on this land, right near this castle, but why was that important?

I read some more until I got bored and decided to go see how Archie was doing.

CHAPTER 31

I could hear him crying before I got to the room and when I came in the day nurse was jiggling Archie trying to get him to calm. "I'm sorry, Your Highness, he's been crying for a while."

"He's got some good lungs on him, that's for sure." His face was red from the carrying on.

"Has Bella fed him?"

"We have strict orders not to bother her, she has a schedule when we're supposed to—" It was very hard to talk over his screams. I put my arms out and the nurse deposited Archie into them and I did a little spinning dance-walk around the room like I had seen Emma do. I motioned toward a bottle and tried to get Archie to take it. He was too worked up to care. "Is he wet?"

She said, "I just changed him."

"Okay, " I hollered, "then I'll dance. When was your last break?"

"I could use one!" She hollered back, so I sent her away and danced, just me and Archie screaming his head off until suddenly he wasn't.

He calmed and I jiggle-danced over to the bottle and fed him while my jiggles turned to mild jostles and finally slow rockings. "What's with all the noise, little guy? You're one day in and already acting like an asshole? Screaming at your nurse? I mean come on, you get more friends by being quiet and—"

His eyes looked up into mine. "Aw, sweetie, yeah, I didn't mean to call you an asshole. I meant it in a loving way." I kissed his cheek and breathed in his scent. "You smell like a baby, not the awesome deep scent of your dad, but you'll probably get there someday. But seriously, it's time to man up, stop bellyaching — how are you going to be big and strapping like your dad if that's how you're carrying on?"

While I spoke Archie looked at me as if he was listening, sucking on his bottle. Then his eyes closed and he was asleep, just like that.

After a few moments I took the bottle from him and sat in a comfy leather chair holding him, content. I didn't have anything to do but stare at the baby. That was enough. I may have dozed off too.

Magnus came to the room a little later to take me for dinner and after dinner, Magnus and I returned to the nursery and the baby was wheeled in from Bella's room. We held him again while we slept and woke to rock and feed him in the night.

In the morning, bleary-eyed, we put him in the bassinet to be wheeled back to Bella's room.

I said, watching the bassinet pass through the double doors. "That was fun."

Magnus joked, "Aye, though I will have tae get my sleep while I am in the meeting this morn."

"You have another one?"

"Not many more, yesterday we discussed border security and military actions. Today we have tae discuss the rights of ascension. Tis the set of challenge rules compellin' me tae fight someone with a claim tae the throne."

I said, "Those are the barbaric rules you're going to change."

"Och, aye. But I canna change them alone, I have tae discuss it with my Board of Controllers first."

"Who is that?"

"Apparently the king has a dozen people who are tae tell him what tae do."

"Do they seem wise and helpful and capable and kind?"

"Perhaps two of them, the rest are nae any of it. But I am the decidin' factor."

"Did Donnan have people tellin' him what to do? If that's guidance, they really need a new system."

"He did. I can call for a dismantlin' but tis frowned upon without allowin' the Board tae opine on it first. Some of them daena have a wise thought on anythin'. Some of them only hold an opinion if tis the opposite of the man beside them. The good part is we can jump and the Board will control the kingdom until I return."

"Speaking of men, are there any women on the Board?"

"Nae."

"You should remedy that. Women make up 50% of the world, and we have some pretty excellent advice sometimes. Replace six of those men with women and let's see if you still have trouble getting opinions."

He kissed me on my cheek. I remembered to ask, "Hey, do you know what Samhna means?"

His brow furrowed. "Tis the day of Samhain."

"Like October 31?"

"Aye, the night and the morn of November. Why are ye askin'?"

"The book said there was a battle on that date in 1557, I still don't understand what the significance is..."

"Twould have been November 1st then."

"What makes you say so?"

He grinned. "Men canna fight in the dark though we might try."

I chuckled. "That makes sense."

He said, "I was thinkin' we might want tae go soon. We could go tae the past tae get your ring."

"I'd like that. I'd like that a lot, but only if this is all under control while we're gone. There were battles just the other day."

"Tis why I have tae go tae these meetings." We kissed each other goodbye and parted at the door.

CHAPTER 32

*W*e did this for almost a week. Meeting in the nursery and holding Archie at night. Parting during the day for meetings and duties and I had them too — meetings with the staff.

I read more in the book, taking it downstairs with me to the nursery in the afternoon and holding Archie and reading. I now knew more about the battle of Inchaiden. The date, Là Samhna, probably as Magnus said, November 1, in 1557. And it read as if Magnus's Campbell ancestors had massacred their opponents, like really, brutally massacred them. In the book it sounded like they had gotten scared by something — 'twas sharp and clangerus crashin a fiery tempest of men in hoods without faces shewn.' During the battle the Campbells gained the advantage and killed them all except one man — who they called simply Tadhg.

I was trying to decide whether to risk waking the baby to ask the room if Tadhg was a common name when the doors slammed open and Bella stormed in.

Her face held a dangerous fury. "What are you doing holding my baby? How dare you? You give him to me right now!" I jumped from my seat and held Archie out towards her. She grabbed him from my arms, spun, and deposited him, now crying, into the bassinet.

She turned on me. She was shorter but so angry she filled the room. She loomed over me. "You are not allowed to touch him with your filthy disgusting hands!" My heart had gone to racing, my hands shaking.

The two nurses backed to the wall. She turned on them, "You let this terrible witch hold my baby? How dare you, did I give you permission to?"

A nurse said, "No, I didn't realize..."

The door behind me opened, more strangers witnessing my shame. "She is not allowed to hold my baby, ever! She is a monster! She murdered Donnan. You saw the photos!!!" I took two steps back.

She pointed at me. "You know she is a filthy witch. She has bewitched Magnus and is keeping him away from me and his son."

"It's not like that — I—"

"She is not allowed to touch him, ever!! Do you hear me? Ever!"

I wheeled around and shoved past Dr Franklin and one of the nurses standing in the doorway and stumbled down the hallway to the elevator. I frantically pushed buttons for the ground floor. I cried big, ugly tears while the elevator descended, clutching my stomach, my body wracked with sobs.

The doors slid open and I pushed out. Strangers stared at me as I passed. I pushed past guards, crying, barely able to see, and raced down the front steps of the castle and across the grand lawn toward the trees to the right side. Racing, I made it most of the way before I heard Magnus's voice long behind me, "Kaitlyn!"

I made it to the woods. I didn't know why but maybe I just wanted to hide there. It made sense to get behind something so no one could see my shame. I collapsed on the soggy dirt floor of the woods and rolled in a ball and sobbed in the dirt and muck of a Scottish forest.

"Kaitlyn!" Magnus caught up to me, dropped to a skidding halt beside me, and lifted the top half of me into his arms. "Kaitlyn, what has happened?" Behind him were two drones and three all-terrain vehicles, forming a circle around us, the drones hovering above, guarding.

I shoved him off. "You! You did this to me! You did it." I scrambled to my feet. "I hate you so much."

He stood. "You daena mean it, Kaitlyn."

"I do." I shoved him on the chest. "I hate you. I hate you so much. You killed me — you destroyed our life. My baby died and now this bitch is calling me—" I couldn't even say it. I sobbed and shoved him again. "I hate you. You did this to me. You brought her into our life and she is talking to me like that?" I pushed my hair back from my face. "She's calling me a murderer in front of all those people? She is such a bitch. God, I hate her so much."

I shoved his chest again. He didn't move. I shoved him again. He just took it. I balled my fists and pummeled his chest and pushed him once more. "I hate everyone so much." I devolved into tears, crying into my hands, desperate and so so so sad. He reached for me and I shoved him away. After a really long time after the tears had stopped coming, I added, "She doesn't deserve you. She doesn't deserve Archie, that sweet baby, she is so mean."

The look on Magnus's face was dark and scary and my heart dropped. "I'm sorry."

"You daena have tae be sorry."

"I shouldn't have said that, I didn't mean it." Tears welled up again, "I do sound terrible. Like a terrible person. Don't be mad, please, I — I'm so sorry. I didn't mean it." He took me in his arms and held me.

My tear covered face was pressed to his shoulder. "Please tell me you forgive me. Please, I'm scared. I don't want to lose you."

He held his lips against my forehead. "You arna losin' me, mo reul-iuil."

"I didn't mean it about hating you."

"I ken it." He wrapped his arms tighter. "I am nae angry with ye."

"I'm so sorry."

"Tis because ye are worried, ye have had a rage and now ye are scared." He pulled me from his chest and pushed a bunch of matted wet hair from my face. "Fear follows rage, because ye have gone off your head and when it includes your family — one time Sean and I came tae blows in the Great Hall at Kilchurn and Baldie shoved us intae the courtyard. I wanted tae kill Sean. The men were laughin' at me, and I had a great fury buildin' in my chest. I drew my sword and challenged everyone, my uncle, anyone who wanted tae fight. I called them something like, maggot-headed sheep-hole muckwallers..." His smile was sad. "And when they stopped laughin' they all walked away. Like I wasna important anymore and I remember the fear, mo reul-iuil, but ye daena need tae fear me. I am nae leavin' ye."

"What were you fighting with him over?"

"He said somethin' about our dear mother." He shook his head. "I was on the wrong side of it."

"What are we going to do?"

"I was hopin' ye would ken it." The buzzing drone right over his shoulder was disconcerting while we stood in the woods somewhere in Scotland.

"I don't. I don't know how to be a queen and a stepmother and a wife. I want to go back to being Kaitlyn. Where I can just worry about whether you're okay and whether our friends are okay."

"Och aye, tis a great many things tae be worried on. What does grandma Barb say on it?"

"I don't know." I thought for a moment. "Maybe: I have nothing to fear only things to do?"

"We need ye tae make a list. What is the most important one?"

"Your son."

"I would say, you."

I chuckled. "You're just saying that to make me feel better." I smiled. "But thank you."

"What is next on your list?"

"Having sex. It's been over a week and, " I cut my eyes at him. "It's making me act like a just woke bear."

He laughed. "That sounds like somethin' I would say."

"That's why we're perfect for each other."

"Next?"

I sighed. "I miss our family in Florida."

He said, "Bella will be released from the hospital in two days. I will send her home with a nurse. I will make sure my Board kens how tae direct the kingdom, Hammie is capable and will—"

"You called him Hammie."

"Tis the perfect name for him. Then you and I will go tae Florida."

"We can't."

"Nae, we can. I am the king if I say tis what I must do then tis what I will do."

"God, I'm pretty hot for you right now." I pretend sighed, "What about Archie?"

"We will have tae say goodbye tae him for a time."

Tears welled up. "Well, that sucks."

"Aye." From the castle another vehicle headed toward us, fast.

It was Hammond. He pulled the vehicle right up to where

we stood. "Your highness, I urge you to return to the castle. This area is not yet safe enough, you're unprotected."

Magnus agreed but refused to ride. We walked, the vehicles spinning to follow us, the drones hovering near our heads. The castle, the gigantic multi-storied palace of brick and glass loomed ahead of us, long lawns, a grand stair, stately columns. It reminded me a little of the Getty museum in Los Angeles, modern and commanding, but also big and stately. It seemed judgmental, like I wasn't important enough to live there, not worthy.

"I'm so mortified, what do they all think of me?"

He took my hand in his. "Have you considered they might think ye are their new queen and they mayna have formed an opinion on ye yet? They might think ye are verra kind tae spend your time dotin' on your husband's son. They might think ye bore Bella's rage with grace and humility. They might think ye have been gracious tae everyone ye have met so far. I wouldna worry on how they view ye, I think."

"She said the rumor is I've bewitched you. Yet another time period thinking I'm a witch."

"I have a minister of information. I was thinking I will have him release a report ye arna guilty of murderin' Donnan. Twas self-defense, we will announce it."

I grinned. "Now see, that's the public relations I'm needing."

"What are public relations?"

I kissed the back of his hand. "It's unimportant. What's important is we're going to see our friends soon. I'll come up with a plan tomorrow."

CHAPTER 33

*W*e returned to our apartments and I curled up with the book again while Magnus went to speak to Bella. I stared at the pages watching the letters spin on the page wishing I knew how to turn on Netflix in the future.

A while later Magnus returned for dinner.

I asked what he said to Bella and he replied, "I told her tae never speak tae ye in that manner again. I also told her if you hear the bairn wailin' without its ma, ye will pick the bairn up — tis your way. I told her tae keep the bairn in her room if she daena want it comforted. She was shocked and told me I was heartless. I told her the bairn was hers tae care for unless twas mine tae care for. If twas mine I would be includin' my wife in it. There were a great many tears."

"So you don't get to see him anymore?"

"The nurse will bring him here tonight. Nae matter how angry she was, she wasna happy tae have tae be awake all night with a mewlin' bairn."

"Good," I grinned happily. "We get to be awake all night with a mewling bairn. And now I'm so glad I didn't start drinking in despair."

~

Magnus invited Hammond to dinner and it was my first time seeing Hammond so well-rested, smiling, at ease. His red wavy hair combed, his beard trimmed, his uniform fresh.

The war was still raging but he was growing confident that we would win so we relaxed a bit and I asked him important pressing questions like, "How do you get the news of the day?"

He spoke to the computer showing me how to manage our room projections but all the sample news stories were freaking terrifying.

That brought me to an even more pressing question, "How do you watch a movie? Or better, and more necessary, mindless entertainment?" He promised to send us a list of the year's best movies and shows.

Then I thought to ask, "Can I get a book translated?" I pushed my now empty plate away, retrieved the book, and placed it in front of me.

He had no idea who could translate it for me, but we started talking about the history of the time vessels. He explained what I mostly knew already: one of the kings, Donnan's great-great-great-great-grandfather, fought aliens, and won the vessels. Then, wielding epic power, he came to the future and took over.

"Could it have been Johnne Cambel?"

"No, never, the first king was Normond."

"Weird."

"The founder of our glorious kingdom, King Normond the First in 2167. We learn it in school. What we don't learn in school is that King Normond came from the late 1600s because most people don't know about the time travel vessels, only rumors. You have to be in the upper levels of government or in the king's inner circle to know the truth."

"The late 1600s? Not earlier?"

"I was told they came from the 1600s, I'm certain. 1686 or something."

I looked at the intricate detailing of the cover. "I thought this was the origin story of the vessels. I was sure of it." I took a sip of my wine.

Hammond asked the computer for the history of King Normond and we listened to a synopsis while large photos on the wall showed us his kingly portraits. The story began from his rule, in 2167, and there was no mention of how the vessels came to be. Or time travel. Or definitely nothing about the original battle or the aliens.

Hammond said, "The Tempus Omegas like I said aren't common knowledge, but they're anecdotally talked about, rumors and stuff. Donnan made the rumors worse by spreading one about how, unless you had royal blood, they would burn your skin if you touched them. It was effective in keeping people from wanting to."

"They do burn every cell you have with a hot poker when you use them, but then again I don't have royal blood."

Magnus said, "I do and tis much like havin' your skin seared off."

Hammond grimaced.

Magnus asked, "How did you ken of them?"

For the first time that evening Hammond looked as if he was guarding his words. "I was Lady Mairead's advisor for a time. She told me."

I leaned in. "You were her advisor? Do tell, everything you know."

Magnus poured him a whisky.

"I think you probably know more than I do, as you've used them."

I laughed. "I meant, do tell us everything about Lady Mairead."

"Oh. There isn't much to tell. She confided in me when she first arrived at the castle but that was a long time ago. She was lonely and thought Donnan brought her here to be his wife. He proved that he didn't."

My eyes went wide. "That's so sad."

"I don't know, she was better off without marrying him. He was an evil man." His face flushed as he spoke.

"How did your relationship as her advisor end?"

"She grew tired of having no power and wanted me to kill Donnan so Magnus could rule."

He spoke to Magnus, "You would have been quite young. She wanted to be regent and rule on your behalf."

Magnus said, "It sounds like her."

"When I refused she had me exiled. I came back under Samuel but learned quickly he was a worse ruler than Donnan. Donnan was malicious, but smart. Samuel was brutal and stupid."

He said to Magnus, "My apologies, Your Highness."

Magnus scowled. "My wife and I have killed the men ye speak of and twas because we had tae. I daena mean tae raise my glass tae murder, but tae winnin' a war I will, and twas a war that I and Kaitlyn Campbell fought and won." He raised his glass. Hammond and I raised our glasses too.

I asked, "So the other day, when you moved us here for the coronation, that was the first time you've seen her?"

He chuckled, "Yes, it was awkward to be serving Magnus when that was all she ever wanted."

"She must have been very surprised."

Hammond said, "Everything about the last few weeks has been surprising."

I said, "That's what happens when the world is one big shitstorm."

He chuckled. "I haven't heard that turn of phrase before."

"What, shitstorm? It fits: Wars, battles, rogue time-traveling generals, bitchy mother-in-laws, it's a full-blown tornado of poop."

Hammond laughed. "Yep, it's apt."

I remembered to say, "One more thing, Hammond. Magnus promised to introduce you to a singer for helping me, what was her name — it was a one-name name, she's very well known?"

He said, "Shona."

"Yes!" I turned to Magnus. "Your future-self promised, so you have to fulfill that promise and introduce them."

Hammond chuckled. "I'll take that promise, she's gorgeous."

Magnus said, "I haena any idea who she is but I will figure out how tae make it happen after we return from Florida."

Hammond asked, "When will you leave?"

"Day after the morrow."

I said, "If I can figure out how to get us there. The General Reyes guy has a way of knowing we're jumping into Florida."

Hammond said, "You don't know how he monitors you?"

"No."

"It might be a locational, like a sensing tripwire, one situated over an area. Usually they cover about fifty miles but this could be much bigger. You could travel to another place and move along the ground to get there, but you should leave the vessels somewhere safe while you test it. You don't know if it's your body or the vessels 'tripping the wire'. Then you need to look for the tech and dismantle it. I'll do some research on it tonight." He spun his whisky glass. "I wish I could go with you. You need the protection."

Magnus said, "I need ye here, watching over the kingdom. I have a man named Quentin there, who I am goin' for. But if ye are wantin' tae time-jump I will take ye sometime."

"Thank you, Your Highness." He stood. "I must say it's been a better dinner than I ever had with Donnan. You haven't once clocked me with something you had on hand."

Magnus winced. "He hit me with the sticks, what are they called, the ones with the game...?"

Hammond said, "Billiards?"

"Aye, he hit me with those."

I said, "Ugh. That guy was such a creep. I can't believe we have to live in his house." I put my hand on Magnus's. "And I'm sorry about the whole hitting you with sticks."

Hammond said, "It's your house now."

I said, "I can not get used to it. It's like living in someone's parent's house, and not a cool parent, a psychopathic abusive parent. I need a hazmat suit and a therapist just to go into the closets."

After Hammond left, Magnus asked, "What are ye thinkin' of?"

"The origin story of the vessels, but also..." I took a deep breath before saying it. "Your origin story — Hammond said Donnan didn't marry Lady Mairead. Did you know this?"

Magnus shook his head slowly. "I dinna..." He adjusted the dirty silverware on his plate. "Come tae find out I am a bastard, Lady Mairead has never thought tae mention it."

"That complicates things, right? About your crown?"

"Everythin' about my crown is complicated. But aye, twill complicate it more. Donnan did choose me as his heir though and I have been crowned already the king—"

The sound of a baby crying filled the apartment, then a nurse wheeled in a bassinet with a screaming baby inside.

Magnus joked, "Och, tis a joyful sound."

It wasn't. Archie was positively ballistic. Magnus scooped him up into the crook of his arm and seemed oblivious to the noise, while I bounced from one foot to the other with anxiety. "Do you think he's okay?"

"Aye, listen tae the lungs on him, he's remindin' us tae make room. He be too small tae take the space he needs, so he's doin' it with his voice."

Magnus and I traded off the baby: walking, rocking, dancing, feeding, singing, teasing, brushing our own teeth and getting ready for bed. We were hopeful we would get some sleep tonight though it was looking very bleak, until finally almost suddenly he wound down. Magnus said, "I am verra tired, mo reul-iuil."

"Me too." I pulled the bassinet to the bed with the side down, and I lay on the bed beside it and held his little sleeping hand. Magnus cozied up behind me his arm draped over my side. He raised his head to look past me to the baby in the soft darkness of our master bedroom. "Och, he makes a loud noise for a bairn that can sleep so sweetly."

"True that." I held Magnus's hand and kept my other hand on Archie and though I was tired for the longest time I listened to them both breathing in their sleep.

CHAPTER 34

Magnus met with his doctor to have his stitches removed and then with Hammond for last details and to determine what we needed to take with us back in time.

I spent the morning reading more of the book. I skimmed over some battle scenes, Johnne Cambel was really into writing about his glory in vanquishing his enemies. I slowed when the pages described the scene after the battle. There were bodies everywhere, and Johnne Cambel and his brothers went from body to body emptying pockets and findin' "a grete manies ingeny and aparatus of..."

This really seemed like the origin story of the vessels. The more I read the more I was sure, but it was the wrong date by a century. I couldn't figure out why.

I asked about Johnne Cambel from 1557 in Kenmore Scotland. The first entry said, "John Campbell of Glenurchy, Argyllshire, Argyll and Bute, Scotland, United Kingdom, born January 6, 1532 and died on November 1, 1557 in Inchadney, Kenmore, Perth and Kinross, Scotland, United Kingdom."

He died on the battlefield in 1557 and he wrote about in this journal in 1558.

Johnne Cambel was the first time traveler and he was from freaking 1558.

I knew it. I figured it out.

Me.

Of course I didn't know why the century wasn't right. And I didn't know how in the world Johnne Cambel who couldn't even write his own name figured out how to use the Tempus Omegas.

I asked the room. "How in the hell would a 16th century man figure out how to use a machine?" The computer answered, "In the 16th century the compound microscope was invented as well as the thermometer, also notable, bottled beer."

I said, "See, exactly my point," but then I remembered there had been a man alive at the end of the battle. The man, Tadhg. I re-read in Johnne Cambell's journal, "...being a man left with spirit we gathered him to the castle."

I flipped through pages and found one, deeper in, with a drawing tight to the inside. The drawing looked like a vessel. Sort of. Close enough to think I was right. There was another drawing, of a circle. Writing beside it identified it as, "Nae liquid nor solid." I thought that was the neck cuff and the wrist cuffs, the metal that I had been bound with more than once. There were other drawings too, things I hadn't seen yet. I read for two hours with paper beside me for notes. Sometimes I had to write the words that confused me in my own hand to decipher them. Many times that didn't help.

I asked the computer to direct me to the room Magnus was meeting in. I left our apartment followed by two guards and pretended like I knew where I was going. I found the room and knocked quietly.

Magnus was alone, at a desk, leaning back in a chair. "I was about tae return tae ye."

"I couldn't wait, I wanted to show you this." I opened the book on the desk in front of him and pointed at the drawn image. "That's the vessel. There's the metal thingy Lady Mairead put around my neck. There's something else, see? I can't tell what that means. There's another something. Can we see the vessels? Maybe Donnan has more tech than you realize."

At the back wall there was a sliding door that opened onto another room. This one was filled with antique weapons, knives and swords encased on shelves lining the walls, like an ancient armory stored in a high-tech manner: white walls, fancy lighting, metal shelves, glass displays. There were doors at the long end of that room with an elevator that went down, down, down, deep somewhere in the middle-inside lower levels of the castle.

We exited the elevator into a vault of a kind. "This makes me a little claustrophobic."

"What does that mean?"

"Scared of being trapped in a confined place."

"Me as well, and this lower level is where Donnan kept ye imprisoned. I have asked it tae be closed off but the lack of people in the outer rooms has me feelin' verra vulnerable down here."

"How do you know where this is?"

"Lady Mairead shewed me the other day."

"Where has she been lately?"

"She said she needed tae do some travelin'."

Inside the vault was dark and old like a castle dungeon. There were wooden ancient-looking crates — five. Most of them were closed but one had the lid shifted off. Inside were vessels nestled in straw.

"Are vessels in all of these?"

"Och aye, tis many more than I originally thought."

"Anything else?"

He lifted the lids on all the boxes, some were half-full, some were almost empty. It looked like twenty-three vessels in all. Inside a smaller box was a coiled ball of the gold metal that had once bound my neck. I gingerly poked it. I found another two boxes of the gold metal. A box with an apparatus that... I opened the book and turned to the pages with the drawings, this was not much like it, but could be... Johnne Cambell wasn't a very good artist.

But there were at least three drawings in the book that weren't here. And there was an empty box.

"Lady Mairead once said Donnan was watching your coming and going, that he knew you were figuring things out with the vessels — where's that tech?"

"I daena ken, I haena seen anythin' in the drawers of his desk or the safe." He lifted another lid on another empty box.

None of this helped much but at least I knew the book was about the vessels and my guess was the missing machines were part of the reason why Lady Mairead wanted the book.

"Why do you think the boxes are empty?"

"I think someone has been pilferin' the boxes. I canna ken for certain, but I can proffer a guess."

"Your mother?"

"Aye."

"Which means she can track us, probably, and who knows what else." I sighed and asked, "Should we take the vessel we need for traveling tomorrow morning?"

"Nae, I have two upstairs. I also have a collection of weapons and some gear."

"Nicely done."

On the way upstairs in the elevator Magnus said, "Hammond and I have agreed on a date we will return."

"And we have a plan. We land in Georgia, then we get in touch with Quentin."

Magnus put his arm around me and kissed me on my forehead. "I will try tae be capable of fightin' as soon as we land."

"I will try to get up too. If General Reyes is there, we'll be ready. And next jump we'll have Quentin with us."

Magnus said, "After that I winna worry as much."

CHAPTER 35

That night Archie was calm, watchful, and barely cried. It was like he wanted to be kind because he knew I needed some baby to fall in love with, but also it was an unkindness because he was a serious sweet quiet baby I was falling in love with. Magnus too, it was in his eyes, a love that held him enraptured. I readied for sleep for another night with my hand on Archie's, my other wrapped in Magnus's. "Can we do this?" I whispered.

Magnus's voice came from nestled in the hair behind my ear. "What?"

"Can we leave him?"

"We must."

"But he's so wee."

"Och aye, nae much more than a haggis."

I giggled and turned in Magnus's arms to my back. He rolled onto me, our lips met, and we kissed.

"We should have a son Kaitlyn."

"I know." I ran a finger through a lock of his hair, pulled it out long and watched it spring back. "But what if we had to leave him?"

"I daena ken if we could."

I nodded looking into his eyes. "Then we have to wait."

"I ken it but tis hard tae."

"It really is. So hard."

He kissed me again and we cuddled together spooning, watching Archie sleep.

There was banging on our apartment doors. Magnus was already gone from the bed. I scooped Archie from the bassinet and went to the bedroom doors to look out. Magnus opened the door and soldiers rushed in, Hammond just behind. "Your Highness we have to move you to a safer location."

Magnus and Hammond were discussing the danger. Roderick's men were coming, there was an attack on the castle. Three spies were found within our household, they knew we had been out on the grounds. They knew Archie had been born here. They saw a sign of weakness. I spun with Archie in my arms, what would we do? I considered the closet as a hiding place. My heart was racing and Archie began to scream.

I said, "Shhhhh, shhhhhh, shhhhhhh, Archie," Magnus called from the living room, "Kaitlyn, stay clear of the windows."

I heard Hammond say, "We are decided?"

Magnus called, "Get dressed, Kaitlyn."

"Where are we going?" I rocked Archie in my arms right and left up and down.

Magnus rushed into the room and began to dress in his clothes, a shirt and kilt, strapping on his belts and weapons, his sword across his back.

"Dress," he commanded. He rushed from the room calling over his shoulder. "Be ready when I get back."

I put Archie on the bed and hovered over him dressing. "Shush, baby, Kaitlyn's trying to think." I dumped my underwear and shirt and pulled on a pair of slacks and a shirt with a jacket. I had my 17th century clothes in a backpack. I put knives on my leg, all the while, shhhhh, baby, shhhhh." I picked Archie up and raced into the bathroom and combed through my hair, peed super fast, jiggling Archie in my lap, ran back to the bedroom and grabbed my backpack, strapped it on, and ran to the living room. There were guards everywhere.

Magnus ran back into the room. "We are going." He put a hand on Archie's cheek, briefly, then said, "Pass him tae the guard."

"Wait, what? Where's he going? Where are we going?"

"They're taking him tae a safe house. We are leavin'."

"No, he should stay with us, we should all go to the safe house, make sure he's safe before we—"

"Kaitlyn, daena argue. He's goin' tae be okay."

"But—"

Magnus's voice raised, his words were clipped. "See all these men, Kaitlyn? They will guard him. If I remain they will have tae guard me as well. Dost ye understand?"

"Yes. Yes, I understand." I passed the screaming, needing to be comforted, baby into some strange soldier's arms and watched him writhe and scream and, oh god — Magnus pulled my arm.

"I'm sorry, Archie, be safe, okay? We'll come back, I promise. We're coming back."

Hammond said, "The west lawn is the direction they attacked from, you need to go to the east rooftop."

Magnus pulled me down the hallway while Archie kept crying.

We shoved out of the doors to the rooftop. In the distance I heard guns firing. An explosion shook the ground. Magnus said, "Stand behind me." He pulled a vessel from his sporran. "Hold on."

"How are they getting Archie from the castle?"

He said, "Car. They'll use our storm as cover while they escape." He began reciting the numbers we had picked. I had been so focused on Archie I forgot to brace myself for the pain and anguish that came crashing into me a second later.

CHAPTER 36

I woke in a field, forcing myself up, get up get up get up, Magnus was kneeling beside me, clutching his sword, watching all directions. "Are ye awake, Kaitlyn? We needs be from this open space."

"Yes, let me get my bearings, hold on." I pushed my hair from my eyes and looked around with bleary eyes. We were on the edge of a wide lawn, near some flower beds. Across the way was a building, but the storm that came with us rushed everyone inside.

I clambered to my feet.

"Head this way, this is the botanical gardens, just like I planned." I ran crouching behind all the bushes to the front gate and the parking lot. Magnus jogging behind me, looking around cautiously as we hustled. "Now we just walk to the restaurant."

"Will food be happenin'? I am hungry as a bear."

I laughed. Our paces slowed to walk beside each other on the grassy slope along the two-lane road. "You often describe yourself like a bear."

He rubbed around his head standing his hair up in all directions and play lunged at me. "I am like a bear in my appetite. I am also happy tae have things just as I want them much like a bear."

I chuckled. "I don't think of you that way at all, you seem pretty easy going, taking things as they come."

"Tis because ever since ye met me, everythin' has been a'comin'. I can either argue or accept it. I suppose I have learned tae accept it in a way though I would verra much like tae live with ye here in Florida. Ye ken it, I say it all the time."

"That's true I suppose you do. Okay, I'll agree, you're most like a bear. What animal would I be most like?"

Magnus thought for a moment and said, "The iora rua."

"And that is?"

"A splendid creature, known for living wild in the highlands and forests of Scotland, but they are also cousins of animals ye have here in the New World and I would guess in the future as well."

"Really? The iora rua, and they're splendid? Is it like a deer or something?"

He grinned. "They are verra splendid and they arena a deer."

"What are they then?"

"They are adaptable and hardy, they have good vision, and are verra intelligent. They also make a nice home, tis much like ye."

"Tell me what it is!"

"I am nae goin' tae tell ye, you will have tae learn Gaelic tae ken it."

"Fine, but it's splendid? Wait, here we are."

The road opened next to the off-ramp of the I-95 freeway and to the right the Cracker Barrel restaurant. "We haven't been followed."

"Nae, there haena been any trouble."

Magnus faced me and I smoothed his hair after his dramatic

bear impression. "You look good, considering you just jumped 300 years."

"As do ye."

We passed through the front porch and entered the restaurant.

CHAPTER 37

First, I borrowed a phone from the front desk and then I called Zach; I had memorized his phone number years ago.

The phone rang and rang.

I texted: Pick up, it's Katie."

Then I called back.

He answered, "Katie?"

"We're at the Cracker Barrel in Savannah."

"What? Okay, need a ride?"

"We need Quentin." I turned my back so no one could hear me. Magnus stepped close to block me. "We can't jump into Florida for some reason. There's a guy, have you had any trouble? Anyone looking for us? Anything?"

"Nothing. It's been very quiet and we kind of forgot danger was imminent."

"Good I'm glad, but also danger is imminent. Tell Quentin to come. We're waiting at the Cracker Barrel." Magnus mouthed something. I added in a low whisper, "Bring weapons." Magnus said something else. I added more, "Bring all our 18th century gear. And Quentin's. Oh and there's a piece of paper in the safe, folded, it's got a list on it, handwritten. Can you bring that too?"

I passed the phone back to the hostess and profusely thanked her. She didn't need to be thanked though, she was perfectly happy checking out Magnus, batting her eyes, giggling as he looked around at the decor, totally entranced by the kitschy, quaint, southern, general store vibe.

"You hungry, Highlander?"

"Och aye, I could eat a muc a'by m'self."

We followed the hostess to our table, "What's a muck?"

"A pig, mo ghradh."

"Oh they'll have that, definitely." We dropped into our chairs, Magnus making sure he could see the front door and through the windows to the outside. I ordered two large Cokes. I assumed there was Coke in the future, why on earth would they have stopped making them, but I hadn't been offered one which kind of seemed like what was the point of being a queen?

We looked over the menus. I said to Magnus, "I think you should order the Country Fried Steak, none of your chefs will ever cook it for you and it comes with corn muffins plus three vegetables. I'm thinking if you sweet talk the waitress she'll bring you buttermilk muffins too. Also you need this Bowl of Turnip Greens, that's your style for sure."

Magnus stared at the menu, "Dost they have any dessert?"

"Oh Magnus, just you wait: pie and ice cream. Coca-Cola chocolate cake and ice cream, yes, dessert. And we have at least two hours to kill and our next stop is the 18th century so we need to eat more than enough."

After we ate, we leaned back in our chairs. "Och, I need tae sleep like a bear now too."

I grinned. "Me too, will they mind if we sleep here? Course I'm still horny as hell, we have got to have sex soon."

Magnus raised his brow with a grin. "We haena room here tae do it proper."

"True that, this needs acrobatics. We'll have to wait for our 18th century bed." We grinned at each other. "Will it be at Madame Greer's house or back at the castle?"

"I daena ken, I will need tae make amends tae Sean and beg his forgiveness."

"What are the odds he'll forgive you? You said you used to fight?"

"I have never had him hold a grudge against me, so if he has made peace with Lizbeth then we will be back in graces."

"So we are glad Lizbeth is alive and in charge of him still."

I leaned forward and sucked some super thirst quenching ice cold sparkling Coke through the straw. I leaned back and sighed. "Is Archie okay?"

I wanted an immediate answer but instead Magnus seemed thoughtful about it and that kind of scared me a little. Finally he said, "I hope so."

He very quietly added, "I need ye tae guard your heart, mo reul-iuil. I ken tis nae somethin' ye do, ye feel things verra much, but ye need tae try."

"What do you mean?"

"With Archie—"

"I don't understand, he's your son, I..."

He reached for my hand. "He is Bella's and we mustna forget how dangerous she can be." His thumb stroked back and forth on the back of my hand.

"So you're warning me not to love Archie? That Bella might have some way to get between us?"

"Nae, Kaitlyn, Bella has nae way tae get between us, but if ye lose your heart tae her baby she will be dangerous tae ye."

I huffed. "First, dear husband, I can't guard my heart. You know this is true, and I mean, I can try to be a grownup and pretend to be guarded, but he's a baby. I know I lost my baby and maybe it's making me... this is making me really sad. You're making me feel like I'm doing something wrong by caring about your son."

"Twas nae my intention. I just dinna consider ye would love him so much, I dinna realize I would. It has come tae me he will be a weakness and..."

I shrugged. "He might be a strength. You love me and it makes you stronger. You're like a big giant bear of love, killing monsters in the 18th century woods because you love me that much. Archie might make us both strong enough to vanquish the bad guys, whoever they are."

I looked around the restaurant. "But you're right. I know it. I do. I will try. But just know this, I'm trying. You don't have to keep warning me. Let's try to guard our hearts and be strong, but also let's ask occasionally, 'Is Archie okay?' Without having to worry about sounding weak." I smiled. "He is really cute. He looks like a little mini Magnus."

Magnus joked, "Och, tis a tough road ahead of him."

I laughed. "You're so handsome!" I whispered, "That lady over there hasn't taken her eyes off you the whole time she's been eating." My eyes scanned the room. "That one too."

"Aye, because I am a bear in a restaurant, they have tae stand guard—"

"Is that what you think it is? Please, you know what it is."

He chuckled.

"I love you. I'm not guarded, but I'm strong. Stronger every day. And we need something to do while we wait or I am going to climb on your lap right here and probably get kicked out of the whole state of Georgia. Plus we already played this little 'jump the pegs' game to death while waiting for our food. Let's go check out the general store."

~

Magnus was delighted by the store. It wasn't a word I could use very much about staggeringly handsome muscular heroic kind of men, but he definitely was 'delighted'. There were shiny, excessive Christmas decorations everywhere and he wanted all of it.

"We'll have to save those for when we come back for Christmas."

"Och." He was disappointed as he put a glitter-covered reindeer skull with horns that were tied with plaid ribbons back on the shelf.

Then he turned to see a Jump the Peg game. "Tis the one from the table, can we take it?"

"Of course."

He wandered around looking at all the striped candy sticks and asked across a display, "Could I buy this, tis candy?"

"Yes, for you?"

"I want tae take it to my nieces and nephews."

My eyes widened. "Oooh, good idea, also..." I surveyed the store. "Let me get some things for Lizbeth too. And get something for Sean. He might like one of those beanies." Magnus's face looked a question, I said, "It's for your head, a warm hat." I held up a dark one.

"Aye, one of those for Sean, wait..." He counted on his fingers. "I want six of those." He picked more candies. "Maybe ten of those beanies."

I picked out rose-scented oil, soap, and lotion for Madame Greer and Lizbeth. And a chocolate bar for Lizbeth. Then two scented candles and silk scarves too. A quilt. Another quilt. I returned to Magnus with my arms full. His arms were full of candies and a checkers game.

I said, "We're going to need to buy some bags." I went to look at their canvas bags and passed the tea and coffee area. I bought some of that. Coffee might finally make 18th century Scotland doable. Plus some popcorn and a tin of cookies.

I put some more chocolate in the pile and once the cashier totaled it, paid with the cash we had procured from Donnan's safe.

We returned to our table. For fun I grabbed a few brochures from near the front door while Magnus went out to the porch and looked for any signs of trouble. I slumped our bags under our table and sat. When the waitress came to check in, I ordered another round of sodas and some appetizers to make us seem less like freeloaders.

When Magnus returned to the table I said, "Check this out." I pointed at a brochure. "St Simon's Island. It looks like there were Scottish highlanders that settled a town called Darien in 1736. And they were protecting Georgia from the Spanish in Florida. This is so interesting. I had no idea there was a Scottish history to the area."

"Would there be Scottish highlanders still livin' there?"

"No, probably not, I mean, their great grandchildren possibly, but I don't think anyone would speak Gaelic if that's what you mean."

"Aye, tis what I meant. I forgot the amount of time that has gone by in the one place and the other. Tis a burden to have it go so slow and so fast, I forget tae make sense of it."

"Well, it's rather senseless isn't it? You're a Gaelic speaking Scottish highlander and you're here, why shouldn't more be here? Speaking of, what month should we go back to? It needs to seem plausible we went to the West Indies and back. We were last there in December I think and I don't want it to be cold."

"If we return in the Spring, I might help in the rebuildin' of the castle."

"Okay, good, then we'll be warm too."

Magnus chuckled, "If ye want warm, mo reul-iuil, ye daena want the Spring. Ye want three days in August."

"So a cold Spring, that's fine. I forget the crazy northern country you're from with its endless nights and freezing summers. Spring sounds good. How about May?"

Magnus's eyes drew to the parking lot. "I think Quentin has arrived." We stood to go meet him on the porch.

CHAPTER 38

Magnus and Quentin clapped their arms around each other, a giant bear hug of friends. I laughed happily. Hayley jumped out of the passenger side of Quentin's truck and hugged me and then I hugged Quentin too. He was already dressed in his kilt and linen shirt. He laughed at our excitement. "You guys have only been gone for two weeks."

I said, "It feels like a lifetime. For Magnus it's been two lifetimes. Plus he's a king now."

"A king? Shit, what do I call you?"

Magnus joked, "Either your highness or sire or Magnus the Magnificent or—"

"Boss then."

"Aye, boss is what I am used tae."

Hayley said, "I'm still calling you Mags, it fits you better than any of it."

I hugged her again as a second car pulled in beside us. It was Zach. And we started the round of hugs over again. Quentin told Zach, "Come to find out Boss is a king now."

Zach said, "Really? I'm a fuckin' royal chef? I might need a raise. Two things, one, Magnus doesn't look old at all. And two, you're really taking Quentin again?"

I said, "I found Old Magnus and he made me go to the future to get Young Magnus. He also said to get Quentin. I'm just following his orders."

Quentin joked, "Well, he is the boss. But if he's the boss, who's this guy?"

Magnus said, "I'm the king."

"Oh, that's right, this is fucking confusing."

Quentin opened his truck's tailgate and pulled out backpacks. He had a kilt for Magnus in green and blue tartan. It would be a better fit than the one he was wearing. He had another sword for Magnus too.

Zach pulled open his glove compartment and retrieved the folded piece of paper.

I told Magnus, "That's the note from Tyler."

"Och." Magnus flipped it open, glanced at the page, nodded, and placed it carefully in his sporran. "Tae read it later."

I said, "Let's go into the restaurant and feed you, Quentin, before we go." So we packed everything back into the truck and went inside to eat a second meal.

After we were done eating, Hayley and I went into the bathroom with my dress to change.

I pulled my future-pants off and passed them under the door from the stall and she passed me my shift over the door and I pulled it on. It was freshly laundered. "Will you tell Emma thank you for washing this? It smells amazing. And I'm sorry I didn't get to see her before we left again."

"Definitely, so has it been death-defying?"

"A little. Not as much. I have something to tell you." I gestured over the door for the skirt.

"This sounds bad, are you pregnant?"

"No, and that wouldn't be bad, Hayley, get a grip. But I want you to stay cool and hear me out."

"Okay."

"Magnus had a son with another woman."

"Jesus Christ, I'm going to kill him Kaitlyn."

"Hayley, you aren't going to kill him. You're going to—"

"He had an affair on you? He got her pregnant? I'm fucking going to—"

The bathroom door opened and Hayley hushed.

Someone entered the stall beside me, but once the door clicked, Hayley started again yell-whispering through the door. "What are you going to do about it? Because I'm going to kill him."

"Hayley, listen to me, he was imprisoned and this woman, well, she kind of—" I said, "Pass me the bodice." She passed the bodice over the stall door. "She kind of forced him." The toilet in the stall next to us flushed.

The woman adjusted her clothes and stepped from the bathroom stall.

Hayley joked with the stranger, "Do you hear my friend? She's making excuses for his lying, cheating ass."

"Hayley, I am not." The woman washed her hands and left the bathroom. I stepped from the stall and turned so Hayley could lace my bodice.

She said, "That stranger who heard it agreed with me, I could tell by her shocked expression."

"I'm not making excuses for him beyond the truth. He has never lied to me about it. And he was hundreds of years in the future at the time. She really did force him. She threatened my life."

"He's a freaking lethal weapon. He could have not. I can't believe you're listening to his bullshit reasoning."

"Oh yeah? Well—"

"First James, then Cameron, now this, you deserve so much better." She pulled one of my laces tight.

I turned around and put on my most stern look. "My husband slept with another woman and I learned about it a while ago. I have already been dealing with this. I have to live with it. I mourned my marriage and hated the sight of him, but every day in every way he has been making amends to me. Every minute. It's precisely because I have had my heart broken by other assholes that you can trust me on this — it's not a pattern of abuse. It's Magnus. He had something awful happen to him and he broke his vow to me, he told me, and begged my forgiveness. And I know it won't happen again."

She huffed. "Because he told you?"

"Yes, but I also have proof." I held the sides of her face. "Because his son, Tyler, the one he made with the other woman, told me Magnus lived in another lifetime alone for twenty-five years without me, loving me, mourning me. So yeah, Magnus will never cheat on me again. Ever."

"Wait, Tyler was Magnus's son? What?"

"There was literally a time-loop vortex of crazy and don't get caught up in all of that. Tyler was Magnus's son. Magnus raised him while he was alone. That's all you need to know."

"That's some crazy wackadoodle time-shit there."

"True that, welcome to my world."

"Okay, turn, I'll finish your laces." I turned. She added, "So you don't want me to kill him?"

"Nope, I want you to love him like a brother and forgive him for being human and thank him for saving my life over and over and loving me so completely. That's what you're supposed to do."

"Fine. I will. It helps a lot he's so easy on the eyes and so rich and charming and overall wonderful. But seriously, he has a son?"

"Yes, a baby. The baby's real name is Archie. He was born about a week ago and I spent a lot of time with him and lost my heart a little."

"Wow."

"Yes wow. And how are things with you?"

"Really awesome, I met someone."

I squealed. "You did? Like a real someone? Like a *someone* someone?" I turned around to see her face. She was glowing, I didn't know why I hadn't noticed before.

"Yes, a real someone. He's hot. I met him last weekend, and he's just so... I really really really like him."

I threw my arms around her. "That's so great Hayley, I'm so happy for you. You haven't talked like this about anyone in forever!"

"I know. We all went out the other night. Quentin and Zach really liked him too. James even met him and I suppose Michael knows about it by now, but everyone thinks he's great."

"Yay! When can I meet him?"

"When will you be back?"

"I'm aiming for Christmas, you should have seen how excited Magnus was when he saw the ornaments in the general store. I really want to see his face on Christmas morning when Ben is opening presents, Santa is going to blow his mind."

"Okay, come back at Christmas and I'll bring my new guy to meet you. Maybe the day after because we've been talking about going away for the holiday."

I pulled on my boots. "That's the kind of guy he is, going away? Wow, that's like a grownup thing."

"I'm a grown-up. I have a career, a man; I'm barely a train wreck."

"Yeah, me too. I'm sorry I'm leaving again. I'll come back soon and we'll catch up for real." I smeared on some Burt's bees lip balm and checked myself in the mirror. "18th century, castle Balloch on the River Tay — here I come."

CHAPTER 39

When I returned to the dining room Magnus had left for the porch. I found him sitting in a rocking chair with the letter open. The day was beautiful, cool and sunny, plus the porch had a nice shade to it. I sat in the rocking chair beside him.

"We ought tae buy some of these chairs. They are verra comfortable for thinkin'."

"You read the letter?" I wrapped my arms around his elbow, leaned on his shoulder, and looked down on the letter. The opening read, "Dear Da..."

"Aye I read it. Tis difficult tae understand some of it, as it haena happened. Dost ye think twill happen?"

"I don't know, we might have changed everything, but then again, nothing big might have changed. The you that raised Tyler fought General Reyes. The you I met in the 17th century fought General Reyes. I think we have to move forward assuming General Reyes is going to cause us trouble. Did Tyler have anything helpful?"

"He said I figured out General Reyes is able tae track us when we jump in and out of northeast Florida. Tis faster than watchin' for the storms. He can be there almost at the same time. It makes him verra dangerous."

"We kind of knew that already, does he explain how?"

"Nae but he only says Florida and ye met me in Scotland, so Balloch might be safe…"

"You did think I might have been followed. It's why we left for Kilchurn."

"But did I ken we were, or was I guessin'?"

"I have no idea. What else does it say?"

Magnus looked at the paper. "It says a great deal here." He pointed midway down the page. "General Reyes is from Barcelona, Spain. Have ye heard of it?"

"Yes."

"He was born there in 1535. He traveled to Scotland in the 1500s."

"Wait, the 1500s? In Scotland?"

"Aye."

"That's when the vessels were found."

"Och, he might have been there from the beginnin' which makes him verra dangerous."

I added, "And that would explain their clothes."

"Twould. He has also lived in Florida. He has a home in… Dost ye ken this word?" He tapped the place.

"Saint Augustine."

"Dost ye ken of it?"

"Oh yeah, Saint Augustine is a very old city in Florida, pretty close to Amelia Island. Which might help us understand the boundary of the tracking device. It didn't extend here, to Savannah. Maybe it only works for eighty miles or something."

Magnus kissed my forehead. "Maybe."

Then he said, "I also ken he leads with his left arm and takes a half step tae the right. He leans because of a past injury."

"That's not very helpful."

Magnus looked down at my face. "Tis verra helpful if I am fightin' him, man tae man."

"Anything else?"

"There is some strategy — he has two ways he will battle. One, a larger army will descend on us, but sometimes it is a verra small war party, and if tis small it will only have five men. If I only see two there are more men I canna see." He pointed at the letter, at a small hand-drawn diagram in the corner. "He often uses a left-flank maneuver. If I canna see the other men, I should expect them from the left. I only fought him once personally. I dinna win, but I also dinna die."

"Will all of that be useful?"

"Aye, and Tyler said I believe Lady Mairead is involved with him."

"Of course." I added, "We kind of knew that because of how frantically she was looking for that book after I said his name."

"You still have it?"

"In my pack, I haven't gotten very far in it yet but I'll keep reading." After a moment I asked, "Did he say anything else?"

"He said he loves me and thanked me for bein' a good Da. He daena regret savin' your life and he told me tae take care of ye and..." His voice cracked. "I wish I would hae spoken on it with him, thanked him for it."

I squeezed around his arm. "I know you do, my love. I know."

He said, "The whole time I was with him I thought he was goin' tae win ye, and I wasna verra fair. I raised m'fist tae him and..."

"I know." I nuzzled into his shoulder.

He held the side of my face, against his arm, like a hug. "We ought tae return tae our family."

I kissed his jaw. Then I took the letter, unbuckled his sporran, and placed it inside. "Let's go eat some more dessert that always makes you feel better."

CHAPTER 40

A while later we drove the small highway to a deserted side road. Magnus and I climbed out of the car. Quentin passed Hayley his truck keys to drive it home. We did a last check of our bags and collected everything into a pile. It wasn't much this time, but we had lots of presents. It was nice to not be chased for once.

I hugged Zach and told him to hug Emma for me and Ben.

He asked, "When will you be home?"

"Where is home, by the way?"

"We're still at the same place, the round house on the beach."

"I wish we could be at our last place, or the one before it, but I guess this is life on the run. I want to be there for Christmas, but we would probably land here again. I don't know why it is, but for some reason we can't jump into Florida. Maybe don't bring Hayley or Emma when you come get us, because we don't know if we'll have to fight our way across the border."

"Okay, I'll be waiting for your call. Try not to come on Christmas Eve though, we have plans with family."

"All right, December 23rd. I'll see you then."

Magnus was speaking very solemnly to Hayley, then they hugged.

When I hugged her goodbye with a kiss she said, "I told him I wanted him to explain himself."

"Seriously Hayley, I told you—"

"Don't worry, I'm not going to tell you what he said, but it was enough. I've forgiven him."

"What did he say?"

"I'm not telling you."

"It must have been good if you've forgiven him that easily."

She laughed. "Oh it was good, you know how he is, but I'm not telling you what it was."

"I'll get it out of him. Easily. All I have to do is lift his kilt and he'll tell me anything."

"Or you could not be an asshole and let the people who love you have a conversation about you without you being involved."

I grinned. "Fine. But it was good?"

"Yes."

"Good. I love you."

"I love you too and I'm sorry I called you an asshole."

I shook my head with a sad smile. "I said that exact same thing to Archie just the other day."

"Who the baby? He probably deserved to be called one — screaming their heads off, pooping all over the place."

I joked, "Someday you'll make an excellent mother."

She joked back, "Hey, I'm not the one calling babies assholes to their faces. I do it behind their backs like a nice 'Aunt Hayley'."

Quentin, Magnus, and I stepped away from the vehicles to our pile of stuff. We stood in a tight circle while Magnus pulled the vessel from his sporran. I said, "Thank you for coming on such short notice, Quentin."

"Aye I have been missin' the ol'castle."

I laughed. "The broken-down 18th century castle?"

"Nah, I kinda missed the girl."

Magnus said, "You'll be seein' her soon enough. Dost ye have your weapons in hand, in case we are met?"

Quentin nodded and patted the sword on his hip, the knife on his ankle, and the gun holstered under his arm.

"Good. Are ye ready, Kaitlyn?"

"Kind of, " I patted my leg, where a knife was strapped and between my breasts where a small one was nestled, "but not really. Man, I hate jumping." I jiggled from foot to foot nervously. I shivered, shook out all my limbs, and rolled my head. "I hate to say it but I have to do this." I moved between Magnus's arms, pressed against his chest, clutched his shirt in my fists, and closed my eyes.

Magnus checked to make sure his sword belt was buckled. "Ye ready, Kaitlyn?"

I nodded my head.

He joked, "Dost ye need a hug tae go as well, Quentin?"

Quentin said, "No boss, think I can do it on my own."

I said, "Fine, whatever, I can do it on my own too." I pushed away from Magnus and stood alone for a half beat. "Nope, can't do it." I clung to his chest again. "I'm plenty brave enough, I just—"

Quentin said, "I know it Katie, you've done this a lot more than me."

"Thank you for noticing." My voice was muffled in Magnus's shirt.

Magnus began to count and twist the vessel. I clenched every muscle in my body and tried to ready myself for the unbelievable pain but it still hit me like a baseball bat to the stomach and the head all at once.

CHAPTER 41

I forced myself up as soon as I was in command of my senses, but Magnus was already crouching above me. He pressed a finger to his lips. I looked around, Quentin wasn't there.

A few moments later Quentin returned. "No one."

We were in a clearing but surrounded by trees, a pine scent in the air. It was a cool day, but not cold. It looked near noon. I swooped my hair into a ponytail and pulled the tartan around my shoulders. I moved the brooch, so it was perfect.

Magnus said, "We are goin' tae a tavern. Twill take a few hours tae walk it."

"Ugh," I groaned. "We have to carry all this stuff? I didn't think about that when we picked out all the presents."

I carried my pack and two bags. Magnus carried four bags. Quentin had a heavy backpack with a lot of gear and also a couple of bags. We walked. Luckily it was a beautiful day. We were within trees for some of it, but a lot of the walk was up and down hills, along a worn path that skirted around a mountain, past a creek and along the banks of the river.

After an hour we stopped to relieve ourselves and eat some food, drink water, and then we walked some more.

Magnus watched behind us. At one point he made us stop in the shadow of the trees, totally quiet, while he climbed the bank to check in every direction, but when he returned he said, "We arna bein' followed."

It was a relief, but we were never completely sure.

We walked some more. Quentin asked, "So when do we get to the fun part, Boss?"

"Tis the fun part."

"Nah I mean, when do we get to castle brawls and me tasing highlanders?"

"You liked doin' that? I may need ye tae soon enough. We will inquire at the tavern how the castle and the village are farin'. If the castle inhabitants are amenable, I will set a meetin' with them. If Sean will come and we can talk of the matter, twill be good." He switched the bags to his shoulder. "If he comes and daena want tae talk then ye can drop him with your taser."

"See, that's what I mean, the fun part," Quentin joked. "What about Katie?"

"We'll have Lizbeth come tae meet with Kaitlyn, they will greet each other warmly and talk as sisters do, and they will make the men around them behave less like barbarians. They will make it so we daena have tae brawl or use your taser. We can share a beer instead and talk of it as if twas merely a distraction."

"I don't know Boss, he wanted to kill you pretty dead."

"Och aye, he did."

I watched the side of Magnus's face. He was stoic and thoughtful, with his bag of candy over his shoulder trudging to the tavern instead of to his home, wondering if he would be welcome at all.

But it was hard to blame his family if they didn't forgive him — we had seriously messed this place up.

Quentin noticed Magnus's down-turned mood.

"Sean will be sensible. He should really say he's sorry to you. He saw you lay down your sword and get arrested. He saw Kaitlyn get arrested. Commander Davis and his men all left with everything and there's been no more trouble, right? Maybe you should walk in there and tell him to apologize to you. I'll back you up."

"Nae. Tis my family."

"Sure. So yeah, it's probably going to be easy to forgive everything. Plus you have candy. Plus you have all those sodas I made you buy. Those are going to make them all really happy."

CHAPTER 42

*I*t had been close to three hours. We rested along the way and traded off bags but I was still exhausted when we made it to the Taybourne Tavern.

The building was half-timbered with a high pitched roof and was three stories high. When we entered the large downstairs room, it was very dark inside. There were three big tables and about ten men seated in groups of three and four. We dropped our belongings against a wall and Quentin and I sat at one end of a long table beside the pile to guard it.

Magnus spoke with the man who ran the place and was gone for about twenty minutes. He returned with a round of ales and placed them on the table in front of us. "Dougie says all the Campbells are back at the castle. Rebuildin' has begun. He told me Liam has been here in recent days and says they have renewed fightin' against the MacDonalds and arna worried much on Commander Davis."

"That's great, right?"

Magnus took my hand and smiled. "Aye, tis verra good. I

daena ken if I will be forgiven but I am glad of the family bein' in harmony with each other."

I took a slug of ale. "So when do we meet with them?"

"He will send a messenger tae the castle tae notify them I am here, but it daena look like they will come until the morn."

"Good, then we get to drink. I've been needing to just relax."

Magnus's eyes flitted to a man at the far end of the table. Quentin glanced that way too. I guessed relaxing wasn't really possible with all these 18th century men around.

I took another swig of ale and wiped my arm on my mouth. Quentin hunched forward on his elbows. A half-second later a man approached us and loomed over our table. "Your man here is dark as night. He the one causin' the trouble at Balloch?"

Magnus grunted and stared straight ahead. "Nae."

"What business have ye got with the Campbells?"

Magnus tensed. "We are Campbells. Tis nae business, tis family. We are simply restin' for the night afore we go home." Magnus took a long sip of his ale and lowered it to the table. "Dost ye have a problem with a man and his family havin' a rest or will ye walk tae the other side of the room and leave us be? Because I am willin' tae discuss either. I would like tae enjoy my drink with m'wife and m'brother, but I haena held my blade in a few days — I wouldna mind the interruption so verra much. I could return tae m'drink after."

The man glared. "I am charged with watchin' for MacDonalds."

"You can tell from our aroma we arna descended from mucs."

The man grunted.

"But I tell ye I have reconsidered and daena want tae fight ye. I would much rather enjoy a drink with m'wife and converse with m'brother than fight ye over some reason I daena ken. I will get ye a drink and one for your men and we can enjoy our evenin' without havin' tae bother each other again."

The man said, "Aye," and Magnus went and arranged to have him served some more ale, clapped him heartily on the back, and returned to our table.

"We must be cautious, he haena the good sense tae ken he was spared. He may try tae start somethin' again."

Quentin said, "I've got my eye on him."

In all of that I kept my eyes down and forgot to drink from the stress of it. Now I swigged long from my ale. "Oh man, that tastes good. There's a lot about the 18th century that's hard, but there's ale and, of course, Magnus Campbell and his family."

Magnus grinned.

I asked Quentin, "Did you ever think, growing up, that someday an 18th century, Scottish highlander would be calling you a brother?"

"I did not, but then again, he's not really an 18th century Scottish highlander anyway."

Magnus said, "What dost ye mean, Black MacMagnus? I was born in a castle. I have the brogue of a highlander. I have on a kilt and a sporran. I swing a two-handed sword and most of my family resides here in the land of Scots. How can ye say I am nae a highlander? I have the scars tae prove it, from the battles a highlander will fight."

Quentin raised his mug. "True that boss, but I have the brogue of a highlander as well if I be wantin' tae. Arna I wearin' a kilt? Daena I sleep in a castle of a time? Have the scars of a fight?" He pushed up the sleeve of his shirt and pointed at a scar on his upper arm. Then he pointed at a large scar on his knee, "Wait, that's from skateboarding. But this one, this is from here. He pointed at a small scar on his shin.

Magnus laughed. "Tis verra wee, ye might want tae keep that one tae yourself." He drew up the front of his shirt and showed his surgical scar, purple, raised, still marked and dotted from the stitches that once held it together.

Quentin said, "Dammit man, why do you always have to win everything? Wait let me show you the skateboarding one again." They both laughed. Quentin added, "What I'm trying to say boss, is though you might share the same clothing as these medieval motherfuckers you don't have the same mindset. I think you're a modern man, trapped in the dark ages of history."

Magnus smiled, "Ye daena consider me a barbarian, Black Mac?"

Quentin said, "Nae, ye are too civilized."

"Och, tis a welcome compliment. I thank ye."

I grinned, a little misty-eyed looking from one to the other. Then I hiccuped. "Uh oh, I think I have a buzz." I hiccuped again. "What time is it?"

"Tis time tae retire tae our room."

"Our room, all of us?" I was really hoping not because I missed my husband, really really missed him and didn't want to sleep in a bunk room or in a pile of smelly highlanders.

"We have our own room. Quentin will sleep and guard in the hallway outside the door."

Quentin joked, "I suppose my compliments didn't work to win me a warm bed? I'll remember this."

Magnus chuckled. "Aye your bed will be warm. You can sleep along the crack under the door and the heat from our fire will warm ye."

CHAPTER 43

*M*agnus and I carried all the bags up the creaky steps to the second floor. Remembering the rats that had eaten my lip balm, I spent time moving all the food into one bag, zipping it closed inside another, then wrapping it with a third and tying it closed, while he built a small fire in the hearth. The room was simple, but the bed was bigger than the one we were given at Madame Greer's house. It looked lumpy, but there were blankets so that was good.

Magnus threw back the covers and investigated the mattress. He did a little brushing move which kind of freaked me out. "What was that?"

He sat on the bed to take off his shoes. "Nothing but the local fauna here tae welcome your arse, mo ghradh." He rummaged up my skirts and pinched my butt. I squealed.

Quentin's voice clear as a bell asked, "Everything all right boss?"

I said, "Oh my god, Quentin, can you hear everything we're saying and doing in here?"

"Yup."

"Shit." It was all I could think of to say.

Quentin said, "Of course I've been y'all's night watchman for years, you don't always close your doors."

I said, "Oh my god."

Quentin said, "Don't worry I'm putting in my earbuds. I came prepared."

I called, "Okay, good night, we're going to sleep now, nothing going on."

Quentin added, "What? I can't hear you, but keep in mind everyone else in the tavern can."

"Crap."

Magnus shook his head sadly. "My wife has forgotten she is in the 18th century. Tis a place where tis common tae hear your neighbor in the night. Tis nae somethin' tae worry on."

I whispered, "None of the women here have sex, Magnus. They're all too pious. Too busy with farm work and survival at the hands of the Campbell men."

"Aye, " he pulled off his second boot. "Tis true. Tis why I traveled tae find ye, for the sex of it."

"Ah, finally, you admit it." I dropped my skirt to the ground and whispered. "I'll welcome you to my shores if you'll help me get out of this bodice of bondage."

Magnus untied my lacings while I watched the fire in the hearth leap and dance. "I do love a fire in the bedroom. Can we have one of these installed in your castle?"

The scent of burning wood filtered through the air. "I would imagine it winna be easy, but I will ask for it."

He yanked my bodice, sliding it up and over my arms.

He sat and I stood between his legs and wrapped my arm around his head, my other hand steadying his jaw. I brought his chin up and kissed him. And kissed him. And kissed him until my knees were weak. "Hello Master Magnus. Are you ready for this?"

His hands slid slowly up my calves around the back of my thighs. Up up up. His lips pressed to mine he whispered. "Och aye, Madame Campbell, I am ready." His fingers glanced between my legs, up... in... around...

I moaned and held around his head while he massaged around and around my thighs, my ass, my hips. I whispered against his hair. "I don't know whether to go slow or fast, I missed you so much."

His head nestled against my chest. "I have missed ye too."

I sighed and relaxed in his arms. "Slow then."

I kissed him more, my tongue exploring between his lips, tasting the breath of him, strong and sure. The breath that had been weak and wanting was now returned, his health restored, even though his skin held so many scars, it also held that scent. I drew it into my lungs.

His jaw was stubbled, I ran my lips along it, sharp and rough, to his ear. I nibbled and breathed whispered sighs there as he scooped my shift up and off my body and tossed it across the room.

"I am naked, dear sir, and you are still fully clothed."

He grunted. He ran his hands in a massage, up and down my back causing me to shiver in his arms. I climbed on his lap and pressed across his kilt planning to tease him and make it last, but it was just so freaking sexy sitting naked on his wool-covered lap. I groaned as his mouth found my breast and I rose to meet his lips. "God, please take off your clothes." I was panting, full-blown-breathless.

"As ye can see, Kaitlyn, I canna undress because ye have me pinned."

His hand moved between my thighs and a finger went up and explored. *I have to get up to...* my voice and thoughts left my mind — *what?* I held on tighter around his head. *Were we...?*

Magnus said, "Shhhhh, mo reul-iuil. You daena have tae

speak." He stood with me wrapped around his waist. I pulled his linen shirt up and off his arms, over his head and away. I dropped my feet to the floor and ran my hands along his chest and his stomach while he unlatched his belt and allowed his kilt to fall to the ground. He turned me around, my back pressed to his chest, he rubbed around my breasts, my stomach.

Then we both kneeled and he, with hugs and caresses, leaned me over the mattress and with his wide chest spread along my back and his mouth near my ear, his breath on the nape of my neck, his hands wrapped around mine — he pushed inside of me and paused, pressed, pushed...

My breaths worked in and out with his, *oh god,* we rocked against each other. Our movements synchronized and small and seductively slow. In my moans were words. *I love you I want you...* He exhaled against my skin, and it was much like a dance, warmth and shiver, press and pull, within and without, *ohgodohgodohgodoh.* I pressed against him and sat back on his lap, knees spread wide across his. His hands caressing up and down and over all of me, *ohgodohgodohgodooooohhhhhhhh.* I collapsed forward, my face pressed into the rough fabric of the mattress, gripping the blanket's woolen folds.

Magnus rose up, held my hips steady, and it was a lovely intense ride full of slapping skin and *oh god, oh Magnus, oh, oh,* and he was hard and fast and powerful and then *och, mo reul-iuil.* He collapsed on my back and clutched me to him, wrapped and holding, gathering me up from my gravity pressed down on the hard bed. He lifted me to his chest, his arms under and repeated a simple, *och.*

I said, *I know.*

We remained there panting. Magnus wrapped around me and inside me at once. His sweaty cheek pressed to mine, his gentle pressing, his body's weight, the gravity. I could have fallen asleep, right there, half on half off the bed with firelight dancing in the half-light of a spring night in Scotland.

He kissed my cheek and pulled off me gathering me to the bed, climbing on beside me, and pulling a cover over us. I curled alongside his arm, my lips on his shoulder. "Goodnight, my love."

CHAPTER 44

*W*aking was blissful — a bird outside the window chirped us awake, but then the noises rising from the ground floor, men clomping around downstairs, reminded us it was time to rise. We kissed and caressed and agreed it was time.

I peed in the chamber pot and then Magnus and while I pulled on my skirt, I saw him chuckle as he pulled on his kilt. "What?"

"My tartan smells like my wife."

I batted his shoulder. "It does not."

He raised his brow. "Och aye, tis a blissful scent of her." He put the kilt to his nose and inhaled.

"Magnus, you cut that out. I do not have a 'scent'."

"Aye, ye do. I have told ye this, ye smell of osna, a sigh or a breeze."

"Okay, that's better. So your kilt smells like a sigh, I can live with that."

He laughed. "Nae, my kilt smells like your castle gates."

"My what?!" I chuckled. "Magnus, I am a proper Campbell

wife, and a freaking Queen, I'll have you know. You best speak about me with more due respect."

He buckled the belt around his waist holding the whole thing together. "Your Highness, I ken ye are a queen, tis why I dinna call it your stable gates."

I batted him on the shoulder again with a giggle and Quentin from outside the room asked, "Boss, you almost ready to go eat? I'm hungry."

"We'll be dressed in a moment, Master Quentin."

The tavern kitchen passed around bowls with a paste like porridge and a small cup of milk. I was given another large mug of ale, which seemed bonkers so early in the morning. The milk was good though, warm, which was unexpected. I knew there was some coffee upstairs, but didn't want to ask the barkeeper for hot water.

Magnus directed us to one of the tables and before we finished our breakfast, there was a commotion outside — horses and men's voices. Magnus stood. He said to me, "Kaitlyn, please be quiet on the matter, allow me speak."

I said, "Of course." I wouldn't have known what to say, anyway.

To Quentin he said, "You will be watchful?"

"Yes boss. Will you ask about Beaty though?"

Magnus leaned on the table his expression intent. "You are serious about her, Master Quentin? Tis the young Beaty Campbell, dost ye understand the difficulties of the coupling?"

"The coupling? I — I just wanted to see her."

The door of the tavern opened. Magnus said, "We will speak on it later—"

I turned to see his Uncle Baldie, his brother Sean, his brother-in-law Liam, and about seven other men I recognized.

I wished Lizbeth would have come but guessed she probably had no place here in this meeting, but neither did I. I was simply here because it wasn't safe for me to be anywhere without Magnus and Quentin.

The men moved into the tavern taking all the space, pulling chairs to the central table roughly, spreading out like no one else was there.

Baldie said, "Young Magnus come speak with us." The men all had a way of appearing to be relaxed and sitting sprawled, although their hands rested close to their weapons. The air was tense with the suspense, they could just spring into action. This was a lot more men than I expected. I couldn't tell if they were being friendly or if Magnus was in deep shit.

I really hoped he wasn't in deep shit. Quentin had a gun, but he wasn't planning on using it against the Campbells. His fingertips itched near it, anyway.

I clasped my hands in my lap, stared at my fingertips, and tried to hear what was said.

I was shocked though and from the looks on their faces they all were, too, when Magnus, big strapping Magnus, dropped to his knees in front of his brother and very quietly began to beg his forgiveness.

I wasna used tae begging on m'knees in front of other men, but as of late I had been on my knees most days prayin' tae God for forgiveness and on m'knees in front of Kaitlyn, beggin' forgiveness, and I guess I had grown used tae the posture. Twas a great deal of wrong I did in my life, and was sometimes hard tae explain I kent I had wronged.

But if I drew m'self in and became small, twas easier for the person I had wronged tae forgive me and twas a lesson I had been puttin' tae practice.

When Sean crossed intae the room tae the table, he was bound up with anger and wouldna sit. I could see he wasna goin' tae reconcile without a real gesture of contrition.

The truth was, I had brought real damage on my clan. I hadna any choice at the time, I was chased and needed their protection, but I had brought death too near tae m'family.

It had been a hard night, tae nae be able tae go home. Tae be sleepin' in the tavern. Those men had approached me last evenin' and I had claimed tae be a Campbell, but I couldna tell them I was Magnus, nephew of the Earl, brother of Sean, nephew of

Baldie, because I hadna known what my standin' was and so, without standin', now, I decided tae kneel.

My brother had a look of shock tae his expression.

"Sean, my brother, ye have lived and breathed and fought alongside me since we were weans and I ken I have brought death and destruction tae our family and the gates of our castle. I have fought alongside Liam and Baldie but I also took up arms against yerself... I ken ye were doin' what ye thought best tae protect your family. Ye may have been right in many ways, ye told me tae take the battle tae my own kingdom instead of bringin' it here, but I dinna heed your wisdom."

Sean grunted.

"Since I turned myself intae Commander Davis—"

Sean sneered, "You dinna turn yerself intae him, I turned ye over."

I wanted tae argue but instead I said, "Aye."

"I am surprised ye arna in prison or worse."

"Och aye. I am nae in prison because I killed Commander Davis and all of his men for what they did tae our family. Then I fought my Uncle Samuel and killed him as well. I have been crowned king since I saw you last and wish tae tell ye my family here has nothin' tae fear from armies from my lands. I bring a promise of peace from the kingdom of Magnus the First."

Sean's fist slammed intae the side of my head. The pain jerked my head back and almost knocked me tae the dusty floor. I righted myself and shook my head tae clear it. "I winna fight ye, brother."

With a growl he grabbed the back of my head and kneed my face. "Ye almost killed us Magnus."

The pain tae my nose was terrible, but I kept tae my knees. "I ken tis true, my brother. I am beggin' forgiveness." Blood poured down my chin.

Sean put his hands on his hips and laughed, a big guttural

laugh. The surrounding men joined in laughin'. He proffered a hand and I took it. He pulled me tae my feet and threw his arms around me in a brotherly hug.

"Daena bleed on m'shirt, Young Magnus, my Maggie has woven it for me."

I stepped back with a laugh. "I wouldna want tae ruin it brother, tis the only part of ye that is nae ugly."

"Och, says the handsome younger brother, but see, Magnus. I have broken yer face, now ye art nothin' but a scabby-boggin tarriwag."

I smiled, "Och, now we are twins."

CHAPTER 46

*C*hairs were pulled out and highlanders sat together in a circle to talk. The proprietor handed Magnus a dirty rag to wipe his nose on and I made a mental note to explain germ theory and bacteria to Magnus as soon as I could.

"Phew."

Quentin opened his eyes wide. "Shit, that was scary. I was thinking, 'How the hell am I going to carry him out of here and fight off all those men, plus Kaitlyn?'"

I laughed, that laugh of 'Oh my God We Just Almost Died.' "Would you be fighting me or carrying me?"

"I have no idea, you are always a wildcard."

I looked over at their table. "Wish I could hear what they're saying."

"Yep, me too. I seriously don't think Magnus should have groveled, but I guess it worked."

"He had to help Sean save face. Sean was an ass, but he has to live here and take care of people, so Magnus was helping him by acting like Sean was the one who was in the right. I'm super proud of him."

"Me too. He's a good big brother."

We grinned at each other.

"I was about to say you're older than him but he is older by 300 years. So speaking of old people — you know this whole seeing a Campbell woman is a big deal. You like her?"

He nodded.

"What could you possibly have in common?"

"Katie, seriously, coming from you?"

"No, really, tell me, what does she do?"

"She works on her dad's farm."

"A farm, wait, how old is she?"

"I don't know, probably 18."

"Probably eighteen! She's just a — Quentin has something happened with her?"

"Yeah, but I like her, she likes me. I told Magnus to help me see her."

"Quentin you cannot have a baby mama in the 18th century. You will screw up the whole course of history."

He grunted. "Rich coming from you."

"I'm not wrong."

He said, "I'm not talking about a baby mama. I wear protection. I'm not stupid. Look, I just want to see her. And she's not too young for me, her family already thinks she's getting too old, her father told her she was hard to marry."

My eyes widened. "Why is she hard to marry?"

"Because she's funny and she speaks her mind."

"Oh lord, these Campbell women are as much trouble as the Campbell men." I handed him my mug. "Will you get me another ale, we needs be drinkin' more than this."

When he approached the proprietor to get me an ale. Magnus

with his bruised face, whose focus had been on the conversation, kept an eye on me the entire time. Quentin returned to the table a few minutes later and Magnus returned his attention to the conversation at his table.

I said, "You know there's a possibility you'll have to marry her? You understand that right? I mean, if her family can get past the part where you're black. I have no idea how that works."

"I think you might be confused about how sex works, Katie. You can have sex and not be married, do I have to show you diagrams?"

"Do I have to hit you upside the head with a bible? I get you can have sex with a girl in the 18th century and you can be a scoundrel, but do you understand the ramifications of being that kind of a scoundrel?"

He spun his drink. "I don't want to be a scoundrel."

"Good, well I won't say anything more. I think Magnus will know how to handle this, I hope. But whatever you and he decide, I want to tell you the older Magnus said he needs you. He asked me to get you. He made it seem like that was the first thing on the list: Get Quentin. I know you deserve a life and happiness and a warm bed but Magnus needs you."

He squinted at me with a grin. "I take Boss's need for me seriously, Katie. He's like a brother. He can count on me."

"Good, thank you."

A while later Sean called to our table, "Join us, Black Mac."

Quentin went to the table. A rough-hewn chair was offered to him between Baldie and Sean. The men greeted Black Mac rowdily, and there were pats on the back, and some jeers and insults passed. It seemed like the trouble was over except I was too far away to hear what they were saying.

Magnus turned in his chair enough to have me in his peripheral vision, but didn't look over at me.

So I whiled some time mostly ignored, which was fine, because there were men here I didn't know and just an hour ago the possibility of us all being in extreme danger. I kept my hands folded and glanced occasionally at Magnus while the men talked.

Then a man at Magnus's table banged his mug on the boards and announced to the room he needed another drink.

I ignored him since it had nothing to do with me, but then Magnus startled me by commanding, "Kaitlyn, ye needs rise and fetch Ailig an ale."

All eyes were on me. "Oh." I glanced at Magnus's face. There was still blood around his nose, accentuating the sternness he held there. He refused to look at me. I crossed to the table and asked, "May I get you a drink as well?"

He grunted and passed me his mug with his jaw set.

Another man grunted and held his out for me too. So I swallowed my humiliation and asked the barkeeper for three ales. When I brought them back to the table I even bobbed a little curtsy as I placed them in front of the men. I bobbed another curtsy when a fourth man handed me his now empty mug and a then a fifth.

When I returned to the table a second time I heard Sean say, "...her obedience is verra flatterin' tae yer authority, Mag—" I realized from all the eyes on me that it was me they were talking about.

I flushed, curtsied, placed the ale on the table and crossed back to my own lonely seat. I tried to behave as demurely as I could, my back straight, my hands folded in my lap, my eyes cast down. I didn't know what kind of test that was but I prayed a little I passed it, for Magnus's sake and my own.

Magnus kept his attention away from me and never looked over at me once.

CHAPTER 47

The meeting over we were all to go back to the castle and though there were horses to carry our bags, we, Magnus, Quentin, and I, would have to walk.

The men on horseback rode away down the path and we all collectively breathed out.

I turned to Magnus. "Your poor beautiful face."

"Och, tis verra painful all over here." He gestured toward his entire head.

"I saved out a few things from the first aid kit. First, please wash with this." I handed him a wet wipe.

He winced as he wiped his face around his nose.

"I'm super proud of you. I want you to know it. I'm sorry you had to bleed to do it, but you handled that really well." I passed him a painkiller and some water from a bottle I was carrying.

"Thank ye for jumpin' when I called on ye. Twas necessary for ye tae do it."

"Why was it necessary?"

"Ailig said ye were the one that ruled in m'house. He said twas the story they are all tellin' of us. So I had tae tell him ye submit tae me without question. He challenged my side of it and I am verra glad ye followed m'orders. He is a rough man and would have wanted me tae correct ye."

"Holy shit, that would have sucked."

We packed it all and Quentin slung the pack over his shoulder.

We were returning on the path we followed yesterday, through the same trees, along an uphill route that soon left the sparse trees and ascended into hills.

Walking uphill I asked, "Can't we follow the river?"

"Nae, I am still concerned we are bein' followed. If we are elevated, we will spot them."

"Oh, that makes sense."

Quentin kept checking behind us as we walked.

I added, "At the tavern I followed your orders because you never give them. I'm simply pointing that out in case it seemed fun and you liked it or something. And I don't need correcting."

Magnus said, "I dinna think twas fun and I wouldna correct ye, I think I have proven it."

"Thank you." I wrapped my hand in his as we walked.

We stopped by a small stream for a rest and agreed to save our treats for the castle. We ate some bread and drank water.

Magnus said, "I spoke tae Baldie of Beaty Campbell, Master Quentin. He says she is broodin' for ye. She is verra young and has been speakin' of ye tae anyone who will listen."

Quentin groaned.

Magnus looked at me mischievously then continued to Quentin. "He also wants me tae warn ye she winna make a good wife; ye are tae ken Beaty Campbell has too a sharp a tongue tae bow gracefully tae ye when ye are her husband."

"I'm her husband now?"

Magnus chewed a hunk of bread and swallowed. "Ye have bed a Campbell cousin of a marryin' age. Ye bed her and the Campbell men ken ye have bed her. What dost ye mean tae do on it?"

Quentin stared at the horizon for a moment. "I guess just dating her for a while and seeing how it goes is too much to ask?"

Magnus chuckled, "Aye, once ye pulled your kilt up ye lost the battle."

"Well why the hell do you guys wear these things, anyway? No underwear, you're at the ready."

"Och aye, tis a curse."

"It's not like I got her pregnant."

"Tis maybe worse, if she was pregnant her father would accept ye more readily than he is inclined tae now. I have been warned he thinks ye may have run off and disgraced her. We will have tae make it a'right."

Quentin ran his hands up and down on his face. "So you were a virgin when you married Katie?"

Magnus's eyes twinkled. "Nae, but widows are nae nearly as much trouble."

"*This* should have been something you told me."

Magnus said, "So you daena like her?"

"No, I like her a lot. I'm looking forward to seeing her again. She's pretty and she made me laugh, and I just would prefer a lot more time to think about it before I marry her."

"Aye, ye will have tae do the thinkin' in the long days after ye are bound."

Quentin groaned.

Magnus said, "The only other option is ye never return and ye choose tae bring a disgrace on her. Twould be easy for ye as ye arna of this time."

"No," Quentin shook his head. "No, I don't want to do that."

Magnus clapped heartily on Quentin's shoulder. "Then you, my friend, will be wed!"

"I don't know if this is at all what I—"

"Will ye live here and start a farm?"

Quentin glanced at me. "Can I still work for you and travel? I mean it's a little like going off to war, right?"

"Aye, you can leave as long as ye provide well for her." Magnus stood to walk.

Quentin said, "How the hell will I do that? I don't have piles of gold."

"I am now a king. I will elevate ye tae the rank of Colonel. As such ye will be able tae bestow upon her family some wealth. I will speak tae her father on it tonight."

Quentin groaned. "Speak to her father — will I have to speak to her father?"

"Aye, ye will have tae afore the wedding."

Quentin groaned again.

And we all trudged toward Balloch Castle.

CHAPTER 48

The front wall was still busted. But the piles of rubble all over the courtyard had been cleaned and straightened, stones piled according to size ready to be used in the rebuild. When we arrived through the front gates, Sean met us to take Magnus and Quentin to meet with the Earl.

And then there was Lizbeth rushing across the courtyard — "Kaitlyn!" She hugged me and held me out to have a long look. "I hae never seen ye look so fresh and well. Our Young Magnus has had a blow tae the face, I see, trouble has followed him, but ye are neither frantic — or is that almost a glow? Are ye with bairn?"

"No, it's only the first time you've seen me that nothing dramatic or awful has happened. Nothing bad is happening, not really, we're simply home to visit for once. And no baby, not yet."

She hooked her arm through mine. "Twill happen in time. Young Magnus has reconciled with Sean I see."

"He has, he got on his knees and begged Sean to forgive him."

"He is a good boy." She led me into the castle. "And Black Mac is here, has he come back for Beaty?"

"Yes, definitely. Absolutely."

"Good because she is chirpin' like a pea hen about him, and we are all verra tired from the listenin' on it."

"Perfect, because he is eager to marry her so we'll arrange it soon."

Lizbeth laughed a merry laugh. "And once she is married, she will fast lose her insistence he is 'the verra best of men'. Tis nothin' like wakin' in the morn with them snorin' and smellin' tae ken the true worth of them."

I laughed. "I missed you so much."

"I missed ye too, sister, I am verra glad tae have ye home."

"I'm relieved it is your home, Magnus and I weren't sure what we would find."

"Once the machines and Commander Davis were gone, Liam and Baldie met with Sean and the Earl. It dinna take them long tae decide the family was safer inside the walls than without so we returned. I told Sean he had behaved like a howlin' gimcrack, and we made up because he agreed with me on it."

"And how's your baby?"

"He is a verra good baby." The corner of her lip turned up. "Or so the nurse tells me."

"One last question, are there still rumors about me? That I'm a—"

She pressed her finger to my lips. "Nae, Madame Greer has handled the rumors, she has spoken tae everyone on it. After we saw my midwife accused, we have all become more sensible on it, and we are a fortunate village our minister haena the kind of darkness tae his sermons that some have. Ye are safe, Kaitlyn, and I pray ye are always safe from now on."

We entered the Great Hall and found there a platter of bread with ale to wash it down. We stood by the table and ate. "What's taking them so long?"

"I suspect the meetin' with the Earl has now included Beaty's father. They wouldna want tae wait. The family has been verra concerned Black Mac wasna returning."

CHAPTER 49 - MAGNUS

*W*e were led intae the Earl's upper chambers, intae the small room where he received visitors. Twas stone walled but lavish with furnishings. He was quite proud of this room and I found it amusin' tae think his sister, Lady Mairead, had filled coffers with much more than this in a single trip.

The Earl sat in a large carved chair, wearin' a towerin' wig and rouge-stained cheeks. I bowed and apologized for the trouble my war had caused him and—

"The men have told me ye are a king now, Young Magnus? You have ascended tae Donnan's throne?"

"I have."

He sat for a verra long time watchin' me, spinnin' the ring on his long fingers.

"Lady Mairead told me of wondrous riches there..." His voice trailed off.

"I do rule over a vast kingdom, but the wealth is nae more than Scotland's wealth, your grace."

He waved my words away. "Seems I should be addressing ye so. What of your coffers — have ye much gold?"

"I have some, dost ye need gold, Uncle? I thought ye in command of great wealth as well as the favor of the queen?"

"I am stretched, of course, far beyond what is my fair burden. There have been many battles fought tae protect our lands, and there has been much damage tae my walls... I have been protecting ye without asking for anything in return."

"Of course. I have some gold with me, and ye will have my assistance, Uncle. I will speak with my advisors as soon as I return."

"Would ye be willin' tae sign a covenant on it?"

I said, "Aye. Will ye have your advisors meet with me on the morrow? We will negotiate favorable terms."

"Good good, and now what of this other matter, this matter of your friend," he nodded toward Quentin in the corner, "and our Beaty Campbell?"

One of the Earl's advisors entered the room approached him and whispered.

The Earl said, "Let him in."

Twas Beaty's father, James Campbell. We all called him Jimmy. He was verra old, stooped and gnarled. I kent him tae have verra many children, most of them daughters, from verra many wives, which meant he would be amenable tae a marriage for his youngest child.

The Earl introduced us and then I introduced Jimmy to Colonel Quentin Peters. Jimmy said to Quentin, "Ah, you are a Colonel though ye art a black man?"

Quentin said uncomfortably, "Yes, sir."

The Earl said, "Jimmy, Magnus is now a king, he has taken his father's throne." He spoke loudly as if Jimmy was hard of hearing.

218 | DIANA KNIGHTLEY

"Ah, a king." Jimmy bowed low and for a moment I wondered if he was able tae stand again.

I said loudly, "Colonel Quentin Peters, would like tae marry your Beaty. He has a large purse and can take care of her verra well. I can vouch for him that he is a good man and will do much tae further your family's fortune."

"What's that you say?"

The Earl said, "Colonel Peters wants tae marry Beaty. Will ye agree?"

Jimmy scoffed. "Beaty? She is verra useless, she daena have the makin' for a good wife, your highness, ye must be mistaken."

Quentin looked confused by the conversation.

I said, "Nae, he wants Beaty."

Jimmy said, "I haena a dowry for her."

I said, "He inna askin' for a dowry, he is offerin' tae take her and provide for her."

"My niece, Mildred, would make a pleasin' wife, she makes a—"

"He wants tae marry Beaty. Your daughter, Beaty Campbell."

"Beaty? Why does he want tae marry Beaty?"

I looked at the Earl tae assist.

He said, "Jimmy Campbell do you give this man, Colonel Quentin Peters permission tae wed your daughter, Beaty?"

Jimmy, sensing the importance of the situation, straightened his back and said, "Aye."

The Earl summoned his secretary tae bring the paperwork.

On a side table with a quill pen, Quentin signed the contract. Then Jimmy signed with a shaky scribble, I signed my new signature, Magnus the First, and the Earl signed last.

When I looked intae Quentin's face tae congratulate him he looked terrified.

～

We found Kaitlyn and Lizbeth in the Great Hall. I hugged Lizbeth hello and kissed Kaitlyn and jokingly presented Quentin. "He is bound, tis official."

Lizbeth laughed a high spirited laugh. "How much did ye get for takin' her?"

I answered, "A lighter purse, we dinna bargain for her. Colonel Peters has offered tae provide for her father."

Lizbeth said, "Och, tis a terrible deal, ye will be regrettin' it once she is bossin' ye around, Black Mac. You had the freedom of a bachelor and now ye will hae the sufferin' of a husband."

We all laughed.

I said, "Has Kaitlyn told ye of our purpose?"

"Nae, she has told me ye came tae see me!" She laughed merrily.

"She left her ring at Madame Greer's house when she was here last."

"Her ring! I have it hidden and safe, I will bring it tae ye tonight at dinner."

CHAPTER 50

*W*e were all talking when Quentin's eyes locked on a young woman across the room. She was pretty, blonde, fair, and petite and when she smiled she had dimples. She was smiling, a lot. Like a whole lot.

She ran squealing into Quentin's arms. "I kent ye would come for me. They told me ye werna goin' tae and I told them my Quentin would come for me. And ye did!"

I watched as Quentin looked into her eyes. "Of course I came for you." They kissed. "I asked your father if I could marry you and he said yes and—"

He glanced at me and Magnus, then around at all the men watching. Then Quentin got down on a knee in front of her.

He held her hands. "Beaty Campbell will you do me the honor of becoming my wife?"

"Aye!" She jumped up and down and threw her arms around his head and repeated, "Aye! I kent ye were goin' tae marry me. Nae one would believe me, but I kent it!" He stood and they hugged tightly rocking back and forth.

I laughed. "Finally someone in our family that makes me look mature."

Lizbeth joked, "You look positively matronly beside that one, Madame Kaitlyn." We both laughed.

~

After dinner, the crowds of people were dispersing and we had only Sean, Lizbeth and Liam, Baldie, Quentin with Beaty sitting in his lap kissing his face whenever she could, and me and Magnus left so we decided to open our bags and pass out some gifts. We let Magnus have the fun of it.

Baldie joked, "Nothin' will buzz around our heads and try tae kill us?"

"Nae, but twill be a funny tickle in yer throat when ye drink." He passed a soda bottle to each of them. "They each have differin' flavors. You can read it on the label if ye want tae." Most everyone turned their bottle to investigate the labels.

Magnus said, "Och, I daena have one of the fancy—" He performed a gesture for opening the bottle.

I said, "A bottle opener, we forgot a bottle opener."

Quentin groaned, "I had one on my keychain and gave it to Hayley. Wait..." he gently dislodged Beaty, stood, and took the first bottle. With the handle end of his sword, he pried the cap off with a pop. "Mandarin lime flavor." He passed it to Beaty who took a dainty sip spilling some of it into her cleavage. Her eyes went big. "Tis a..." She seemed at a loss for words and took another sip.

Quentin circled the table popping bottle tops off, but then Sean had to try to do his own and he and Magnus competed to see who could get their bottle top off first. Then they all raised their bottles, said, "Slainte!" and swigged.

Sean said, "Tis awful," he licked his lip, "tastes of honey and..." He swigged again.

There was a lot of spillages when Baldie and Lizbeth could not get their mouths to work, but there was a great deal of exclaiming and excited gasps at the taste. Even Liam smiled and I hadn't ever seen him do that before.

I said, "We have candy for the children too, but also these..." I brought out a tin of cookies and handed it to Beaty. "Since you're new to the family, this is for you."

For Lizbeth I made a small pile on the table in front of her, lotions and perfumes, soaps and candles. "Smell it." I showed her how to open the lotion and waved it under her nose. Her eyes lit. "Tis so pretty, like a flower!"

She waved it under her husband's nose. "Och, tis a rose."

I said, "It's rose scented for your skin if it's dry, you can rub this in and it will feel better." I rubbed a tiny bit of lotion on the back of her hand. She rubbed it in and sniffed it again. Then sniffed it again. And again.

Magnus passed around beanie hats to Liam, Baldie, Sean, and one for himself. Quentin said he didn't want one, but I guessed it was because Beaty was kissing him and twirling her fingers through his hair. Sean and Magnus were snickering about it.

I gave Lizbeth the quilt next. "I shouldna be takin' so many presents, Kaitlyn."

"You should, but you can share if you want to."

She wrapped in the quilt. "I daena want tae share!" Then she teased Liam, "Ye can have some if ye are kind about it. You will want tae since I smell of roses." She laughed and he chuckled.

CHAPTER 51

On our way to our room I stopped at the window where we had made love decades before this. "Here," I said. I ran my hand along the window sill, remember being perched on it while he—

"Och." He said. "I have always wanted tae have ye here."

"Really? Like, you think about it? Having me at times you aren't having me? In places you haven't had me?"

"Och aye, I think on it."

"Really? And this is one of those places?"

He nodded.

I asked, "Do you want to...?"

"Nae, I daena..." He shook his head. "Maybe another time."

"That's okay, it is weird I've done something with you that you have no memory of." We continued up the stairs. "But seriously, you think about having me in other places? Name one."

"I have named ten places in m'head between the Great Hall and this floor of the castle."

"Really, just now? So we had dinner with your family, and now we're headed to our room and you're looking around at everything thinking about having sex there?" I teased, "This is all so scandalous."

"Aye, see that table? Your arse would look verra beautiful bent over it."

"Master Magnus, I believe you are drunk!"

"See that corner? I could spread your legs there. I think ye wouldna argue on it."

I laughed. "You're right, I wouldn't. But we should get all these leftover presents to our room. Let's have me properly in a bed."

"Aye, on a vermin filled mattress on a proper bed in the 18th century. Tis creaky tae alert our neighbors but sturdy tae keep us from fallin' tae the dirtier ground."

I laughed happily. "Just what we need."

We stopped at the garderobe to pee and then went to our room.

I walked through the door of our bedroom and stopped still in my tracks overcome with emotion. "Oh I didn't..." I walked to the bed and ran my fingertips along the rough fur of the bearskin cover and — "I didn't realize it would bring it all back like this, Magnus. You and I, we were so broken the last time we were here." I dropped onto the bed and curled into the fetal position running my palm over the bedding. "You were here with the oxygen machine and I was so scared you were going to die—" I rolled onto my back and lay spreadeagled. "And I was here, losing you, and I was too broken to be able to—"

Magnus dropped our bags. He climbed beside me and lay with his chin resting on my tummy. "You have never lost me, mo reul-iuil. Nae once."

I put my hand on his jaw. "In other lifetimes I lose you over and over again."

"Nae here. I am here, ye are here. We are together. You

haena lost me and ye winna allow it. You are a terrible arse, ye would fight tae keep me."

We both laughed. Mine was a little sad though.

His smile drew down. "You are bein' so sad again, mo reul-iuil."

"My heart broke right here on this bed."

"Aye, but we patched it here on this bed too." He wriggled up and kissed me right on top of a breast above my bodice then he rested his head there. I ran my fingers through his hair and looked at him.

He grinned with a twinkle in his eye. "Can I show ye a place where I have always wanted tae have ye? Tis nae here on our sad heartbreak bed and is nae in the hall or on the stair, tis a better place."

I nodded. "Yes."

He hopped from the bed, a lumbering bear light on his feet. "You will need a blanket. Perhaps more than one."

I stood and he gathered the wool blanket from our bed. I pulled a quilt from our bags. "Where to?"

He took me by the hand and led me through the halls.

CHAPTER 52

We arose from the stairwell on the high walls of the castle. I crossed to the edge and looked. The parapet was partially crumbled from the battle we brought here months ago. The ground was a long long, four stories down.

"Lay out the blanket, mo reul-iuil. I will dismiss the guard."

I glanced over my shoulder as I spread the wool blanket and saw a man on the far edge. Magnus spoke to him briefly and passed him something. Then the guard left. "What did you give him?"

"I gave him a piece of candy. It should keep him for some time." He sat on the wool blanket beside me. "Turn around and I will work your lacings."

I sat in front of him, pulling my hair from its band while he untied my lacings in the moonlight. It didn't take long before my bodice was over my head and off my arms to the ground beside us. My loose linen shift was now a comfortable nightgown after the binding of the bodice.

I lay back and he lay beside me and offered his bicep to rest my head and we both looked up. Stars were flung from one side of the sky to the other, the Milky Way stretching through the middle like I had never seen it before, bright and twinkling and diamond-encrusted. It was breathtaking.

"See this sky, Kaitlyn? Tis always the same heavens wherever we are."

"True." I wrapped my hand around the curve of his bicep, feeling the strength there in his bent arm. He was at rest but still so strong. "But here's the thing about the heavens, Magnus — what do you see?"

"The stars laid out for us, tae guide us, rionnag. Tis majestic and comfortin' that they are always there in every time, stalwart and eternal."

We both stared at the sky. "What does 'runak' mean?"

"Star."

"Oh."

We were both quiet for a time.

I added, "I see something totally different."

"Ye do?"

"I told you once we send spaceships up, but did you know, Magnus, we have sent ships out to see what is out there and they just go? It's endless — billions and billions of stars flung out. What I see are the stars blown apart, not in one layer, but deep, moving and shifting. We will never know even a small bit of it. It's terrifying actually that the eternal sky is so big. It proves we are insignificant. We mean nothing."

"Och, ye are in a mood."

He chuckled and I giggled into his chest.

"So what ye are saying — there is a man in a ship and he is explorin' the skies? He must be the bravest man God has ever created. He sees this black night and says, 'I want tae go see what lies inside it'? That man is nae insignificant. The men who built the ship, the men who steer it? They arna insignificant. They are warriors. The stars daena prove we are unimportant, they are there for us tae prove our courage in every century."

I looked at his face. "Jesus Christ Magnus, you are—"

He grinned at me. "I am what, right?" He put on a falsetto voice. "'Master Magnus ye are absolutely right, this sky is majestic and I winna argue on it anymore.'"

He laughed, his chest jiggling under my head as I laughed along with him.

I said, "Master Magnus, you are perfectly right, let's wave up at the man." I waved. "Hello, courageous man exploring the universe."

Magnus kept watching the stars. His breathing slowed. I watched them for a moment then I curled onto his chest and watched his jawline, where it met his neck, the tendons and sinews under his skin, the stubble of a new beard growth, the lobe of his ear with the jagged scar from the battles after our wedding... I could see his breaths, the beat of his heart, all contained within this small space, everything that kept him living, right there.

While he watched the infinite sky, I watched the up-close bit of him, finite and human and fragile. I wriggled up and pressed my lips to that spot, feeling the thrum of his heart against my mouth, breathing in the scent of him.

Then after a long moment he pulled me onto his body, loose gown, warm under the quilt. My lips met his and we kissed with our bodies pressed along the full length of each other, a thin layer of fabric between. His hands rumpled my shift in fistfuls and without breaking our kiss I struggled his kilt up.

I kissed him, my fingers wrapped through his hair, while he explored me and then settled me down on him with an exhale into each other's skin. I peeked at his face: closed eyes, concentration. "We are outside, under the stars," I whispered.

"Och aye, tis a good place tae have ye."

My breaths were fast and panting. "You're in my castle on a castle, it's very funny if you think—"

Magnus chuckled, his hips working against mine. "You arna usually so talkative durin' m'takeovers of your fortifications."

I giggled, a quiet laugh kept just between us. I ran my hands along this chest, up his arms, pushing them above his head, where I held them, my body spread deliciously along his length as we rocked together. My temple pressed to his cheek, a lovely friction. "I'm just happy. I really like you," after another beat I added, "and your cannon." I laughed against his skin.

"Och, I ken ye do, mo reul-iuil, tae come with me tae the high walls."

"This?" My voice was breathy near his ear. "You, my love, can always come into me in my high walls."

We both laughed. His chuckle shaking my chest. "Tis nae what I said, though twill work for what I meant."

Our laughs entwined, vibrating the ether, rising into the clear sky, sound waves rolling on and on ever-expansive. I rose up, sat fully down, and arched back with a breathless moan. I rode him — my hands pressed to his wide chest. His hands directing my thighs, breaths and moans and linen fabric veiling and surrounding me. Linen stretched across his torso and yet we were unclothed and wrapped in the quilt — the cool air on our faces and hands, the warm heat where we were pressed together. And then after a long — lovely — slow — time I shifted my body and energy and finished on him hard and fast and *oh. God.*

I collapsed on him pulling my arms in for warmth, nestled against his chest his arms around me.

His hands wrapped through my hair. He slid from inside me and slowly I rolled to his side, and we lay there, our breathing resuming a normal pace, our heartbeats slowing. His body grew heavy.

I mumbled, "Are we sleeping here?"

"Nae, mo reul-iuil. But I am nae ready tae go downstairs. Go tae sleep I will get ye tae our room."

My last glance before I fell asleep was Magnus's eyes open watching the endless sky.

CHAPTER 53

I woke to a light day and a warm bed. The wool blanket on me and the quilt. I had no idea how he got all of us from the roof in the night, but he did and it made me feel so taken care of like a child with all my needs met. I pulled the covers to my cheek. Heartbreak bed felt a little like secure and comfortable bed now. I looked up at Magnus. He looked down, his brow lifted, he grinned.

"Did I do good, mo reul-iuil?"

I nodded and pulled the covers up more.

After a few moments of wordless comfort he said, "But we must rise, Quentin will be married this morn."

We were fully dressed by the time there was a quiet knock on the door, and Lizbeth's voice, "Kaitlyn?"

When I opened the door, she entered with a basket over her arm. "I have brought ye presents." She looked at Magnus. "What are ye still doin' here Young Magnus? The men are risen, ye arna the newly married ones, ye have tae be the ones that run the place while the newly married couples do their couplin'."

Magnus chuckled, kissed me on the cheek and joked, "You heard her, Kaitlyn, she is an auld hag now, nae wantin' anyone tae be in love anymore."

Lizbeth laughed and batted his arm as he left.

She put the basket on the small table near the fire and uncovered the contents. "First, ye be wantin' this." She held my ring.

"Thank you thank you thank you." I threw my arms around her, kissed her cheek, and put it on my finger. I looked at it, back in its place, the garnet shimmering, the gold glistening. "Thank you."

She patted my forearm. "Nae, thank you, sister. You saved m'life, I am sure of it."

She pulled out the first aid kit I had left in her room. In her basket I could see the flashlight and other pieces of equipment we had left when we were captured. "Much of this is verra dangerous."

"I agree." I took the two-way radios and the flashlights from the basket. "I think though, this kit is important for you to keep. I don't think it will cause you any trouble. You have a safe place, right? I'll show you what it's all for." I showed her how to use the alcohol to clean the implements, how to apply the antibiotic cream, and how to put on the bandages. "If there was a deep cut and it was relatively clean, you could use this, making sure it's very very clean, to stitch the wound."

"The skin, Kaitlyn?"

I nodded. "It's what I did with you. It's what the doctors did with Magnus's side. Ask him to show you his scar and you'll get a feel for it. But keep this clean, and I'll bring more next time I come."

We put everything she was going to keep back in the basket

and I took the other stuff, the unsafe things, and packed them into my backpack.

She asked, "Are you ready tae help this young child get married? She is all a'fluster with worry and excitement. Tis quite a lot of carryin' on."

Lizbeth and I went downstairs to what was to be Quentin and Beaty's room. We knocked and entered. Beaty was in the middle, her face flushed red, her hair sticking out, still in her shift, bright, red rouge on her cheeks, a weird dark red lipstick on, white powder on her skin.

Lizbeth said, "Beaty, what means this, ye arna dressed? Where are your helpers?"

"I sent them away, they weren't helping! I daena think my makeup is right. I am supposed to be beautiful and they were clucking about me like I was ugly and I'm so worried." Beaty clutched her shift and just about tore it. Her eyes were wide with fear. "What if he daena come tae the church? What if he daena want tae marry me?"

I placed an arm around her and patted her shoulder. "Poor, poor Beaty, of course he is coming to the church. He has traveled all this way to get to you." I directed, "Put your arms up, sweetie."

Lizbeth pulled the bodice over her arms and snugly down around her middle and matter-of-factly laced it. I held Beaty's hands. "I know you just met me but I went through this same thing with Magnus. I was terrified he wouldn't show and—"

"Did he?"

"Um yeah, he showed up at the church and we got married. That's why I'm Mrs Campbell now."

"Och, tis right, he married ye and he is a king and ye arna much tae look at..."

"Excuse me?"

"Nae, I am sorry. I dinna mean it that way." She burst into tears. "I just meant ye arna a queen. Ye daena make me avert m'eyes. Ye daena have a crown, tis what I meant."

"Now see, you're right, I am just a plain ol'woman and Magnus married me. Quentin will be there at the church to marry you because you are beautiful and young and you make him laugh."

"He has a verra wonderful laugh, daena ye think so?" Lizbeth began to wrap Beaty's blonde hair up on her head.

I found a scrap of cloth and dipped it in water and smudged and wiped at her makeup. "Yes I do. We've known each other since we were bairn and when I was first married and Magnus had to go away for a while Quentin and I became very close friends. He's a great guy and he's very loyal. If he says he will be at the church, he means to be there."

Her hands were shaking. "How do I look?"

I had her makeup much less clown-like. "You look beautiful. Doesn't she, Lizbeth?"

"You look quite a beauty, young Beaty, he winna ken how tae behave he will be so overcome with the beauty of Beaty." She laughed merrily.

Beaty looked around the room. "This is my new room. I had tae move here tae the castle and it..."

Lizbeth asked, "Where did ye sleep at home?"

"In the kitchen. I used tae share it with m'sisters but they have all gone away tae be married and now there is a dog and a pig and some other animals and there is an excessive noise from them..."

Lizbeth smoothed the tartan on Beaty's shoulders. "Well, that must have been verra lonely for ye last night." She pulled Beaty's chin up. "But now ye will be sharin' the bed with your husband and soon ye will have bairn about your skirts and ye will be dreamin' on that one night ye had of peace and quiet."

Beaty shook her head. "I daena think I will ever want tae dream on it, twas verra quiet and frightenin'."

Lizbeth grinned. "Trust me. I am an auld hag as my young brother just reminded me this morn, I have a wisdom about me in my ancient years."

"How auld are ye?"

"I am a score and eight, my dear, a decade or more beyond ye. I ken the way the world works, if ye need me tae explain it, ye just come and ask."

Beaty nodded.

"You can ask Kaitlyn about the world as well, but she only kens of Magnus, och Magnus, och och och Magnus. I love ye Magnus." She grinned at me.

I laughed, "While that may be true, I figure Beaty might just want advice from me about love."

Lizbeth waved a hand at me. "Och, love tis only tae give ye more babies—" She cut herself off and gave me a sad pout. "Dear sister, I am sorry I said it. I should watch my tongue."

"It's okay. I hope to have a baby someday soon."

Lizbeth squeezed my hand. "Well, let's go get this girl married, shall we?"

Beaty burst into tears.

When we arrived at the church, I glimpsed Magnus standing behind the building. I waved him over and spoke to him privately. "She is in tears. She's so scared. He's here right?"

"Aye," Magnus grinned. "He has some terrible fears as well."

"Well yeah, he would usually be planning to spend some time before he wed her."

Magnus shrugged. "It worked okay for us, mo ghradh." He noticed, "Your ring has returned," and kissed my knuckle.

"Lizbeth had it just like you said she would."

"I am always right, mo ghradh."

I laughed. Then added, "Will you tell him to say something nice to her when he sees her, to tell her she's beautiful or something? Last night was her first night away from home. I mean, Quentin always surprises me, but this may be beyond him. She's really young and she's getting married and please tell him to be nice to her, like romantic. Should I talk to him?"

"Nae, ye are bein' too nervous. I will speak tae him on it."

Magnus disappeared around the corner to speak to Quentin and I went to speak to Lizbeth and Beaty and we were all called into the church for the wedding and then Beaty's face went ashen and a moment later she crumpled in the dirt in front of the church.

The men looked around to see what happened and when Quentin realized it was Beaty on the ground he rushed to her, as Lizbeth would say, 'like a good boy.' He knelt beside her and patted the back of her hand and brushed her hair back. "Beaty, wake up, it's me, Quentin, are you okay?" He looked at our faces and then back at Beaty as she was beginning to revive.

"Quenny?"

"Yes Beaty, I'm here. We're about to get married. You look very beautiful by the way."

She brushed the hair from her face with a dirty hand leaving a streak on her forehead. "Do I?"

"Aye. You look very pretty." He helped heave her to her feet. She held onto his arm to steady herself. "Lizbeth am I set tae rights?"

"Nae, dear Beaty, ye have a bit of dirt..." She took the edge of her tartan to wipe the smudge from Beaty's forehead. Then Lizbeth and I both dusted her skirts until she was deemed clean enough to enter the church.

This was the same village church where we had attended the wedding last Lammas Day just before all hell broke loose. We sat in the same pew and I watched Lizbeth again for cues on how to behave. Quentin was nervous but stood with the straight back I recognized from his football days, the anthem stance: wide feet, unmoving. As the ceremony went on his right leg jiggled nervously. It filled my heart. I wanted to rush up there and tell him how proud I was he was this kind of guy. How honored Magnus and I were to have him as a friend.

There was a handfasting and a lot of prayers. The ceremony was long and so boring. My hands folded, I couldn't wait for doing the next thing, celebrating.

Finally the priest declared it over and we all rushed out of the church to the open air.

I was pretty overcome. I hugged Quentin. "If your mama was still alive, she would be so proud of you."

"You think? Not sure how she would feel about me marrying the white girl in the dark ages."

I brushed some lint off his jacket, a loaner from one of the men so he would look fabulous on his wedding day. "You are a commander in Magnus's army, somewhere in the future, and you just married Beaty and are now a full member of the Campbell Clan in the 18th century, she would be very proud of you. I know I am. Magnus is."

Beaty rushed over eyes only on Quentin. "Quentin, we are married!"

His face broke into a smile. How could it not? She was all sweet dimples, a big smile, fair and silly and so so in love.

"Yes Beaty, we are." He threw an arm around her waist, lifted her from the ground and kissed her cheek. She threw her arms around him with a giggle. Magnus and I beamed proudly, a stand-in for his family in every age.

CHAPTER 54

The party went through most of the day. There was food and so much drink. Magnus passed all the candy sticks we had left to everyone there. They were amazed by it all. There was exuberant dancing. Bagpipes were being played and a regular ol'mosh pit as the day wore on, drunken folks dancing in a riotous kicking mess.

When we needed a break from dancing, we collapsed into chairs and watched, leaned on each other, poking fun at their moves. I said, "It's just like the nightclub in Jax."

"Tis verra alike, yet this is without the tiny dresses, the bright lights, and the terrible loud music."

Right then a bagpiper made a particularly loud sound. We both laughed but then our eyes were drawn to the doors at the far end. Two of the young men were walking from man to man urgently telling them something. Then they were all moving to the next man and then —

Magnus said, "Pardon me, Kaitlyn. I will be back." He went to find Quentin. They all met at the far end of the Great Hall, every man in the party except the drunken cousin who was already passed out in the corner. The music died. The men all left the Great Hall for the courtyard.

I asked Lizbeth, "What's happening? Can we go listen?"

"Nae, Kaitlyn, just take a chair. The men will tell us of it when tis time for us tae ken."

This was easier said than done. All the women were quiet. The long table was cleared, most of us sat and watched. One of the rough parts of being in the 18th century, there wasn't much to do while waiting. And the waiting took almost an hour.

Magnus, Sean, Liam, and Quentin came into the room at the head of the other men. They headed straight for our chairs.

Sean announced, "Tis a battle on the morrow."

I turned to Magnus. "Who?"

"A small army comin' from the direction of Delapointe's castle. The Earl has told us we must ride out tomorrow tae meet it. He has paid tae raise an army. We will meet them with a strong force."

"But—"

Magnus said, "Let us speak of it in private, Kaitlyn."

We went a little away from the group.

I asked, "Who is it, could it be General Reyes?"

Magnus looked down at me. "I daena ken. It might be Delapointe's son, as the Earl suspects, but it may be General Reyes. Delapointe haena caused any trouble in a verra long time, I suspect this might nae be what it seems."

"We could leave?"

He shook his head sadly. "I canna leave when the Earl has given orders tae ride against an army. Twould be desertin' my family. And Quentin has tae fight, he is a new brother. He must prove himself." He ran his hand through his hair. "I would greatly like for this trouble tae be caused by Delapointe instead of caused by some evil I have brought upon us."

"Me too. And you're injured, you just had a surgery, how can you fight?"

"I will fight okay. I will put the tape on my scar and wear the compressin' band the doctor gave me. I will be careful."

"How long will you be gone?"

"We will ride at first light and will meet them on the field the followin' day, we will return soon after we defeat them."

I sighed. "So like two days, maybe three? We should decide who will have the vessels." I watched the far end of the room, the men and women all discussing and planning for the men to leave. "I will take one, you will have one, but do we go to the future?"

"We daena ken for sure if tis safe there. What if the castle has fallen? Hammie told me nae tae come back for three weeks but he couldna guarantee it would be safe, tis a risk if we arna together."

"So we go back to Georgia and meet there?"

"Aye, but Kaitlyn, daena go without me. If ye can wait, do. Tis verra dangerous for ye tae travel alone right now. There will be guards here, just wait for me tae return, and then we will jump together."

"Don't worry, I don't want to jump alone. I'll have a vessel but I'll wait for you. Seriously though maybe this is just Delapointe's son trying to avenge his father and you will vanquish them and that will be the end of it."

"I hope tis true." He added, "I canna come to the room tonight, I have tae help load the weapons and pack the horses. I will need tae take Quentin's share in it so he can spend the night with Beaty, tis important tae consummate the marriage before he goes in case somethin' happens…"

"God, don't say that." I shivered. "Nothing is going to happen, but yes, let Quentin get lucky tonight. I love you."

"I love ye too." He put his arms around me and squeezed.

The wives said good bye to their husbands so the fighting men could prepare to leave just before dawn. Quentin was allowed to go to his room with Beaty and there was a massive lot of joking and teasing as he left the Great Hall. Beaty was hugged, advised, and encouraged by all the women and when they left he led her by the hand.

Lizbeth said, "Well, tis done, she is an auld married woman now." She sighed. "Was I ever that young?"

"How old were you when you married?"

"I was fifteen when I chose Liam tae marry, but he had tae marry someone else so I had tae marry Rory, my dear late husband. I was sixteen. I was verra lucky tae win Liam in my middle age."

"I'm used to people thinking I'm very young and immature at my age, twenty-four."

She laughed. "You art ancient, my sister, tis a wonder ye arna an auld hag like me."

"Will you ever forgive Magnus for saying it to you this morning?"

"Nae, I will tease him on that for the rest of his auld age. And I mayna call him Young Magnus anymore either, I will call him Auld Magnus, the other haena been around in enough years, we can consider him long gone I think."

I gulped in some air at the idea.

She continued, "Would ye like tae come tae m'apartments tonight?"

"I actually would but Magnus might come to the room to pack some things and I want to be there when he does."

She kissed me on my cheek with a hug and we said goodnight to everyone left in the Great Hall.

CHAPTER 55

The night was awful. Every sound had me shivering and so freaking scared. The room was so dark even with the fire. Plus there was a scurrying scritching scratching sound along one of the walls. Also my left leg was itchy as hell, which meant a bite of some kind from something here in the bed. I tried to pep-talk myself. I named everything in the room: *That's the chair. That's the candlestick. That's the chamberpot. That's the pointy thing I need to ask Magnus what it's called. That sound is the rat, no worries, don't freak out, just a rat. It lives here too.*

I finally fell asleep for about twenty minutes while the fire died down which meant no warmth and no light except the flashlight — all the way across the room in my pack.

I pulled the covers over my head.

After many hours, finally, the door opened and Magnus came in. He whispered, "Are ye awake, mo reul-iuil?"

"Yes." My voice was tiny under the covers.

He chuckled. "Where are ye?"

"I'm hiding in the bed from the rats."

"Tis verra cold in here, are ye tryin' tae turn it intae a refrigerator?"

I sort of pretend wailed, "Maybe the rats'll turn into popsicles and won't be able to make a nest in my hair."

He crouched beside the bed holding my hand under the covers wrapping an arm around my head. "We are packed, we leave verra soon."

His face was very close to mine in the dark. His breath smelled of beer and food, but not bad, his skin held that musky scent I loved, a bit of salty sweat from the work, a little of horses, not great, but not awful — real smelling like I wanted it to climb on me and fill me with it. Like a man had entered my bedroom and was crouched at the edge of my bed because he missed me, awesome like that.

"Be safe okay? Don't be too much of a hero, stay alive. I need you." Tears welled up. "Archie needs you. And Quentin and Zach and Me and Ben and Emma and Me and Hayley and Hammie and Me and James and..."

He chuckled. His cheek pressed against mine. "Och, tis a lot of people needin' me." His lips brushed down my cheek to my lips and he kissed me long and slow and sweet. "Ye canna stay here, mo reul-iuil. Tis too cold for ye. I fear ye will turn tae an icicle and even the rats winna be able tae keep ye warm. Get ye up, I will take ye tae Lizbeth. Bring yer quilt."

I climbed from bed with the quilt wrapped around me and shoved my feet into my boots. It was so dark there was no way I could see so I bumped against Magnus and he put an arm around me and led me out of our room and down the halls to Lizbeth and Liam's apartment at the other end of the floor.

Magnus knocked quietly. Lizbeth's voice, "Aye?"

"Tis Magnus, can I leave Kaitlyn with ye? She winna survive the night on her own, she inna able tae fight off the vermin."

The door opened and Lizbeth said, "Of course, come in

Kaitlyn."

I padded in, penguin-like, my hair sticking from the top of the burrito-wrapped quilt. "Thank you." I said.

Magnus said, "Goodbye, mo ghradh, I will see ye in two days."

I said, "Three at the latest."

"Three at the latest, " he agreed and kissed me on my forehead. He said goodbye to Lizbeth and left me standing in the middle of her apartment. She had a robust fire going in the hearth though, already it was an improvement on my own room. She knew how to do things like survive a Scottish castle at night alone.

She said, "The chamber pot is there, because I daena want tae go tae the garderobe tonight. Dost ye need tae go?" I gratefully and a little sheepishly peed in her chamberpot and then she said, "Ye can sleep on my side of the bed, tis nae so uncomfortable."

"I'm just so grateful. I'd sleep on the floor if you wanted me to."

She said, "The legs on the bed be there for a reason." She climbed onto her side and slid in between the covers. The soft quilt I gave her was closest to her body. I climbed into the covers, still wrapped in my own quilt, thinking happily there would be enough warmth to get through the night. "Good night tae ye, Kaitlyn."

"Goodnight, Lizbeth."

The fire gave the room a soft glow and the small pops and crackles of the flames were a comforting sound.

After a few moments when I was just on the edge of falling asleep, Lizbeth's voice broke the silence. "Kaitlyn, I have been wantin' tae talk tae ye of somethin'."

I could only make out the barest shimmer of light on her face. She was looking at the ceiling.

"Sure?"

"I want ye tae take her with ye."

"Who, Beaty?"

"Aye."

I stared at the ceiling for a moment. "You mean to the West Indies?"

"Nae, I want ye tae take her with ye tae your time."

My eyes went wide. "I don't know what you're talking about... how do you...?"

"Years ago my dear mother told me about it. She brought me a great many presents — paintings and clothing and perfumes, and asked me if I wanted tae go."

I rolled onto my side facing her. "Lady Mairead told you *what* exactly?"

"That she was able tae travel tae a different time. She shared with me the most amazin' foods and asked me tae accompany her. She said the future was full of wondrous inventions and twould be safe for me there, but I chose nae tae go."

"Why didn't you?"

"I couldna leave Sean. Lady Mairead said she wouldna take him because he wouldna understand. I kent Magnus would be safe in the future. He dinna need me, but Sean does. If I went with Magnus, we would be leavin' Sean all alone and he wouldna survive without me tellin' him what tae do. But I tell ye, Kaitlyn, I dinna really believe her. Twas too much like magic tae fly through the air and end in a different year. It dinna sound like twas real."

"When did you begin to believe her?"

She pulled her covers to her chin. "She told me she was taking Magnus to his kingdom and when Magnus returned and his story was much the same, I suspected twas true. Then you came along, and you were nae at all like the girls here. But twas the machines that convinced me."

"They were shocking even for me. I'm from the future, they're from the future-future."

"The men are all takin' them as normal, because they daena ken what tae think of them, but I kent Mairead was tellin' the truth. What year dost ye hail from?"

"Right now in my time it is the year 2018 and Magnus's kingdom is in the year 2382."

"And is it as magical as Lady Mairead told me?"

"I would say yes, definitely, very magical compared to this time. You should think about coming—"

"I couldna leave my bairn, but that is what I am urgin' ye, Kaitlyn. Please take Beaty with ye. I was talkin' tae her tonight, her father beats her verra soundly and she is afeared of him. Her sisters have all left tae be married and she is a great deal lonely and scared of him. She is just married and if Quentin leaves her tae go with Magnus, she will be all alone here in this castle. Her father might think tae come and take her back tae work for him again. I daena think she has the strength tae be waitin' for Quentin for long months and years. And she canna be a widow around these Campbell men, she daena have the wit tae manage herself. I need ye tae take her or I fear somethin' terrible might happen tae her and she is too sweet and silly tae have such a tragic end."

I could see Lizbeth's chin tremble a little while she spoke, something I didn't think I would ever see.

"I didn't consider it before because we thought we shouldn't tell anyone here. We thought you wouldn't understand and — I didn't know about her father. Quentin would want to protect her. I do think you're right. She's just married and Quentin shouldn't leave her behind when we go. Thank you for talking to me about it. I'll talk to Magnus. I'll do my best to persuade him."

"Thank you Kaitlyn. I appreciate it verra much."

"And thank you for confiding in me. Here I thought I was so good at keeping secrets."

She chuckled, "With your outlandish shoes."

"Oh it was my shoes that did it? I figured it was the wacky dress I was wearing that one time."

"Och, twas also that 'wacky' dress, and the word 'wacky'."

There was a soft knock on the door. Lizbeth said, "Aye?"

Quentin's voice, "Madame Lizbeth, it's me, um, Quentin, I mean, Black Mac, and um, Beaty is afraid to be left alone. I didn't know what to do. She said you might let her stay with you in your rooms?"

Lizbeth looked at me with a raised brow and a nod then climbed from the bed. "Och aye, Colonel Peters, Queen Kaitlyn is already here as well. I am a safe harbor tonight." She opened the door and Quentin was standing there with Beaty clinging around his neck.

Lizbeth said, "Now now, dear Beaty, you will needs be lettin' go of your husband. Set your back straight and tell him tae travel safe and God speed."

Beaty pulled her arms from around Quentin's neck and mumbled what Lizbeth told her to say.

Quentin said, "I love you Beaty, I'll be back in just a few days."

She said, "I love ye too."

He said, "Madame Lizbeth, thank you," he whisper-called over her shoulder, "Good night, Katie."

"Good night Quentin, keep him safe, and you stay safe too. Don't be a hero."

"Aye," he said, and rushed away.

It was a tight fit all three of us on the bed, but so much more comfortable and warm and safe-feeling than my own bed, even with Beaty beside me sniffling as she tried to cry herself to sleep. After a few moments Lizbeth laughed, "What are ye cryin' on, dear Beaty?"

"He has left me."

"Of course he has left ye, tis the way of it for a warrior. He has tae protect ye and he canna with your arms around his neck."

"I ken. I just daena want tae be alone."

"Ye arna alone, ye have us and ye have your baby if he has done the deed correctly. Are ye carryin' a bairn now?"

There was a pause then Beaty said, "I daena ken if I — how would I...? Tis just when your middle grows round..."

"Nae, ye can tell. When he was finished beddin' ye did he shudder and groan and collapse on ye like he was havin' a fallin' down fit?"

Beaty said, "Aye, he did a bit. Twas much like that."

I giggled.

"Well then ye may have a bairn a'comin' so ye have that nonsense tae look forward tae."

Beaty was quiet then she asked, "Queen Kaitlyn, if I promise nae tae be a bother would ye take me with you when ye go?" She jumped up to sitting and clasped her hands as if in prayer. "I wouldna be a bother. I would be verra quiet and I would do anythin' ye ask of me."

I said, "It's very far away and it's dangerous and very hard to do..."

"I daena care. I daena care if it takes half my life but I canna stay here without Quentin."

"I will think about it and I will talk to Magnus and Quentin about it."

"Thank ye kindly, Queen Kaitlyn." She lay back on the bed and pulled the covers over her head. Her muffled voice said, "Thank ye, so much."

CHAPTER 56

*M*adame Greer came to visit Lizbeth and me the following morning, all plump, bustling, and carrying a basket of bread and eggs from her kitchen. I was so grateful she brought something to eat because the castle had barely any food prepared for breakfast after the men cleared out the larder to take with them to battle. The kitchen wasn't much interested in feeding the women and bairn. They sent a meal to the Earl in his apartments, the rest of us were to fend for ourselves.

Trouble was I didn't have any idea what that meant — the food looked like something needing a lot of work just to become a basic ingredient. And the recognizable things, like meat, needed a gravy. Pudding would be good with spice. Bread would be good with sweetness. And there wouldn't be a drive-thru for a few hundred years.

I boiled some water, poured it over my coffee, and gave a small cup to Lizbeth and Beaty, but without food this was just one big caffeine buzz.

I hugged and kissed Madame Greer as she spread out her edibles. I gave her a cup of coffee too.

She said, "Well, Madame Kaitlyn, ye have done a fine thing. Your sister is standin' afore us as if she wasna about tae pass through the gates. Have ye considered midwifery might be your callin'?"

Lizbeth said, "Daena start with her, Madame Greer, she is too young and in love tae be spending her life in service tae the whims of all the women of the village. 'Madame Kaitlyn, I have got the pains! Madame Kaitlyn, I have got the winds! Madame Kaitlyn, I need a remedy tae get m'husband off me.'"

I joked, "As we say in the West Indies, 'I do not have the skill set' or let's face it, I don't have the temperament, but I am very happy I was able to help my sister."

"Me too." Lizbeth and I hugged.

Madame Greer said, "You have spent some time in prayer I believe, for ye are healthy and all a'glow. Have ye a bairn a'comin'?"

"No, not yet."

"Continue tae pray, if tis in his wisdom ye will be answered." She took a big bite of bread and asked, "What is this I hear of a weddin' yesterday? Twas Beaty Campbell, the daughter of that barmpot Jimmy, married tae the black man?"

Lizbeth answered, "Yes, Beaty Campbell has married Colonel Peters."

Madame Greer said, "I heard it said the father has beaten her and she may be near ruined. The women in the village can only guess at the dowry Jimmy paid Colonel Peters tae take her. Some are guessin' twas a fair amount."

She said it like a statement though clearly she wanted to know.

Lizbeth said, "Colonel Peters wanted tae marry young Beaty

Campbell verra much. Please tell the village he made a large offer tae her father for her. She is now an Officer's wife."

Madame Greer said, "Good good, I wanted tae ken the truth of it. I will tell the ladies that their story is mistaken."

She sighed and said to me, "Have ye ever heard so many unbelievable tales? If I daena spend m'every wakin' moment listenin' tae them chitter on — I must be searchin' for the truth and then dispellin' the half-truths or the village would be a'stirrin' with witches and harlots and godforsaken men. I spend most of my life talkin' on it."

Lizbeth said, "Well we are so grateful, Madame Greer, that you have shewn us the good favor of tellin' the truth about Kaitlyn."

Madame Greer patted the back of my hand comfortingly.

Lizbeth said, "Did ye hear Kaitlyn is a queen now? Our Magnus Campbell has risen tae the throne of his father's kingdom and so the flyin' machines winna come anymore. He has taken them under control."

"Och, excellent, and our Kaitlyn is a queen? Tis wondrous. I am sure ye are all dignified in your duties. I canna wait tae tell the ladies of it, my sister especially. She has the gout in her leg as ye ken and it has put her in a nasty way. She has been particularly unkind tae me, refusin' tae visit because I canna make her comfortable. I look forward tae tellin' her I made a queen comfortable in my guest room, dinna I?"

I grinned. "Very comfortable. You can tell her if I need to stay in the village I will stay at your house again."

"I will."

"Oh! I have presents, wait here."

I rushed to my room and dug through the bags and rushed back with it. I put the whole bag in front of her and urged her to look through it. "This is lotion, smell." I unscrewed the lid and waved it under her nose.

"'Tis lovely!"

I showed her the candle and the oil and the soap and she was so overcome she started to cry. Wiping her tears on her tartan she said, "'Tis so lovely, I canna—" and she cried some more. There were three pieces of candy and a quilt but I wished I had brought more. She dabbed at her eyes with the edge of the cloth and opened a piece of candy and took one small lick then closed it carefully.

She said she had so much to tell her sister about her visit and I remembered an extra lotion I had brought so I raced up the steps to retrieve it. I gave it to Madame Greer for her sister.

She said, "I kent I was right about ye, Queen Kaitlyn. Twas an honor tae have ye as a guest." She did a slight bow towards me and then kissed Lizbeth on the cheek and took her leave.

Lizbeth said, "Well that did it. There will be no trouble from the village ever again. Madame Greer will be lordin' over them all about her visit with the Queen and they winna ken how tae believe anythin' else.

*M*ovin' the men and the armaments intae place took most of the day. Messengers were sent ahead and we kent Lord Delapointe's army would meet us on the field. Many of the men were irritated and tired from celebratin' the night before and there was a great quantity of grumblin' and anger at unnecessary things. If ye told a man tae move, he was liable tae fight ye for it.

Sean, Liam, Quentin and I had guard duties and then slept when we could. At just before dawn the men began tae stir, tae gather their weapons and their wits, tae prepare the horses, and soon we were all gatherin' tae hear Baldie tell us of the battle plan.

I called across the heads tae him, "Where are the rest of the men the Earl promised?"

"We had about a score join us."

Sean said, "He promised us more than twice that. Tis nae enough."

Men all through the crowd said, "Aye!" and, "Twas promised!"

Baldie said, "The Earl of Breadalbane, in his infinite wisdom, has promised us soldiers and given us instead an assortment of field hands and farmers." He asked the crowd. "How many of ye have a sword?"

Almost all the men raised their weapons. Baldie directed his attention tae one man, without a weapon or a horse. "Ye daena have a sword?"

"Nae, I have a shovel and a dirk."

Baldie met my eyes and shook his head but said, "Tis nae matter, we are Campbells. We will fight and win."

I said tae Sean, "Tis nae enough men, nae enough weapons."

He answered, "Aye, some of these men are here tae die."

At the close of Baldie's speech, I explained it tae Quentin as many of the words he used would be confusin' and Quentin's life depended on understandin'. At the end of my explanation I asked him, "Dost ye ken it, Quentin?"

"Aye boss, it's the same battle plan we used in Afghanistan in 2015, just with horses and swords and wearing a skirt and lining up where they can see ya to shoot ya. I'm the blackest man here. I'm feeling like I have a target pinned to my ass."

"Ye have a better gun than anyone else, ye will be fine." We rode out of the woods tae form a line on the field.

CHAPTER 58 - MAGNUS

*B*aldie sounded the charge and a roar of "CRUACHAN!" went up from our line as we charged across the field in a cloud of dust, horse hooves makin' a thunderous sound. My breathin' quickened. As with all fights I sharpened on what was before me and became more aware of m'surroundings. Twas the way I fought — focused on what was before me, the end of my blade and m'enemy and an urgent need tae make the two meet. Somehow outside of that focus surroundin' sounds and smells heightened. I could feel a man approachin' and could kill him without losin' a step.

I was sword tae sword against a Delapointe soldier, protectin' my injured side while aimin' tae kill him in three swings, when I heard Quentin behind me. His gun fired.

The man I was fightin' clutched his chest and dropped tae the dirt of the field.

"Sorry, Boss, he was yours but I got carried away."

"Aye, he was about tae be mine, but twill be another." I looked over the scene unfoldin', blades and dust and yells. "Get tae Liam, he has three men on him." He galloped through the ragin' battle. I could hear it, without needin' tae see, as a soldier bore down on me.

The full fight lasted for almost two hours until the army, what was left of them, retreated.

When twas done, there was much death upon the field. I surveyed the standin' men for Sean. He was there on the far edge, shovin' a man from his sword with his foot. Then Quentin who waved from across the field. I sighted Liam also standing. Twas then I looked for Baldie.

I turned, lookin' left and right and then met eyes with Sean who was also eyein' the battlefield. Liam, Sean, and I began tae pick through the corpses and half-dead men layin' on the ground.

Finally Liam crouched and called, "I have him!"

Sean and I rushed tae find Baldie layin' mortally injured. *Och nae.*

Sean asked, "Uncle, what say ye?"

Baldie dinna reply. He managed a cough and then took his last sputterin' breath in Sean's arms. We remained there huddled for a long moment.

I said, "Och, why did it have tae be Baldie? We haena got a better man."

"I ken tis true," said Sean. "He was like a father."

"Aye."

Quentin stood above us. "What's with this man's clothes, is he a for-hire soldier or something?"

A man lay on the ground beside Baldie. The way he was positioned, holdin' his sword, twas clear he had been the one tae cause Baldie's death. The soldier wore leather armor, belts with strange markings, clothes that were different from highlander clothes, different from British uniforms I had seen, and different from the French who fought here some.

But though the uniform was different, twas eerily familiar tae me.

"The garb is similar tae the soldiers that fought me on the dock in Florida." I shook the man tae see if he had any life tae him. "Look tae see if other men are here, wearing the same—"

Liam was looking through the bodies on the field for survivors.

Quentin began lookin' for men in the same armor. A moment later he called, "This man — he's still alive."

I rushed tae the man and lifted him by the leather strap across his chest. "Who are ye, where did ye come from?"

The soldier's eyes opened briefly. He looked me in the face. "Who sent ye?"

He croaked a sound.

"What did ye say?"

He coughed and looked close tae death, unable tae speak.

I shoved him tae the ground. "I daena ken. Find their horses, look for more men with the same armor plate." We searched through all the dead and dying men and couldna find anymore but we found their two horses and uncovered coins within their saddlebags. I shewed one tae Sean. "Tis nae English."

Sean said, "Tis French?"

Quentin said, "Nah man, this looks Spanish, like the stuff in the museums on Amelia Island."

I said, "Gather our horses, we must ride with great haste."

CHAPTER 59

"Dost ye want tae take a turn on the grounds, Kaitlyn?"

"I'd love to."

Beaty begged to go with us and so we walked arm in arm around the fields surrounding the castle. It was a beautiful day, a high sky, but though it was spring, it was cold as shit outside.

We walked out, enjoying the grassy slope in front of the castle, and turned north to climb an outcropping of rocks. It was warm on their surface so we paused and enjoyed the sun. Beaty picked flowers and Lizbeth told us about one of the women in the castle who was always so mean. She mimicked her to perfection, "'I am Beileag MacCumasgaigh and I daena want tae tell ye yer business Lizbeth but yer bairn are always yellin' and runnin' through the castle halls and givin' me a fright.' But winna happen anymore — I told m'bairn tae smell the air first, if they have a whiff of a muc, tae run and yell the other way." We laughed and laughed.

We wandered to the river's edge, and I splashed my hand through the water and thought lazily about Magnus, old-style, joking about my 'trout arse', and had there ever in history been someone like me who could love a man at the age of 28 and then go back in time and love him again at 24? Beaty thought we were crazy to be so close to the water, she was terrified of water edges which might cause trouble if I took her to Florida. This would need to be considered very, very carefully.

We traipsed back to the castle by way of the stables, notably quiet because the men had taken every single horse, except two, tied outside in the sun, with all their gear on, and what was weird, noticeable really, was they looked different — different from all the other horses here, but also noticeable, they looked shockingly familiar. Eerily familiar.

I started backing up, "Lizbeth, Beaty, come with me."

"What is it Kaitlyn, you look as if ye've seen a spirit?"

I pulled them away. "We need to get to the castle, fast."

The three of us began to run.

CHAPTER 60

$\mathcal{W}$e made it through the small door within the gate. Lizbeth asked, "What did ye see?"

"The horses, they are dressed like men that have been chasing Magnus, oh crap, and he isn't here."

Lizbeth urgently asked the guards if anyone had entered. They said no. She made them close it all and guard it more and men came from the walls and there was a general uproar as everyone went on high alert.

We raced up the stairs and told everyone to go to the Great Hall. Lizbeth went to warn the Earl and Beaty went to warn the women in the nursery.

I called, "Come to the wall when you're done," and I climbed to the top of the wall to watch for Magnus. There were a few guards along it but not the usual amount. An older man nodded.

I said, "I'm here to wait for Magnus, I want to see when he's coming."

He grunted like that was fine with him.

I asked, "Have you seen anyone, sneaking around or coming in?"

"Nae," he said. I edged past the broken part of the wall and got a view of the stables. There were men near the horses. "Who is that?"

"Our men."

I knew Magnus would be coming from the northeast so I faced that direction, watching for him. It was something to do to keep me from jumping down and running toward wherever he was. Where was he? Some battlefield in the 18th century, fighting people who didn't matter, while General Reyes, or at least a few of his men, was here.

Two of them.

Which meant three of his men were somewhere else.

CHAPTER 61

*L*izbeth and Beaty came to the top of the wall. We all sat leaning against the inside brick. Lizbeth said, "Why do ye think they are here, if Magnus is nae here?"

"Maybe me?"

Beaty looked at me with wide eyes.

I added, "I don't know, but where are they?"

"We might be better hidden in one of the lower rooms, Kaitlyn, ye should come away from the walls."

"It just feels so blind. I need to know what's happening, to be able to see." I crawled across the stone and peeked over the outer parapet. The horses were still there. Right in the open. Anyone could see them. So where were the men?

We sat on the high wall hidden within a shadow. Occasionally I crawled out to peek over the parapet checking for Magnus. But there was nothing to see for the longest time until suddenly there was something — two men, hunched over the necks of their horses, galloping across the fields. One of the men was much darker and so before they were close I could tell it was Quentin and Magnus, racing to get to us.

"They're coming. Oh thank god they're coming."

We all hugged. Then I went back to watching a dust cloud coming off the back of their horse's hooves as they raced. "Let's go down to meet them."

We clambered to the bottom floor and ran out into the court-yard and raced to the gates. Lizbeth said, with a lot more calmness than I was capable of, "Two of our men, Young Magnus and Black Mac, are approaching. Open the gates for them." The gates creaked and groaned as they swung open. Then there was an uproar above us on the walls. A gun fired above us, then another.

The gates crashed closed. The guards locked the door again.

"What's happening?"

Lizbeth listened for a moment, men were rushing along the walls and racing up the stairs and—

"They are fightin', tis Magnus and Quentin fightin' someone just outside." A louder gun fired, from outside, twice. Beaty screamed.

A moment later Magnus and Quentin came through the door within the gates, Quentin with a limp to his step.

Beaty wailed in dismay and rushed to him. "Are ye well Quentin? Oh nae, please daena die."

"I'm fine, I have a cut on my leg, sweet Beaty." He peeled his socks down to see the cut. It was a small gash and would heal well enough.

Magnus came directly to me. "Are ye okay?"

I nodded. "There were two horses and we didn't see the men."

One of the men on the wall announced, "There's a third horse at the back of the castle."

"Kaitlyn, get tae the women in the nursery and lock your-selves in."

The men were signaling to each other and spreading out to search the castle while we rushed to the staircase, to the third floor, and into the nursery. There was a guard outside the door but we were quickly let inside. The rooms were full of women and children, but very quiet, eerily quiet, as everyone sat waiting for the all clear. There were older women in the chairs so we sat against the wall. I raised my knees and tucked my head and tried to be as quiet as I could be.

And we waited and waited and waited.

A baby cried after a while and it unsettled the room. A search for someone possibly inside the walls of the castle, and the baby was inconsolable. Beaty pressed her hands over her ears.

Men fanned out checkin' all the rooms in the castle, twas a great many dark spaces and corners and would be possible for an enemy tae hide for a long time.

I went tae the Earl's Chambers and knocked.

He called me in, sitting at his desk, wearing his most magnificent wig. He said, "Magnus, I was thinkin' ye were away in the battle, have ye just returned?"

There was a man in the room with him. A man dressed in the leather armor we had been seein' often this day — a man we were just now searchin' the castle for.

"Is this man a guest of yours?"

The Earl said, "Why yes, this is Captain Alfaro. He has been offerin' his services as a—"

"We are upendin' the castle searchin' for him as he is a Campbell enemy, and I daena ken what he is about, but I do ken he is a dead man." I drew my sword.

The Earl backed to the wall. Captain Alfaro drew his sword.

I said, "What is your business here?"

"To kill you, Magnus Archibald Caelhin Campbell, or would

you rather, Magnus the First, crowned just recently in the year 2382?"

I charged him and swung, blade meeting blade, we clashed and fought knocking a table over with a crash.

I had him against the bookcase but he shoved me off. I lost my footing and slammed against the desk. The Earl cowered.

The Captain shifted his sword from hand to hand. "Or do you prefer, Magnus Campbell, the year 2018?"

I righted myself and studied him for his weakness.

"Living on Fletcher Avenue with Zach Greene and his lovely wife, Emma, and their son, Ben, right now preparin' the house for your return..."

I roared, charged him, swinging left and right, arcing down. He miscalculated my left swing and overstepped givin' me a chance tae slice his arm. I grabbed his jaw and with the heel of my hand against his throat shoved him against the wall. "Who sent ye?"

"And then there's your wife, Kaitlyn. She hasn't been to see her grandmother for their usual visits — such a shame. She is so lovely. She killed Donnan for you, she's strong, though she is not invincible."

I stabbed him through the stomach, deep, with a twist. Shoved him to the ground and yanked my sword from his body. I turned on the Earl.

"How dare ye invite this man intae this castle?"

The Earl straightened his wig and smoothed his coat. "I wasna aware he was your enemy, Young Magnus. I have been deceived. Twas a mistake."

"You have made many grave mistakes, Uncle. Ye dinna send enough soldiers, we were outnumbered, ye have killed Archibald John Campbell—"

"Baldie is dead?"

"Aye, " I held my sword up and aimed at him. "As well as

many other men, and ye are responsible. You were tae send men, instead ye sent field—"

"I paid from my own coffers for soldiers—"

I interrupted, "Using my gold."

"If they dinna appear tae fight, tis nae my fault. You are bein' unreasonable, Young Magnus."

"I am King Magnus, ye should speak tae me with more deference." I lowered my sword. "You need tae prepare the castle for the dead, they will be arrivin' on the morrow."

"Do we need more guards on the walls?"

"Nae, they are after me and I am leavin' today."

CHAPTER 63

*L*izbeth and I were holding hands leaning against the wall when Magnus rushed in.

"Did you find him?"

"Aye, he is dead. I have news, Lizbeth, tis—"

Her face went ashen. "Liam — Sean?"

He took her hands in his. "Tis Baldie, he was killed in battle."

"Nae, it canna be, Magnus, he was like a father tae us. He canna—"

Magnus put an arm around her and held her for a long moment. "Sean and Liam will be bringing him home, twill take some time."

Lizbeth wiped her eyes. "Did we win the battle?"

"Aye, we won, Lizbeth. I daena think Delapointe will think tae meet us on the field again."

He said to me, "Kaitlyn, we must go now."

Quentin was at the door. Beaty rushed into his arms.

Lizbeth and I hugged.

I said, "I'll be back as soon as I can. I'm so sorry we won't be here for the funeral."

"I understand Kaitlyn. Ye will speak tae Magnus and Quentin?"

"Yes, I'll leave Beaty with you so we can talk."

Magnus and I rushed upstairs to our room with Quentin right behind. Magnus recounted to him all Captain Alfaro said before Magnus killed him. Captain Alfaro, and of course General Reyes, knew everything about our lives. It was terrifying.

We were all panicked and confused about what to do next. Quentin said, "We have to go to Florida, or at least Savannah, we have to warn Zach."

Magnus said, "Aye, we have tae move them tae safety."

I said, "I agree." Magnus and Quentin were both wearing clothes that were filthy and blood-covered. We dug through our packs for anything better to wear, for cleaner clothes, a way to comb hair, to somehow get presentable for America, 2018. We hurriedly packed bags and separated the last of the candy into a bag for Lizbeth to give to the children.

Magnus pulled his shirt up and I checked his wound and put on fresh tape while Quentin stuffed the oxygen concentrator from the last time we were here into a sack.

Quentin seemed quiet and distracted but finally he said, "I want to take Beaty."

Magnus only half-listening asked, "What did ye say, Master Quentin?"

"I want to take Beaty with me."

Magnus said, "I daena think—"

I jumped in. "I agree with Quentin, as does Lizbeth. Magnus, her father beats her and—"

Magnus looked serious. "Dost she have scars? You have paid a great deal of wealth for her—"

"Magnus! She's not property."

Magnus said, "Aye, she is femme covert, he has a legal right tae—"

"What does that mean?"

"She relinquished her legal rights, everything she does goes through her husband. He gets tae decide—"

"What? That is the most awful thing I have ever heard. You're saying she's like his property? Am I property? Holy shit."

"Listen tae me, Kaitlyn, she is his wife and he can decide tae do what he will. Aye, tis much like property, but I daena mean he should treat her as such. I am simply askin' if he wants tae complain on his contract."

"Are you kidding me?" I jammed stuff into a bag. "I am so pissed off at you right now—"

"You are nae listenin' tae me on it, ye are just arguin'."

"He should be fighting for her, protecting her, not bullshit renegotiating his contract."

"Kaitlyn, I have just come home from war. I have almost died three times this day. I daena want tae argue with ye about the contract of marriage as I am the one who negotiated it. I tell ye, ye are mistaken on it. I daena want tae discuss it anymore."

"Aargh!" I crossed my arms and pouted, furious with him for not understanding. He continued packing our things into a bag.

Quentin said, "Um, Magnus, Kaitlyn? We need to get back to the issue…"

"I daena think it wise. Beaty wouldna understand. Twould be dangerous and painful and—"

Quentin said, "I can't protect her if I'm not here and I can't help you if I stay. It's the only solution."

Magnus said, "She's verra young. She would be scared and—"

I said, "She's his property, right? If he wants to take her it's his right, who are we to stop him?"

Magnus said, "If ye will remember I wasna sayin' tae treat her like property. I was sayin' tae use his rights against her father. You are the one sayin' tae treat her like property."

I humphed.

Magnus slung a bag over his shoulder. "Quentin, I think ye should leave her here. Lizbeth will watch over her. She will be protected here in the castle. Twould be for the best."

"I can't leave her. I won't."

Magnus watched him for a beat, then he looked at me, then he nodded. "All right then, bring her, but we must go verra fast."

CHAPTER 64

*a*nd that's how we got out of the gates with Magnus and I rushing and Quentin behind us, leading Beaty, convincing her it would be okay. He told her she would be scared, but he would hold on to her and she wouldn't understand anything she was seeing and other sweetnesses and kindnesses — not enough, because there was no way to truly prepare her.

She was assuring him that as long as she was with him she'd be okay but she had no idea what she was in for.

Also his reassurances were making me a little jealous because here I was — just argued with my blood-splattered husband. And he was, from the blood-splatters, clearly having a shit day. And despite his shit day I argued with him about marriage contracts and whether women were contractually property and while they shouldn't be, I was arguing against centuries of precedence and if I had just listened... Instead I reacted and now we were rushing out the castle gates, running to an unknown future, and pissed off at each other while carrying loads of stuff and really feeling like I needed a rewind button. *Really.*

We came to a field and placed all our bags around our feet. I said, "I'm sorry."

He adjusted a bag that was falling over. "I ken ye are."

I chuckled sadly with a little pout.

"What?"

"You usually say," I put on my 'deep' voice. "'Ye daena need tae be sorry.'"

He grinned a half-grin. "This time ye do, mo reul-iuil."

"God, you are..." I sighed.

He pulled the vessel from his bag. "Have I ever once treated ye like property, Kaitlyn Campbell?"

"No."

"Have I ever once made a decision for us without takin' your opinion on it?"

I shook my head.

"And I think more than once I have let ye make all the decisions in respects tae me, tis nae fair tae argue with me on this point."

I nodded. "I know. I'm really sorry. I don't know why I did it." I exhaled. "This is all just so hard. I got carried away. I'm really really really sorry."

He said, "Ye daena have tae be sorry." And then he grinned and I knew we were going to be okay.

I tucked my head against his shoulder and felt his strong arm around my back. Quentin had his arms around Beaty and held his arm against Magnus's. Magnus twisted the ends of the vessel. It hummed to life.

A moment later the force of the time-jump hit me in my gut and it felt like I was torn into microscopic pieces.

CHAPTER 65

The storm was dissipating when I woke. Magnus's hand on my hip, he crouched over me. I tried to force myself up but there was a lot of wailing going on. Then I realized it was Beaty. I pulled myself to sitting and clutched her hands. "Beaty, shhhhhhh, shhhhhhh, it's okay, you're here. Quentin is right here."

Magnus and Quentin were both facing different directions.

I said to her, "As soon as you can move, we need to move," and then I waited for her to be able to hear me.

She was crying with her eyes clamped shut. "It hurts Queen Kaitlyn."

"I know it does. And it's really bright. Your eyes will hurt and you'll want to keep them closed because everything you see is going to be scary as shit. But I promise it will be okay. Okay?"

I asked Quentin, "Is your phone working, can you call Zach?"

He pulled his phone from his sporran. "I still have juice!" He held Beaty's hand as he called Chef Zach. Magnus and I whispered instructions: Tell him to bring Emma and Ben. Tell him to bring all of his important papers. Tell Emma to call Grandma Barb's home and make sure she's okay. Tell them to add security. Bring his laptop. Pack a bag.

Quentin told him to be careful, watchful, cautious, and to come, now.

He told us not to worry he was on his way. With Emma. With Ben.

We would all meet in this hotel and decide what to do next.

Beaty was sitting with her head buried in her knees.

I asked, "Can you try to stand?"

The day was bright blue, clear and cool, wispy clouds wandering across the sky. The garden we landed in was fragrant and pretty even though it was December. We were behind a grouping of bushes and I didn't really know if we happened to land there or if Magnus had dragged us behind them.

I stood in front of Beaty and held out my hands. "One two three." I hefted her up though she was so petite it wasn't hard.

"First, you're going to see cars, right off the bat, don't freak out. It's going to be weird, but try not to let people know you think it's weird.

She said, "All right, Queen Kaitlyn." But then we turned a corner, she saw a car and shrieked like the world was coming to an end.

Magnus stepped in front of her.

Quentin put an arm around her.

I held her hand. "Shhhhhh shhhhhhhhh, it's okay. That's just the car I was telling you about. That's all it is, lots of them, see. But it's fine."

We got her crying down to a sniffle and then we walked the highway in our bizarro Ren-faire clothes. Luckily by carrying bags in certain ways there were no visible bloodstains, but we were certainly odd looking. Cars slowed and people gawked. They probably wondered if we were some weird religious cult, but hopefully they thought we were re-enactors of some kind. Like I thought back when I first laid eyes on Magnus.

Beaty had to watch our feet while we walked because if she looked anywhere else she spiraled out of control. We needed to get to a hotel; we still weren't sure we weren't being followed.

We passed the Cracker Barrel and crossed the parking lot to the Inn and Suites. So far Beaty was freaked by the parking lots, the inn, the noise, the lights, the cars, and a pigeon. Quentin went inside, with the credit card he thankfully had in his sporran, to book us all three rooms; there was one for Zach and Emma and Ben, too.

This all worked perfectly. We weren't followed. Beaty survived. Zach was still alive.

Magnus and I would buy dinner. Beaty would love a big meal. Wait until she tried American-restaurant-at-a-highway-exit style food. There was even a McDonald's.

Also, and this was cool, we passed a Walmart. I would get everyone into the room and maybe walk back to buy us all some clothes and toothbrushes.

Quentin passed me my keycard and we went up a stairwell to our rooms. Beaty kept her head turned to his chest and he carried her in.

Magnus and I went into our room to rest. We were exhausted. All my plans for walking to get clothes ended up not happening. Instead we would wait for Zach in bed.

*S*he opened our door with somethin' called a keycard and we stepped inside. The room was verra luxurious compared tae the tavern room I had secured for us near Balloch. I asked, "Why are there two beds?"

"I don't really know. It's called a double. I guess if you don't want to share..."

I pulled open drawers on a dresser. "Tis empty." I opened a wide closet.

"We can unpack our suitcase and put our things there, except we don't have a suitcase. We do have this bag with an oxygen concentrator inside, a weird assortment of battery packs and other equipment from the drones and vehicles, and two-way radios."

I opened a wee door tae see a wee refrigerator, also empty. Kaitlyn tore plastic off of two glasses and filled them with water. We both drank.

She sprawled back on one of the beds. "I'm hungry and want clean clothes but I also just want you in my arms."

"Och, tis a request I canna disagree with." I crawled ontae the bed and lay beside her. My head on her curved arm, my arm across her breasts. I could feel the rise and fall of her chest with her breaths. She twirled my hair.

She said, her voice tremulous, "I'm so sorry we fought."

"I am too, mo reul-iuil."

Her lips brushed along my brow. "I'm so sorry about your Uncle Baldie."

Baldie's face came tae my memory. He was leadin' us from Balloch tae Kilchurn, followin' the trail, tellin' the men in the group about the improvements he had made on the castle, excited tae shew us. I had been eight, and was ridin' on my own, but I was listenin' tae him speak about the walls and the furniture and I kent he was the kind of man I would aspire tae be, generous. The men admired him. He liked tae share and wanted tae be surrounded by a big family.

I said, "As ye ken, it never mattered that we dinna share blood, he was always there for me ever since I was a wee bairn, a better father than the one God gave tae me. I will miss him verra much."

"He was a good man. I liked him a lot. If you ever need to talk about him just do."

I nodded findin' it difficult tae speak on him anymore.

She asked, "The things the man at Balloch said really scared you?"

"Aye. He kens a great deal about all of us, we arna safe."

"But what if we do everything differently? New house. No social media. Different stores. We could jump to different places and then travel over roads like normal people. Like we're doing here — coming to Savannah instead of Florida. New habits, new routines. Maybe we'll be safe then?"

I considered it, but I dinna think twould change the course of it. General Reyes kent too much of us. Tae me the battle had just started, but tae him twas almost won. "Maybe. I daena ken."

Her wool bodice was warm under my arm. Her chest rose with a deep breath, an exhale against my skin. I pulled her closer and held her tight. I dinna ken how many more times like this we would have.

She wrapped a leg around my waist. I shoved aside her skirts tae uncover her.

She laughed at my struggle. "Are my 18th century skirts in your way?"

I joked, "Aye, my century is often an impediment tae my happiness."

"I'm your happiness?"

I chuckled. "You ken it, I daena need tae say it again."

She sighed. "Speaking of happiness, I wanted to be home in time to show you Christmas."

I pulled her thigh higher on my waist and kissed the rise of her breast.

She asked, "If I had managed it, and we had been home for the holiday, what would you have given me as a gift?"

I nestled m'ear tae her breasts. I was beginnin' tae think I would like tae bed her now, but she seemed tae want tae converse instead. I felt along the skin of her thigh and around the curves of her buttocks.

She pressed her lips to my forehead. She was waitin' for an answer and I had nothin' I wanted tae give her more than everything she wanted. I had been thinkin' on it as we gained Beaty in our group and worried over Archie and Zach's family. I felt a great deal of regret that I hadna given her a bairn. I was protectin' everyone else tae have their own families, but nae protectin' Kaitlyn, not enough, though I had promised.

I said, "I have somethin' tae talk tae ye of, but I daena want ye tae feel sad."

She breathed in deep and froze. "Oh?"

I reached for her hand tae hold it still and raised tae look intae her eyes. They were full of fear and worry. "I have verra many people tae protect."

She nodded. "It's true, some might say you have too many."

"Och aye, too many, but I will do it gladly, Kaitlyn. I mean tae keep everyone safe and protected, but tis only you I..."

Her eyes glistened. "So are you saying I'm your focus? That doesn't make me sad..."

I clasped her hand tighter. "But all the others... Tis like worryin' on them... they are distractin' me from what is important. You and our..."

I didn't know how tae say it without upsettin' her.

"Our what?"

I tucked my head tae her chest. "Lizbeth has been speakin' tae me on it. She told me ye have a sadness inside of ye and ye canna talk of it, ye winna try, but ye want a bairn, Kaitlyn."

Her voice caught. "I do, but it's not the right time. It's..."

"I daena ken if we will ever have a better time, mo reul-iuil. How can I continue to protect all these people when they are havin' their own families?"

Her chin was tremblin'. "They're our family. Archie is your family. Ben is like a nephew."

"Aye, tis true, and I dinna want tae cause ye distress or sadness... ye are cryin' and—"

She sniffled. "It's okay, I'm a big girl."

I kissed her cleavage just above her bodice. "I daena want tae sound like I daena love our big family. I will always protect them with everythin' I have. And I ken ye will protect them, and love them, but you deserve tae have the bairn ye have been wantin'. So I will protect ye, Kaitlyn. And I will protect our bairn. I can. I daena want tae keep waiting for a better time, tis time now."

I rubbed the tears off her cheek. "Tis what I would give you." Her eyes were so full of sadness. "Would ye like a bairn, Kaitlyn?"

"Yes." Her leg wrapped tighter around my waist. "I really would."

"Good."

She rolled out from under me, and crawled across the floor tae her backpack. She dug and retrieved her wee pills. "I didn't take today's yet." She climbed back tae the bed and wrapped around me.

"I am only a few days from my period and I've been taking it consistently — let's see..." She counted on her fingers. "It would probably be ten days before I would be ready."

"For what?"

"To make a baby."

"Och, I am Scottish highlander, we make a baby whenever we want tae and many times when we daena want tae."

She laughed, a vibration in my arms. "While that may feel true, the science of it is I'll really be ready in ten days and then we can have sex fifteen times that day to make sure it happens."

I chuckled against her cheek. "I like the sound of that."

"Me too and that's basically New Year's Eve. So it's a date. We'll ring in the new year by making a baby."

"What year?"

She was thoughtful for a moment. "2019?"

"And 1704 and 2383"

Then she said, "But with a baby we will have to decide where and when and what time. There's so much to consider."

"Nae." I grabbed her pills and hid them behind my back with a laugh. "We daena have tae consider. I am givin' it tae ye as a Christmas present, ye canna ruin the romance of it."

She laughed with a wee spark of joy in her voice. "I would never want to be accused of ruining the romance."

Then her lips met mine for a long lingerin' kiss. Her tongue explored my mouth, her teeth nibbled my lips. Her breathin' quickened and her hold around my back tightened.

I ran my hand up the inside of her thigh. "Your garden has overgrown, mo reul-iuil."

"We've been in another century, I am not carrying razors to a century where they barely bathe."

I chuckled. "I daena mind, as ye ken, I think tis sexy." I rubbed my hands along the length of her leg from her ankle tae her hip and around the back of her perfect arse and pulled it tight tae my kilted front.

"Oh really? I thought you liked my smooth legs."

"Och, aye, your smooth legs are sexy too, daena make me choose."

She chuckled, her breath a warmth beside my ear.

My hands graspin' the soft flesh of her arse, I could feel her drawing closer. Her body burrowin' toward mine.

Her breaths were quick and gasping as she pulled in air against the tightness of her clothes. I nibbled on the top edge of her breast and she drew closer still, archin' toward me, twas as if she was sayin' it under her breath, *more more more*. She asked with a gasp, "We were just going to rest — isn't there danger and...?"

I rolled her to her back, rumpled her skirt up around her waist and explored with my fingers. "Aye, we were goin' tae rest, and there is danger, mo ghradh, but ye said ye haena stationed a guard on your walls today. So I was thinkin' twould be a good time tae capture your castle."

She smiled. "I don't think a day is enough... I don't know if..." She writhed with my fingers, nudgin' toward my hand, beginnin' tae forget herself, becomin' a moan and a want.

She grasped at my kilt, bunchin' the fabric up and held the length of me, tight, drawin' me close — *I want you.*

I ken ye do, mo reul-iuil, from the sùgh am gròiseid.

God I love it when you speak — what does that...?

In answer I licked her, bringin' her tae moans.

Then I spread her legs wide and climbed on. She gasped as I entered her and as I pushed my way inside she was at once acceptin' but also quiverin' vulnerable, as she becomes, open and wantin' and out of her head, trustin' me, and needing me, all her strength gone away.

I held my mouth on her shoulder and went slow for her, waited for her tae warm tae me. We lingered there, our heat risin', teasin' with our lips, runnin' my hands over her curves and softnesses.

Then she pulled a pillow down and pushed it under her arse, raisin' her hips for me, wrappin' her legs around my back. Twas time tae take her. Her voice a low hoarse whisper, the prayer she repeated as I rode her tae the end. I collapsed on her body, she was soft skin and gentleness but had the strength tae bear me.

She held me, cool linen and dry wool, her legs wet sticky warmth. She exhaled, her breath a sweetness beside my ear.

"Do you think we just made a baby?"

I joked, "I daena ken but I tried."

"We might still need to try fifteen times on New Year's Eve though."

I said, "Aye," though I wasna convinced we would have that many days. While still inside of her though I wanted tae promise it, tae take care of her always, every day.

I thought tae say, "If somethin' happens tae me, if we are separated, mo reul-iuil, I want ye tae ken how much—"

Her body stilled. "What do you mean if we're separated?"

"I daena ken, but in case we are—"

"Well, we aren't going to be."

"But if we are, I need ye tae be strong, tae nae go weak. Tae protect our family and stay alive. Tis the only way I will be able tae fight him."

Her hands tightened on my back. "I thought we were going to keep you from having to fight."

I looked intae her eyes. "I will have tae fight him Kaitlyn, ye ken tis true. Please stay strong."

"Okay, if we're separated, if you're fighting, I will be strong."

"And ken that I love ye."

She nodded. "I know it."

"Where do ye ken it?" I asked with a smile, recalling our first night taegether.

She rubbed her fingers on her lips. "Here because I can taste you." She tapped her ear. "I know it here because you tell it to me." She raised her arms above her head, stretching long under me. "And everywhere because I am filled with you, you're entangled in my fibers."

I placed my hand on her chest. "Inside your heart?"

"I know it there. And here." She reached between us to pat between her thighs. "I am a verra happy wife." She asked, "Where do you know I love you?"

"On the air around me, mo reul-iuil. On every breeze is your sigh, under every sky. Tis always the same stars, ye ken. As long as ye are under them then I can hear ye, *I love ye,* ye say. I can always hear it."

"Good." She added, "I do know it, Magnus, that you love me. You love me so much. I won't ever not know it as long as I'm alive."

"And ye will stay alive?"

She nodded. "Yes."

"Thank ye." I spread her fingers and kissed her palm. Then held my lips there against the strength of her hand.

I rolled off and we both lay on our backs staring up at the ceiling.

I asked, "Now I have given ye a Christmas gift, what are ye goin' tae give me for Christmas?"

"Hmmmm. I already established you have a day with fifteen

different sex acts in your future, I mean, that's pretty good, right?"

I joked, "Och, tis a usual Thursday with ye, mo reul-iuil. I think it has tae be special."

"More special than a baby? More special than fifteen sexual encounters in one day? Man, you're tough, highlander."

She was thoughtful then said, "I will learn to ride a horse and then we can ride together, side by side."

I looked up at the perfect white ceiling, in this perfect hotel for restin', in the perfectly safe state of Georgia, in the perfect time of 2018, wantin' tae believe that I would be ridin' alongside her soon. "Aye, tis perfect."

"Really?"

I took her hand. "Really, Kaitlyn, I will buy ye a horse named Osna and ye will ride her. Tis a perfect gift for me."

"God, I love you. And we can buy you a horse like you had in Scotland when I found you."

"What kind of horse?"

"A war horse. It was black and big and so beautiful."

"Och, a each-cogaidh, I like that kind of horse."

"You named him Shark."

I laughed. "Tis a good name for a strong stallion."

"So we'll get you one," she said.

My stomach growled.

She said, "But your first Christmas present, I'll buy you some McDonald's."

CHAPTER 67

We knocked quietly on Quentin's door.

"How's Beaty?"

"She's doing okay, but we're famished."

"Us too, if we can use your card we'll go get McDonald's."

He loaned us his card and gave us his order and then Magnus and I walked across the parking lot. We ordered so much freaking food it was shocking and everyone in the store stared at us. We were still in our Scottish clothes and looking a little homeless because of the dirt and smell and filth and lack of complete cleanliness.

We were laden with drink holders and bags of food crossing the parking lot when I said, "What if I never bought you McDonald's that first day?"

"Aye, I mayna have fallen in love with ye without the full stomach."

I laughed. "You could have gotten a ride to that hotel with

someone else, like James, and he would have dropped you off at the hotel. Our whole lives would be different."

"I think ye may have been better off, there has been a lot of heartbreak since ye met me."

"I wouldn't trade one second of it, Magnus. Not one. I can't separate out the heartbreak from the happiness, and I wouldn't want to. Like Barb would say, we're tangled up you and I. And it's so true. From the first moment to this moment, everything is so beautiful, the highs and the lows."

"Och. I love ye, Kaitlyn."

"Like we said in the room, I ken ye do, I am a wonderful woman." I grinned, then lifted the drink holder and took a sip from the closest straw in a Coke that was as big as my head. "But seriously, what if we had never met? If you think about it, the strange series of events that brought us together — I mean everyone who meets the love of their life is a marvel, but us — we met each other across centuries and I'm grateful every day the stars and time and vessels brought us to..." I stopped dead in my tracks.

Magnus asked, "What happened, mo reul-iuil?"

My eyes wide, I said, "The vessels brought us together and so... do you see? The book, the book I'm reading..."

"You arna makin' sense."

"Magnus, I haven't been able to figure out the point of the book — it's about the origin of the vessels, but it's really about the battle and there isn't much information in it that seems important. Why was Lady Mairead frantic about it? One of the main reasons it seems unimportant is because it doesn't even have the same date as the historical record, like how important is it if it's wrong? But it just dawned on me, it's *right*. The date in the book is the right date. And the reason why the historical record is different is that it's the most dangerous date in history." The whole time I spoke I stared at the horizon, figuring it out a second before I said it.

Now I turned to Magnus and said, "All it would take is one person with one of those vessels to go back to that battlefield and take it all. Then that person would have all this power. They wouldn't even need evil intent, someone could just want to rule the future world better than Donnan did and boom, they could — but if they were evil..."

Magnus said, "One man with a gun could take all those vessels and there would be nae stoppin' him."

I nodded solemnly. "And Magnus, if someone, whether they had evil intent or not, went back to that date on the battlefield and took all the vessels?"

Magnus nodded, "I ken it, Kaitlyn."

"We would never meet. This whole everything would just..."

"Och," he said. "Nae. We canna let it happen. What is the date in the book?"

I blinked and considered it for a moment. "You don't remember it?"

"Nae, I daena ken if ye ever told me."

"Yeah, maybe not. Um... Maybe I shouldn't."

Magnus's eyes squinted, "Why nae?"

"Maybe the less people that know, the better."

He looked at me, his brow drawn down, "I am nae just people, I am Magnus, and my life may depend on the information."

"But maybe knowing it makes you unsafe — I know it and I feel kind of freaked out about knowing it."

"Aye, ye ken it and ye have tae tell me everythin'." He put on his falsetto voice, "'If we daena tell each other everythin', Magnus, our whole marriage is terrible.' Tell me, I am a big boy, I can take it."

I huffed. "Man, you're using all my words against me. Fine,

the date is November 1, 1557, and now we should destroy the book." We started walking toward our hotel room. Then I stopped in my tracks again. "We can't destroy the book. If we destroy it today, it doesn't help. Someone just needs to go back and get to it before I found it. Shit, my heart is racing. Who knows the date, anyone beyond Donnan?"

"I think if Lady Mairead kent it she would have gone already."

"Probably."

"If General Reyes kent it we wouldna be havin' this discussion."

"We have to guard the book while we figure out what to do. And we need all the vessels under our control or we're never safe."

"Where is the book now?"

"The hotel room."

We walked a hell of a lot faster.

In the hotel room I dug through my pack for the book. Once I found it, Magnus packed it beside the two vessels in his sporran.

He strapped his sword to his back and a dirk at his waist.

Then we hugged for a long time.

From in his arms, my hands on his strong back, my voice muffled against his chest, I said, "You know, this is frightening, but as Grandma Barb told me once, it's always been there — this danger. That we know about it shouldn't make us more scared. We're human, we have brains, we can think our way through anything." I pulled away and smoothed the hair back from my face. "She of course wasn't talking about evil men and time travel, she was talking me through a fear I had when I was young that the people I loved were going to die, but still..." I smiled. "It applies. We'll figure out what to do about the book."

"We could go tae the time when Johnne Cambell wrote it and destroy it then."

"Yeah. That's within our skillset."

"You can make a list of all the vessels and I can secure them."

"List-making, also within our skillset." We smiled. I added, "See, I just realized this ten minutes ago and already we have many great ideas. "We will kill General Reyes for screwing with our family."

"Tis within my skillset."

"Mine too."

"Aye, mo ghradh, ye art a terrible arse."

"So true." I hefted the bags of food and the drink holder full of sodas. "And I'm about to be stuffed full of fast-food too."

$\mathcal{W}$e knocked on Quentin's door again.

"You want to go and sit by the pool and eat? They have tables and it's a beautiful evening."

Beaty said yes, so we all went to the pool area. She kept her face hidden trying not to look at anything as we went.

"How are you?" I asked.

She said, "I am a'feelin' it, tis too bright and I am fearful hungry."

When we got to the pool area, it was already growing dark. We spread the food out on the table and then Magnus and I watched while Quentin sweetly showed Beaty how to eat everything and she sweetly kept her eyes closed but opened them when he teased her. She ate watching him for guidance.

I however had a quarter pounder in one fist, French fries in the other, and the straw positioned right in front of my mouth. Everyone laughed as I set my meal up perfectly and plowed into it.

Then through the lobby, I saw Zach, Emma, and Ben enter the hotel.

I waved them into the pool area and we all hugged.

"And this is Quentin's wife, Beaty Peters."

Zach, still standing, said to Quentin, "What the fuck is happening? How long were you gone?"

Quentin said, "About three days."

Zach repeated, "What the fuck?" then recovered himself and shook Beaty's hand while she was still clutching her face into Quentin's shirt. "I'm very happy to meet you Beaty, this is my wife Emma and little Ben."

She glanced quickly at them then pressed her face back to Quentin's chest. "Tis verra nice tae meet ye as well."

I said, "As you can imagine, it's pretty overwhelming. She had no idea what was happening until she was literally time-jumping, so she could use some calm voices and maybe not so many 'what the Fs' at the top of your voice."

"Point taken." Zach sat down.

"And now you're all chill and not freaking out at all, Magnus has bad news."

Zach turned to Magnus, Emma turned to Magnus. Ben was sitting in Magnus's lap beating the table with his wooden car.

Magnus said, "There is a man named General Reyes who is tryin' tae kill me for unknown reasons, though I would guess tis because he wants m'crown. I ken I have been fightin' him for many long years, but in this time it has only been a few months."

"He's the reason you can't jump into Florida," said Zach.

"Aye, Kaitlyn and I have been tryin' tae get ahead of him, but he is cunnin' and verra dangerous. Tis as if he has more information about us than we have of him, but I found out this mornin' he kens much more than I thought."

Zach said, "What does he know?"

"He kens your name. He kens ye have a family and ye reside on Fletcher Avenue."

Zach kicked his chair out, stood, and said, "Fuck." He

glanced at me, "Sorry Katie, but this deserves it. He's threatening me? My family?"

"Aye, he's threatenin' me, and because I consider ye a brother he is usin' your name tae scare me, but aye, he is threatenin' ye."

Zach said, "I'm so tired of this bullshit. What are you going to do about it? I'm a fucking chef. I know a little sword-fighting but I can't fight an army from Scotland, I don't know how."

"They are from Spain..."

"I don't give a shit where they're from, what are you going to do to protect us? And Quentin, he's our security guard — is he going to live here now, protect us 24-7? Can he? I mean probably, right? But you keep taking him with you. And now he's married?" He turned to Emma and shook his head.

Ben said, "Da-Da!" and waved his wooden car at Zach.

Zach turned back to Magnus. "You're bringing a shitstorm down on me and Emma and Ben and we've got nobody to take our safety seriously."

Magnus said, "I take your safety verra seriously, Chef Zach, you are my brother. I daena want tae put your family in danger."

"Yeah, but it follows you." He huffed and we all went quiet for a moment. "I'm sorry I got pissed, Magnus. This is just a lot to take in. I've never known you to do anything but try to keep us safe."

"Thank ye for sayin' so, Chef Zach, but I am feelin' my failings verra much."

"So what do we have to do?"

Ben pushed the car across the table with a vroom noise then slung the car off to the ground and laughed.

Magnus picked up the car and gave it back then said to Zach, "You will have tae move tae a safer location."

"It's just a few days before Christmas."

I said, "I'm really sorry Zach."

"Fuck." He reached out for Emma's hand across the table. "Anywhere?"

I said, "Yes, just not Florida."

"Fine, where do you want to go babe?"

"I've always wanted to go to Austin. My aunt is there we could stay with her while we get a place."

"Okay then."

"You will have tae go from here. I will send Quentin with ye. You were nae wrong on that, Chef Zach. Twas nae fair tae take the security guard from ye. I will increase your pay so ye are comfortable, but ye will need tae be cautious while I fight this battle against Reyes."

Zach nodded. "I get you."

"I ask ye take care of Beaty, she will probably need some extra attention."

We all looked over at Beaty, glommed onto Quentin's front, her face in a wad of his shirt.

"Did ye have enough tae eat Beaty?"

"Aye, King Magnus."

His brow lifted and he smiled at me. "Chef Zach will make ye some delicious food like this every day. Twill be verra good for ye and ye winna be scared soon. Except in cars they will afear ye greatly for a long time, but twill be okay, they winna hurt ye."

She mumbled, "Aye, King Magnus, thank ye."

Zach said, "We'll get Hayley to send someone to the houses for the computers and I mean, we probably should move the safe again. We'll have to get all the important things shipped to us."

"Speaking of, did you get the parchment appraised?"

"Not yet, but I looked at it under a light and it's totally got a drawing there. If it's a Da Vinci that would be fucking crazy. Do you think she steals it or just asks the artists for it—"

Hayley's voice from the door of the hotel lobby. "Hey girl!!!"

"Hayley?"

She was coming out to the pool area with a man who had to be her new guy. He was very handsome and they were holding hands and both smiling. I jumped from my seat. "I'm so sorry I didn't call you. I was having a meeting with Zach and Quentin and here you are!" I hugged her and said to the man she was with, "I'm Kaitlyn."

"I'm Nick." He had dark hair cut short with a swoop on top and a jawline that was square and excellent. He looked to be maybe twenty-nine, like not too old, but old enough to look like he was in charge of something.

His clothes were very nice, a dark jacket, a pale blue shirt, and dress slacks. Hayley looked beautiful wearing a little dress and tights with tall boots. She glowed.

Best part? He had nice eyes and was smiling. And Hayley looked ecstatic. "Zach said he was coming to see you and I was getting ready to go away with Nick but I really wanted to come see you and so he asked, 'Baby, what's got you down?' And I said, 'My bestie is only an hour and a half away, ' and so here we are because he'll do anything for me." She rubbed her nose against his and then they kissed.

"Awwww, that's so great. I'm so happy for you. Where are you guys going?"

"Atlanta, for Christmas."

"So fun!" I squeezed her shoulders. "I'm so glad you came. I need to introduce you to Quentin's wife."

Hayley shook her head. "Uh uh, no way!"

Quentin said, "Yes way, this is Beaty Peters, my wife."

"Whoa, I was not expecting that." She hugged Beaty and Quentin at the same time. "Welcome to the family, Beaty. Quentin and I have been friends since... when did we start being friends? Like first grade?"

Quentin said, "Yep."

She said to me, "Wow. Katie were you at the wedding?"

I nodded.

"Man I can't believe you got married without me being there, but fine, we just have to have a party now, here, on this pool deck." She looked around. "I see you have McDonald's, did you plan this as a wedding reception, Kaitlyn?"

Chairs were shifted and Nick sat beside Magnus. Hayley sat on his other side, their hands clasped on his knee.

Magnus was jiggling Ben on his knee, but he wasn't focused on him, he was instead fumbling with something in his sporran.

And I probably should have noticed then.

But it took a moment of slow motion for it all to register.

Quentin asked, "What's up boss?" He took his eyes from Magnus, who wasn't answering, and swept his eyes around the fence of the pool.

My eyes followed his. There was a dark sky, a glowing pool, visibility was not good, but across the dark pool area, just outside the darker fence, stood a man. His back was to us. He was wearing those old-fashioned clothes, the ones I was used to seeing on General Reyes's men. A few feet beside him stood another man, and another. My gaze went around the perimeter, men stood about every three feet surrounding the fence.

My heart raced.

I looked back at Quentin, our eyes met.

I looked at Magnus.

His eyes said it all.

"Take Ben." He thrust Ben toward me and one of our vessels and the small book dropped into my lap. I covered them with my skirts as Emma stood to take Ben.

She returned to her seat completely unaware of all the men, the tension, the danger surrounding us.

Quentin glanced at Magnus, a look passed between them.

Quentin said, "So Nick, I know we've hung out before but I think I forgot to get your last name?"

Nick's facial expression was a broad charming smile as he said, "My full name is Nicholas Reyes."

And my whole world went fucking kaboom into teeny tiny pieces.

Magnus's hands were clasped, staring down at them, focused, bound within his body, tensed and furious. His arm about an inch from Nick's arm.

He could kill him, but he couldn't because we were all here, pressed close, people he loved.

The finger on his right hand twitched, gestured, *Away*.

Quentin pushed his chair back with loud scrape and stood.

Nick, no longer holding Hayley's hand, said, "Why don't you sit back down, Quentin Peters? You'll need to be here for this."

Beaty, having eaten more than she ever ate in her life, plus a Coke, plus some tastes of Quentin's milkshake, said, "Och!" And leaned over her knees clutching her stomach.

I said, "Zach, Emma, up." We stood, shoving our incredibly noisy chairs back. Emma dropped Ben into the sling perched on her hip.

Hayley asked, "What's going on?"

Nick said, "Baby, this is nothing to worry about, Magnus and I go way back, and he and I need to discuss some things."

His jacket fell open and exposed a gun in his lap, pointed at Magnus. "Isn't that right Magnus? We can discuss it here with your family around you for support? That's what Hayley tells me, you're all one big family."

Magnus's voice was low and steady. "Nae, let them go, I will stay. I winna fight."

I edged in front of Zach and Emma and we all took a step back. I had the vessel and the book pressed to my leg hidden in a fold of my skirt.

"Oh you won't fight because if you do we'll kill them all one by one while you watch and then we'll kill you last."

Nick shoved his chair back with a clatter so it fell to the ground. He yanked Magnus out of his seat and shoved him to his knees. He pressed his gun to Magnus's temple.

Peripherally the men were all facing us now, half-hidden in shadows. I couldn't tell if they were armed, but I had a guess.

Nick said to Magnus, "Take off your sword, throw it down."

I watched as my husband quietly disarmed himself and tossed his sword with a clank to the ground.

"Your dirk, too."

Magnus pulled the dirk from its sheath and placed it beside the sword.

Emma burst into tears.

Beaty vomited all over the ground. Quentin lifted her, still vomiting, and carried her to us.

Magnus looked up and met my eyes.

Go?

Aye.

I nodded in agreement, every part of me shaking.

Hayley had been frozen looking from face to face. She grabbed Nick's arm. "I don't understand. What's happening?"

"Aw baby, don't be upset, this is just a misunderstanding."

"You're scaring me." She tried to pull his arm back.

He spun his gun in his fist so it was handle out, and back-swung, smacking her face with the heavy pistol. Hayley screamed and fell over the arm of the chair clutching her forehead.

Quentin tried to get his gun from his underarm holster in time but in a flash Nick had his gun back, aimed at Magnus.

"Quentin Peters, I wouldn't do that. Because first, I will shoot Mags." He asked Hayley. "Isn't that what you call him, baby?"

She whimpered from the ground, "No, please don't."

"Then I'll start shooting into your group. Who wants to die first? Or keep your hands where I can see them, toss your gun down, and kick it away."

Hayley was writhing on the ground holding her eye, blood covering her hands.

Quentin un-holstered his pistol very slowly, placed it on the ground, and kicked it across the tiles.

Beaty moaned and stomach-heaved behind me.

I pleaded, "Hayley, come here. Please come to me."

Hayley pulled herself slowly across the ground toward me.

"Come on Hayley, hurry."

Quentin put his hands up and slowly walked toward Hayley. "I'm not armed, I'm not doin' nothing but getting Hayley, see? I'm just getting Hayley."

Quentin picked Hayley up under her arms and dragged her to our group. She was crying and bleeding and—

Nick gripped Magnus's hair yanking his head back. "Now see, I thought you would put up more of a fight than this, Mags the First. When I fought you in 2397, I never could get the upper hand, but you were alone then. Here you're surrounded by people. I think they make you weak."

Magnus growled, "I said I winna fight, just let them go."

"Sure, I'm a gentleman and you're as good as beat. Plus, I know where they're going. When I want them I just have to go get them. Or better yet when I show up as the new king they can submit to me. Your wife *is* awfully pretty."

I had to get us out of here. I twisted the ends of the vessel. The storm rose above us.

Nick and Magnus were buffeted by it.

I yelled over the wind to everyone. "Hold on to me. Okay? Just hold on."

Nick said, "They're leaving you, Mags, deserting you, how's that feel?"

I started saying the numbers, like a prayer, the order memorized, begging the universe to get me and all these people out of here.

My eyes met Magnus's eyes. The wind whipped my hair, the thunder boomed, lightning and storm clouds above us. My chosen family clutching my shirt sleeves, my skirts.

But not Magnus.

I love you.
    I love ye too. Run.

I finished the numbers as Nick yelled, "How can they leave you? You should be furious, Mags. What the hell, I'll just shoot one of them for leaving you in your time of need. That will be fun."

He fired his gun toward us as the wind, the lightning, the thunder all built into a blast and the storm hit me with the full pain of a time-jump.

CHAPTER 69

I pulled myself from my agony, checked myself for a gunshot wound, then forced myself up. I was under the open night sky, on the landing pad at our castle, a helicopter right there, its rotor spinning, a gusting wind, and terrible noise. The security light on the wall over us was way too bright. I listened — far off explosions, the ground vibrated. I scanned around. A soldier was applying pressure to Hayley's forehead, looking into her eyes, asking her questions.

Zach was moaning beside Emma who was still completely unconscious. A child was crying, a loud plaintive wailing. My eyes were drawn across the rooftop where a soldier was crouched beside Ben trying to calm him. Beside me lay the vessel and the book. I stuffed them inside the handbag fastened around my waist.

Quentin was crouched, shaking his head, trying to become fully conscious.

A soldier patted Beaty's back. She rolled to her stomach and vomited onto the rooftop. I stumbled over to Quentin. "You're bleeding, your arm."

He looked surprised. Blood flowed down his shirtsleeve.

A soldier got to him just then. "Sit down sir, let us check you out."

Quentin said, "We shouldn't have left him."

I nodded and patted his leg. A soldier thrust an earpiece toward me. "Colonel Donahoe," he said.

There was a lot of static. "Hello?"

More static. "... I'm at the... helicop...soon."

"Hammond, Magnus isn't with me."

The radio static squawked and I couldn't tell if he could hear me. "...going... tomorrow..."

I shook my head at the soldier, my eyes wide. "I can't hear him. I can't tell what he's saying."

The soldier grabbed the earpiece from my head, rushed away and returned a moment later with a new one. He placed it on my ear, pulling the microphone in front of my mouth. "Hammond, can you hear me?"

"Yes."

"I don't have Mag—"

"Don't say anything to be traced. Get on the helicopter. I'll meet you by morning."

"I have my family with—"

"How many need transport?"

"Everyone." I made a mental count. "Six, including me. Hayley is hurt and Quentin. Ben is crying. Beaty is..." My eyes went back to Beaty, convulsing on the ground. Quentin saying to a soldier, "It's just a graze man, no big deal. Help Beaty." Hayley had a head wound. I couldn't believe that psychopath hit her. Zach and Emma were moving around, but weren't actually up yet.

"Put Major Dell back on," Hammond said.

I took the earpiece off and passed it to the soldier beside me.

My eyes went to the tree line beyond the lavish gardens past the woods, and beyond, miles away to a fiery explosion and rising above it a ballooning cloud. I watched it, terrified, but it wasn't one of our dark storm clouds. It was just a fiery bomb exploding something. I felt a certain kind of relief and that really sucked.

Major Dell finished his conversation with Colonel Donahoe then stood and commanded, "Everyone on the helicopter, now!"

Hayley was pushed by me on a stretcher and loaded on.

I asked Major Dell, "Where is Colonel Donahoe?"

"He's been gone fighting in the Meadows for the last three days."

"The meadows?"

"That's what we call the east side. Magnus's son is trapped in there by the fighting."

"Oh. Crap. Okay. Did he say when he would have Archie? When we would know?"

"By morning, but I have to insist, Queen Kaitlyn, you get into a helicopter now. This area is not secured and we've been exposed for too long."

I ran to get Ben. "Shhhh, shhhh, it's going to be okay." I picked him up and draped him across Emma's chest. She wasn't fully aware, but her arms wrapped around him anyway. Zach was holding his head groaning. "Zach, focus! We need to get Emma and Ben to that helicopter."

Zach clamored up. He wobbled. "Where the fuck are we?"

"Magnus's castle, the year 2382. But we can't stay, we have to get out of here. The soldiers are taking us to a safe house but we have to move." An explosion rocked the ground right then.

"Shit," he said. He and I pulled Emma to her feet and we held on around Emma's back and fought against the wind to the helicopter, Ben screaming the whole time.

Emma stopped, dug her heels in, and pulled against our hands. "I don't want to go in it."

306 | DIANA KNIGHTLEY

"You have to Emma, I'm sorry, but we have to get in it. We aren't safe here."

She struggled against Zach. "No, I don't want to. It's so bright, it's too loud." She desperately tried to pull away. Ben was totally worked up, his little face turning red from it all.

The helicopter was loud and windy and so freaking loud.

"Come on babe, you can do this. Keep your eyes shut like Magnus. Right, Katie?"

"Yes, of course, close your eyes, I'm so sorry it's scary but we have to do it."

Emma moaned. "I don't want to!"

Zach clasped his hands over Ben's ears. "Baby, ya gotta get in the copter. Ya gotta take care of Ben. It's gonna fuckin' be okay. I've got you, I promise."

She let him lead her inside.

Another explosion, this one sounded closer. A soldier began yelling, "Everyone into the copter! Inside, now!"

A soldier, pressing a compress to Quentin's shoulder, and a second soldier carrying Beaty, loaded them onto the aircraft. They put Beaty onto a stretcher and strapped her in.

The rooftop was now devoid of all of us. If Magnus was coming, this is where he would come. I didn't want to leave, but I had to. I had to climb in that helicopter and go with them to safety.

So I climbed inside. Those of us in seats began strapping on seatbelts.

I looked around at this helicopter filled with all the people I loved. Most of them.

Except Magnus.

I gulped in some air.

I had to be the motherfucking matriarch. Because all these people needed me.

I needed to get Archie, make sure he was safe.

I needed to rescue Magnus, but I had no idea how.

I had to kill me an asshole. But I had to find him first.

And I had to Queen Kaitlyn all of this.

Possibly alone.

Starting now.

Our helicopter lifted into the night air.

CHAPTER 70

The helicopter landed on the lawn of the safe house. The night was pitch-black but the house foyer was lit with only a few lights further in.

Quentin said, "Holy shit, that's a big house. Where are we?"

I stood beside a soldier, helping everyone climb from the helicopter. "This is Magnus's country house. Apparently it's safe here. Make yourself comfortable but don't sit on the couch until you get that arm bandaged."

"His country house — shit, that's bigger than the White House." He asked one of the soldiers. "You guys have fluids? She's not keeping anything down." A soldier carried Beaty inside, followed by Quentin, followed by another soldier carrying a large medical kit. Then Hayley scrambled out holding her head with a soldier helping her to the house.

She paused looking at me through her one non-swollen eye. "What's going to happen to Mags?"

"I don't know..."

"I will never forgive myself if—"

"How were you to know Hayley? You couldn't have. None of this is your fault."

Zach climbed out with his arms around Emma and Ben and we all went in through the front door together.

"Fuck," said Zach, "What's up with this smug-ass?" He gestured toward a giant photo of Donnan in his military regalia in the gigantic front foyer.

I said, "That's Donnan, the one who raped me."

"Oh no, that is some serious bullshit." Zach walked over and with a struggle pulled the giant photo off the wall. "We get to do this right?"

I said, "I like that you did it first, asked later. And yes, I suppose we do."

He went to another large framed photo and pulled it down too. He leaned both against the wall. "I'd break them but it seems like too much work. You are not kidding about the pain. That shit sucked, didn't it, babe?"

Emma said, "So much."

I said, "How's Ben?"

Emma lifted her shirt. Ben was cozied up to her breast, nursing, carried in the sling, under her shirt. He looked at me. I looked at him.

"Hey Ben, I know that was awful, but hey, it's all good now right?"

He nursed, watching me, his little mouth moving.

Emma said, "I think the loud helicopter drowned out his crying and he forgot to keep going."

I said, "Well, I guess that's good."

CHAPTER 71

$\mathcal{M}$rs Johnstone brought us food and drinks and another dress for me to change into. I did it quickly, without the full shower I probably definitely needed. Instead I spot-cleaned myself and got out of my 18th century clothes. Beaty lay on the same gurney Magnus had been on a few weeks earlier right in the middle of the room. She had an iv drip of fluids flowing into her arm to guard against dehydration. Quentin beside her on a stool, holding her hand. His arm bandaged now, but still — blood. He was talking to her in low murmurs. Telling her it would be okay. Assuring her.

Zach and Emma were cuddled on the couch, heads back on the pillows. A sweet family moment after all that danger.

All of that was a little melancholy for me.

Hayley was sitting on an armchair with a sheet spread over it to protect the fabric because she had been bleeding a lot. She held a cold pack to her bandaged forehead, tears streaming down her face. Every now and then she pulled the ice pack off to say, "What the fuck?"

Emma would say, "I know."

Or Zach would say, "Fuckin' right man, that shit sucked."

Hayley asked, "So when are we?"

Zach said, "Katie says it's the year 2382."

"So everyone we know is dead?"

"Except us."

I had been sitting on another chair but could not calm myself. My first thought, Archie. My every thought, *Magnus*.

I was surrounded but felt so alone.

I stood, too nervous to sit.

I walked around the room looking at things without actually looking at anything.

I finally paused, my hands on the back of Hayley's chair. "I want to say to you all, Magnus and I are so very sorry about the disruption in your lives, the danger. I never meant to put you in this position, I couldn't think of what else to do and—"

Quentin said, "What else could we have done? Nothing. I'm your security guard and there was nothing I could do. If anyone is to blame, it's me."

Hayley lowered her icepack and raised her chin to look at me. "We all know this is all my fault."

I held her hand over the back of the chair.

I said, "Nah sweetie, it's not at all. How could you have known he was a psychopath? Everyone liked him."

"I hate him so much. And you know what? From this moment I've decided I have amnesia from this head wound, so I don't even know who you're talking about."

I said, "That's an excellent idea but also, tomorrow, I may need to ask you a million questions about what he knows, what he might have guessed, and what he might be planning, so I'll need you to have a good memory."

"Fine, I'll have selective recollection for you and Mags."

Zach said, "I would like to say none of this is me and Emma's fault." He shook his head. "Though I did tell Hayley I thought

Nick was great. I did tell him too much about our lives. I fucking cooked for him. Man, I hate him so much." He gave Hayley a sad smile.

"That being said, we just survived a shitstorm and we're all alive." His eyes took in the pretentiously decorated room. "Apparently we live in Trump Tower now. This is all unexpected."

Emma said, "I'd like to say this is nobody's fault but Nick Reyes's, so let's stop the victim blaming and strategize how to help Magnus." She leveled her eyes on me. "You've been in some dire situations before, and I really really hate to ask this, but do you think he's still alive?"

I took a deep breath. My whole body was shaking. "I don't know, but I... I don't know."

Quentin said, "If Reyes wanted him dead he would have shot him right then. I think he wanted him alive for some reason and that's good news because every minute Magnus is alive he's a minute closer to killing that asshole."

Zach said, "I completely agree."

I said, "Thank you Quentin. Thank you Zach. That really helps a lot. Okay, Emma, yes, he might be alive."

"Good, then tomorrow we need to come up with some ideas for ways to help him and I'll be praying for him, if anyone wants to join me."

I said, "Thank you I really appreciate it."

A soldier entered the room. "Queen Kaitlyn, a call from Colonel Donahoe."

I took the earphones from him. "Hello?"

"I have him."

"Good."

"He's accompanied."

"Yes, of course. Of course. Bring everyone."

When I turned back to the room, Emma asked, "What was that?"

"Colonel Donahoe has Magnus's son. He's safe."

Emma's eyes went wide. "Magnus's son?"

Zach asked, "When the hell did Magnus have a son?"

"It's a very long story and I..." I took a jagged difficult breath. "I can't really talk about it but he's verra wee and he was in the war and he might be all who's left..." I burst into tears and Emma came to wrap her arms around me with Ben sandwiched between us.

"Oh honey, yeah, you have a lot to tell us but you don't have to tell us now." She wiped my tears. "When is he coming?"

"I don't know, it's too dangerous to tell me over the thingy and..." I sniffled. "They're bringing his mother too and I don't know what to..."

"Oh, oh now, okay, let's see. This woman, the mother, we don't want her here, right? I mean, just so I know."

I shook my head.

"Right, I'm going to talk to Mrs Johnstone."

A few minutes later Emma returned. "Mrs Johnstone has told me there is a whole guest area in the east wing. One across the lawn over there." She pointed somewhere. It didn't matter, I liked the idea of 'across the lawn over there'. "Mrs Johnstone wanted to put me and Zach there but I told her we would all sleep here near each other that none of us minded or much wanted our own house and this — I don't know, *person,* can have the other house. She has gone there now to make sure the bed is made."

"Thank you so much."

"You're welcome. Now what?"

"I don't know, but I think I have to go wait on the front stoop for him to arrive because I kind of feel like I can't breathe."

"Do you need company?"

"Not really. It just needs to be silent for a bit." I looked around. "Will everyone be okay if I disappear for a while?"

They all said yes or nodded and so I grabbed a blanket from the back of the couch and I left them there, sprawled in the luxurious living room, and I went through the marble-floored, footstep-echoing foyer to the ostentatious front entrance. I stood on the top step wrapped in the blanket, looking across the gardens and the sweeping lawn. It was dark except for moonlight with a clear sky above. I looked up at the stars.

See this sky, Kaitlyn? Tis always the same heavens wherever we are.

"I love you, courageous man, please stay safe..."

I wrapped the blanket tighter around me as I heard the hum of the helicopter approaching.

CHAPTER 72

Colonel Donahoe dismounted the helicopter and helped Bella out. She looked terrible. Her hair messy, her face with no makeup, her clothes dirty, she looked like a woman who had been through an ordeal. Exiting from the helicopter behind her was a man I hadn't met yet. Then a soldier carrying a baby carrier. Bella looked over the front of the house and her eyes rested on me then she looked away.

I went down the steps to meet them on the lawn.

I said, "Mrs Johnstone has readied the guest house for you." Archie began to cry in his carrier.

Bella refused to acknowledge me.

Her guy put forward his hand and yelled over the sound of the helicopter. "I'm John Mitchell, Your Highness."

I shook it. "I'm Kaitlyn Campbell."

Colonel Donahoe coughed and corrected. "Queen Kaitlyn."

"Oh yes, of course," I said, but how could I be expected to keep all of this in my head with this woman standing beside me on my lawn? "I hope you haven't been in too much danger?" I asked, because I didn't know what to say. Archie was full-blown very loud crying.

He answered, "It's been difficult. We were under siege for the last fourteen hours."

Bella nestled into John Mitchell's arms. "I'm very tired John, can we just go to sleep?"

"Of course."

Colonel Donahoe pulled me aside. "Where is Magnus?"

"He was captured in 2019, by General Reyes."

He winced. "Do you know the exact date?"

"Yes."

"Do you think he's still there?"

"No, General Reyes is a time traveler."

He shook his head. "I'll help them get settled and then I'll remain outside. I'll think of something, but don't tell anyone that Magnus is missing. You and I will talk in the morning."

"Yes, that sounds good, thank you."

I watched Bella and John Mitchell follow Hammond as he set out across the lawn. Archie screamed his head off in his carrier as the soldier followed them.

Emma appeared beside me without her sling, without Ben. Hayley appeared on my other side. I said, "Hayley you should not be walking around."

"I had to see what all that bellyaching was about, figures it was a baby."

"Magnus's baby."

Hayley squeezed me around the shoulders. "I'm so sorry, honey."

Emma said, "You don't get to hold him, say hello, or anything?"

Tears welled up in my eyes. "No, I'm not allowed to, she won't let me unless Magnus is here."

"Oh, well that sucks."

They were all the way across the lawn and we could still hear Archie's cries. My heart hurt from it all. A tear rolled down my cheek.

Emma said, "To quote my dear husband, fuck this shit." She took off jogging after them.

"What are you doing?" I called. She waved over her shoulder and kept going.

I asked Hayley, "What do you think she intends to do?"

Hayley said, "Well she's not going to let that baby cry anymore, that's for sure."

Emma caught up with the group and from way away through the darkness she was speaking to Bella. And speaking to Bella. Then speaking to John Mitchell and Hammond. Then speaking to Bella. And then she gingerly scooped Archie out of the baby carrier and with the soldier just behind her she walked back toward us, carrying Archie, a triumphant smile on her face.

As soon as she got to me she placed a now calmer Archie in my arms. I was full-on happy sobbing. "What did you say?"

"I told her I was a nanny and you hired me to take care of the baby so she could sleep. She seemed skeptical. I could tell she didn't want to deal with the baby but she didn't want you to have him either, but the man totally agreed I should take him so they could sleep. So I did."

I looked at Archie's sweet crying face. "Yay, little baby, you get to stay with me tonight."

Emma grinned happily and hugged me and Archie. "He is such a cutie, Kaitlyn, and oh my he has some great lungs."

The soldier placed the baby carrier beside my legs. Emma carried it into the house. Hayley followed her in.

And then me, with Archie in my arms.

CHAPTER 73

Zach with Ben asleep in his arms asked, "That's little Magnus?"

I held him so Zach and Quentin could see him. "This is Archie Campbell, Magnus's son. Archie this is Uncle Quentin and Uncle Zach and also your Aunts: Beaty, Hayley, and Emma."

I crossed to the big wide comfortable chair with the puffy footstool which was frankly difficult to get to with the mixture of happy-crying and desperate-crying wetness making it hard to see. It was like all the fear and danger and loss and worry of the last hours had hit me with the arrival of Archie. A little guy who needed his Da. Like me. I needed Magnus, I needed him so much. I dropped into the seat cross-legged with little Archie across my lap.

I chewed my lip.

Emma asked, "Do you need us?"

"No, I'm just going to stay awake and hold him."

"Okay, Zachary, we have to get to a bed."

He stood with little Ben. Emma put the baby carrier beside

me. Inside was a bottle and a diaper. She gave me three extra pillows around my elbows and near my head and kissed Archie on the forehead. "Have fun with this little sweetness." She stroked her fingers down his face. "I forgot how tiny they can be."

Hayley said, "I'm headed to a bed too."

I said, "There are two bedrooms through that hallway. Make yourself at home. Quentin, guess what? You get the master bedroom through there."

"Finally, a proper room."

"How's Beaty?"

"She isn't vomiting anymore, so that's good, right Beaty?"

"Aye," she groaned. "That food was disagreeable."

"Shh, Katie thinks it's awesome, but she has awful taste." She giggled sweetly.

I said, "Very funny," as he picked Beaty up and carried her to their room.

They left me all alone with Archie. I clicked off the table lamp throwing the room into almost darkness, except for the glow of outside lights shining through the foyer windows. Light enough to make out the shapes. Dark enough to not be afraid.

Though I was plenty afraid.

I wrapped the blanket around my legs and adjusted the pillows to get comfortable. "Hey Archie, I'm so sorry you were in the war."

He looked up at me.

"Poor baby, it was probably so scary. And you're probably wondering where your Da is... but I..."

I wrapped my hand around his. "I don't know where he is but I don't want you to be worried." I whispered into the soft skin of his tiny sweet little fingers. "He'll survive this because he's never once let me down."

I kissed his little fist. "I thought he had that one time but now you're here and that's something wonderful. You're not a let down at all."

I ran my fingertips along the soft hair beside his ear. "Did I tell you I was going to have a little boy? He would be just..." I tried to think about what age he would be, younger than Ben, older than Archie. "I really wish he would have... because now your Da is not here and..."

My voice cracked apart with my heart.

"It was so scary. I don't know how he lives through it and I... You might be all that's left of him." Tears streamed down my face.

Archie, oblivious, began sucking on his fists. "Hungry?" I reached over the arm of the chair and rifled through his carrier for the bottle. "Here you go."

He took the bottle hungrily with sweet little gulps. "You should tell me earlier, sweetie, before you're this famished."

I sighed. "I don't know if our timing was right. It would be so great to give you a little brother to watch over. You would be good at that, because someday in an alternate universe you will watch over me." My chin trembled. "And I just want to thank you for that. You gave me a little more time with Magnus and I'm forever grateful for it."

Lacking a better choice I wiped my tears on the edge of my blanket. "I'll make sure this is laundered tomorrow," as if Archie cared.

I settled my head back on the chair pillow and waited for him to finish his bottle.

"All done?"

His dark eyes looked right into mine.

"Hi, Archie." I said. "I didn't mean to frighten you about your da. I just miss him so much." He yawned, his face going through like five different silly phases. His eyes began to close. I brushed my fingertips on his soft cheek and whispered, "Your da loves you and he loves me and we're all connected. It's like a big knot of tangled love. If you listen really closely in the quiet spaces near your heart, you'll hear him — he's telling us he's doing everything he can to come home."

The end.

THANK YOU

*T*his is still not the true end of Magnus and Kaitlyn. There are more chapters in their story. If you need help getting through the pause before the next book, there is a FB group here: Kaitlyn and the Highlander Group

Thank you for sticking with this tale. I wanted to write about a grand love, a marriage, that lasts for a long long time. I also wanted to write an adventure. And I wanted to make it fun. The world is full of entertainment and I appreciate that you chose to spend even more time with Magnus and Kaitlyn. I just love them and wish them the best life, I will do my best to write it well.

As you know, reviews are the best social proof a book can have, and I would greatly appreciate your review on these books.

Kaitlyn and the Highlander (Book 1)
Time and Space Between Us (Book 2)
Warrior of My Own (Book 3)
Begin Where We Are (Book 4)
A Missing Entanglement (short story 4.5)

Entangled with You (Book 5)
Magnus and a Love Beyond Words (Book 6)
Always Under the Same Sky (book 7)

SERIES ORDER

Kaitlyn and the Highlander (book 1)
Time and Space Between Us (book 2)
A Warrior of My Own (book 3)
Begin Where We Are (book 4)
A Missing Entanglement (short, optional, between 4&5)
Entangled With You (book 5)
Magnus and a Love Beyond Words (book 6)
Always Under the Same Sky (book 7)

ALSO BY DIANA KNIGHTLEY

Can he see to the depths of her mystery before it's too late?

The oceans cover everything, the apocalypse is behind them. Before them is just water, leveling. And in the middle — they find each other.

On a desolate, military-run Outpost, Beckett is waiting.

Then Luna bumps her paddleboard up to the glass windows and disrupts his everything.

And soon Beckett has something and someone to live for. Finally. But their survival depends on discovering what she's hiding, what she won't tell him.

Because some things are too painful to speak out loud.

With the clock ticking, the water rising, and the storms growing, hang on while Beckett and Luna desperately try to rescue each other in Leveling, the epic, steamy, and suspenseful first book of the trilogy, Luna's Story:

Leveling: Book One of Luna's Story

Under: Book Two of Luna's Story

Deep: Book Three of Luna's Story

SOME THOUGHTS AND RESEARCH...

Some **Scottish and Gaelic words** that appear within the book series:

Chan eil an t-sìde cho math an-diugh 's a bha e an-dé - The weather's not as good today as it was yesterday.

Tha droch shìde ann - The weather is bad.

Dreich - dull and miserable weather

Turadh - a break in the clouds between showers

Solasta - luminous shining (possible nickname)

Splang - flash, spark, sparkle

Mo reul-iuil - my North Star (nickname)

Bidh thu a 'faileadh mar ghaisgeach - you have the scent of a breeze.

Osna - a sigh

Rionnag - star

Sollier - bright

Ghrian - the sun

Mo ghradh - my own love

Tha thu breagha - you are beautiful

Mo chroi - my heart

Corrachag-cagail - dancing and flickering ember flames

Mo reul-iuil, is ann leatsa abhios mo chridhe gubrath - My North Star, my heart belongs to you forever

Dinna ken - didn't know

A h-uile là sona dhuibh 's gun là idir dona dhuib - May all your days be happy ones

May the best ye've ever seen
Be the warst ye'll ever see.
May the moose ne'er lea' yer aumrie
Wi' a tear-drap in his e'e.
May ye aye keep hail an' hertie
Till ye're auld eneuch tae dee.
May ye aye be jist as happy
As we wiss ye noo tae be.

Tae - to

Winna - won't or will not

Daena - don't

Tis - This is or there is. This is most often a contraction t'is, but it looked messy and hard to read on the page so I removed the apostrophe. For Magnus it's not a contraction, it's a word.

Och nae - Oh no.

Ken, kent, kens - know, knew, knows

scabby-boggin tarriwag - Ugly-foul smelling testicles

latha fada - long day

sùgh am gròiseid - juice in the gooseberry

Beinn Labhair - Ben Lawers, the highest mountain in the southern part of the Scottish Highlands. It lies to the north of Loch Tay.

each-cogaidh - war horse

iora rua - a squirrel. (Magnus compares Kaitlyn to this ;o)

Characters:

    Kaitlyn Maude Sheffield - born 1994

    Magnus Archibald Caelhin Campbell - born 1681

    Lady Mairead (Campbell) Delapointe

    Hayley Sherman

    Quentin Peters

    Beaty Peters

    Zach Greene

    Emma Garcia

    Baby Ben Greene

    Sean Campbell -Magnus's half-brother

    Lizbeth Campbell - Magnus's half-sister

    Baby Archie Campbell - born 2383

    Bella (?)

    John Mitchell - Bella's guy

    Colonel Hammond Donahoe

    The Earl of Breadalbane - Lady Mairead's brother

    Uncle Archibald (Baldie) Campbell - uncle to Sean and Lizbeth

    Tyler Garrison Wilson

    Grandma Barb

The beautiful **Robert Burns** poem, O *my Luve's like a red, red rose,* written in 1794 is actually a song. I knew I wanted to use it in this story, but discovered later it wasn't included in Robert Burns's published book, ***Poems, Chiefly in the Scottish Dialect,*** also called the *Kilmarnock Volume,* published in 1786.

    After careful consideration and because it was so important

to the story, I decided to leave it as it is, a world in which the song was included in the book — so that Kaitlyn can find it and she can read it to Magnus.

Locations:

Fernandina Beach on Amelia Island, Florida, 2017

The Dock by a spring on a piece of unoccupied land near Gainesville, Florida. Owned by Zach and Michael's uncle. Used by Magnus and Kaitlyn to hide the vessels.

Magnus's home in Scotland - Balloch. Built in 1552. In early 1800s it was rebuilt as Taymouth Castle. (Maybe because of the breach in the walls caused by our siege from the future?) Situated on the south bank of the River Tay, in the heart of the Grampian Mountains

Kilchurn Castle - Magnus's childhood home, favorite castle of his uncle Baldie. On an island at the northeastern end of Loch Awe. In the region Argyll.

The kingdom of Magnus the First.

The Cracker Barrel off I-95 in Savannah.

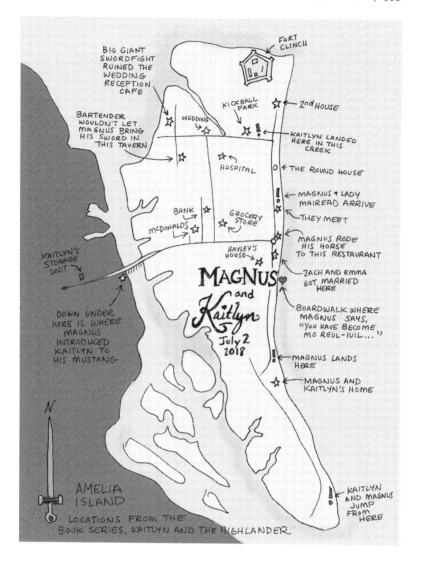

ACKNOWLEDGMENTS

A huge thank you to David Sutton for reading and advising on story threads. While it might be unpopular that you advised me to remove a sex scene (I had them getting busy right after the surgery), you also asked me to add a scene with Magnus and baby Archie. You were so right about both those things. You also found Magnus's horse and mentioned that it might be time for a bedroom scene from Magnus's perspective, which were both great ideas. You have an amazing knack and seem to want the best for Magnus and Kaitlyn; I value your opinions so highly.

A big thank you to Heather Hawkes for beta reading, championing, being a long time friend and supporter, and for saying things like, "So heart breaking! I cried... beautiful too," about the scenes where Magnus and Kaitlyn meet Archie for the first time. It's terrifying to release a book into the wild and I'm so grateful that you've been enthusiastic and sometimes 'on-call' when I'm totally freaking out.

Thank you to Jessica Fox for reading and saying, "I like that Kaitlyn keeps growing up but still manages to be annoying occasionally to remind me that she's still the same person." I like that you say things like this to help me keep it real. Your advice is great and it means a lot that you think this is my best so far.

Thank you to Kristen Schoenmann De Haan for your tireless beta-reading for me and for championing my very first book, Bright. That means so much to me. I also like that you said this, "He is funny, that Magnus. Sometimes he is the most enlightened man, and other times very much that bear." I totally agree.

And a special thank you to Cynthia Tyler, a truly amazing editor, for going through the manuscript with your wit and wisdoms, your attention to detail, and your magical ability to past-participlate the verb 'to lie.' I adore that you 'get' that Kaitlyn doesn't know how the heck to do it and you just want to nudge her in the right direction. I've about given up on her, but you haven't. I'm so grateful you found me or I found you — however it happened, you add an excellent polish to the words. And you do it again and again as often as I need you. I thank ye for it.

∾

A huge thank you to every single member of the FB group, Kaitlyn and the Highlander. Every day, in every way, sharing your thoughts, joys, and loves with me is so amazing, thank you. You inspire me to try harder.

And when I ask 'research questions' boy do you all deliver.

_____

I asked, ***What do you think Magnus would be delighted by in a Cracker Barrel General Store? And what would he and Kaitlyn take to the past with them?***

There were so many great ideas, but these were the ones I used:

Different flavored old fashioned candies - Dianna Schmidt,

Karla Blaise, Jenna Rae Payne, Denagh Lynn McBean, Lauren Ah Sang, Diana Toles, Gail Bissett, Krystal Brazil

Beanie hat - Dianna Schmidt, Lauren Ah Sang

Quilts - Jenna Rae Payne

Holiday displays (ornaments) - Jenna Rae Payne,

Scented candles, soap, lotion for Lizbeth - Tammy Aya Abouelnasr Keener, Patty Wayne, Lindsay Holden-Shannon, Gail Bissett, Sheryl Lee, Lisa Warfield

Coffee and tea - Tammy Aya Abouelnasr Keener

Soda wall - Denagh Lynn McBean, Gail Bissett. Sheryl Lee

Scarves - Denagh Lynn McBean

Flavored tea - Patty Wayne

Chocolate - Patty Wayne

Checkers - Michiko Howard Martin, Lauren Ah Sang, Christine Davis Clinton, Sheryl Lee

Christmas ornaments- Lauren Ah Sang

Jump the Peg game - MaryAnn Meyers, Liza Cook Griggers, Sheryl Lee

Wooden rockers (they didn't buy these but might someday) - Sheryl Lee

Biscuits and gravy - Nancy Graff

Thank you to everyone who weighed in!

I also asked, **"What was the photo that Kaitlyn took with her when she went to 1679?"**

This is the one I chose:

Kaitlyn and I with our horse in the snow in Scotland. Twas the year 1702. We were both smiling.

Thank you for the ideas, Catie Brooks (Didn't she take a photo of them in Scotland on her phone?) and Nancy Graff (I was thinking of them on his horse.) and Kathy Fletcher Bainter

(What about the one she took in the forest in Scotland of the two of them?)

I also asked, **"I need a date. Because something big happened in the 1500s…"**

The winner was Samhain, or All Hallows Eve, and the following day, All Saint's Day, or La Samhna, November 1st. Thank you Margaret Parker, Rhonda Bascle, Heather Story, Dayle Brunson, and Maureen Woeller for helping me pick the day of the battle.

I also asked, **"If Zach and Emma had to move somewhere safe where would they pick?"**

Courtney Wilson picked Austin, Texas. That one felt right to me, unfortunately they didn't make it.

And finally, **"If Magnus and Kaitlyn were to celebrate Christmas in 2018, what would Magnus give Kaitlyn as a present? Also how would he wrap it, present it? Also what would Kaitlyn give Magnus?"**

Magnus and Kaitlyn don't exactly make it back for Christmas, but they do discuss what they would give each other. Thank you for the ideas!

Magnus would give her a baby - Cynthia Tyler

Kaitlyn would give him a horse (or learning to ride a horse with him.) - Denagh Lyn McBean

But there were so many wonderful suggestions, thank you everyone! Michelle Lisgaris, Gloria Michaels-Brown, Julie Napp, Jessica Martin, David Sutton, Liza Griggers, Holley Jewell, Rachael Temaat, Libera Illiano, Riley Walker, Gail Bissett, Diana Toles, Kristen Schoenmann De Haan, Lyn Fox, Denagh Lynn McBean, Tonya Morgan, and Kayla Foster

~

And thank you to Dianna Schmidt for telling me about the Scottish tradition of throwing a man over the side of the boat to bring a good haul of fish. I like Magnus's memory of that day.

~

And thank you to the artist, Nikita TV, for the photos of this amazing model through shuttterstock.com. He is a perfect Magnus and I'm grateful for him...

~

Thank you to Kevin Dowdee for being my support, my guidance, and my inspiration for these stories. I appreciate you so much. And thank you for listening to me as I fleshed out my theory of time travel. That was a big help.

Thank you to my kids, Ean, Gwynnie, Fiona, and Isobel, for listening to me go on and on about these characters, advising me whenever you can, and accepting them as real parts of our lives. I love you.

ABOUT ME, DIANA KNIGHTLEY

I live in Los Angeles where we have a lot of apocalyptic tendencies that we overcome by wishful thinking. Also great beaches. I maintain a lot of people in a small house, too many pets, and a to-do list that is longer than it should be, because my main rule is: Art, play, fun, before housework. My kids say I am a cool mom because I try to be kind. I'm married to a guy who is like a water god: he surfs, he paddle boards, he built a boat. I'm a huge fan.

I write about heroes and tragedies and magical whisperings and always forever happily ever afters. I love that scene where the two are desperate to be together but can't because of war or apocalyptic-stuff or (scientifically sound!) time-jumping and he is begging the universe with a plead in his heart and she is distraught (yet still strong) and somehow, through kisses and steamy more and hope and heaps and piles of true love, they manage to come out on the other side.

I like a man in a kilt, especially if he looks like a Hemsworth, doesn't matter, Liam or Chris.

My couples so far include Beckett and Luna (from the trilogy, Luna's Story) who battle their fear to find each other during an apocalypse of rising waters. And Magnus and Kaitlyn (from the series Kaitlyn and the Highlander). Who find themselves traveling through time to be together.

I write under two pen names, this one here, Diana Knightley, and another one, H. D. Knightley, where I write books for Young

Adults (They are still romantic and fun and sometimes steamy though, because love is grand at any age.)

DianaKnightley.com
Diana@dianaknightley.com

ALSO BY H. D. KNIGHTLEY (MY YA PEN NAME)

  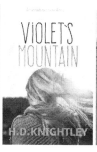 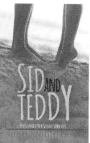

Bright (Book One of The Estelle Series)

Beyond (Book Two of The Estelle Series)

Belief (Book Three of The Estelle Series)

Fly; The Light Princess Retold

Violet's Mountain

Sid and Teddy

Printed in Great Britain
by Amazon